END GAME

BROOKLYN KINGS 2

FELICE STEVENS

DEDICATION

To my family

ACKNOWLEDGMENTS

Thanks as always to my editor, Keren Reed. To Hope and Jess from Flat Earth Editing, you are the best. To Dianne, from Lyrical Lines, I couldn't do it without you. And to Reese thank you for everything.

And to the readers, you make it all worthwhile.

CHAPTER ONE

Brody

How it started…

The crowd was on its feet, their roars and cheers so loud, we couldn't hear the play calls. Our quarterback, Devlin "Devil" Summers, had us hopped up in the huddle, yelling, hooting, and hollering about all the glory we'd get after we won the Orange Bowl.

"Let's do this; let's gooooooo," he shouted, fist in the air. His helmet was on, so I couldn't see his face, but I imagined those bright-green eyes snapping fire, that trademark wicked grin lifting his lips. Tats ran up and down his arms and, as I knew from years of seeing him naked in the shower, covered a good portion of his body as well.

His very ripped, muscled body.

Yeah. I looked. And wished I could touch.

I had a secret.

Me, Brody "Blink" Martin, fastest tight end the Blue Waves had ever seen, All-American, most receptions freshman year, and the NCAA's holder of the record for most yards received three years in a row, liked guys.

At sixteen, I'd made the swim team as well as football. Maybe I'd chosen swimming because I liked to imagine what went on behind those bulges in my teammates' Speedos.

I knew what happened in mine—the time Griffin Waters, superstar senior with a body like carved marble, had walked in on me in the shower when I was rubbing one out.

"You thinking of me, Blink?" His eyes were riveted on my engorged dick. "I saw you checking out my ass."

Shit, fuck. Had I moaned his name out loud? I had been thinking of him. He played the leading man in every one of my dirty nighttime fantasies. I thought I was so damn discreet. Griffin was gorgeous—broad shoulders, a round, firm butt, and his junk, even soft, was huge. I could only imagine how it would feel stuffed up my ass. Or in my mouth.

I freaked and started babbling. "What? No, of course not. I-I—"

The words died on my lips as he shed his towel, pulled the curtain closed, and got on his knees to finish me off. Then, with water streaming down his face and lips still swollen from my cock, he got to his feet, took my hand, wrapped it around his huge shaft, and taught me how to jack him off. He came, splattering hot and heavy over my abs before it all washed away, his teeth scoring my shoulder as he bit me, and I never wanted to let him go.

After that, we'd met every weekend we could at his parents' cabin by the lake, where he'd drive me wild with his tongue and all these toys he'd bring. Never his dick, though.

"Please, Griff. Do it. All of it. Everything. Wanna feel you in me."

"Nuh-uh. I like to play with you and watch you fall apart."

And no matter how hard I'd begged, he wouldn't give me that ultimate pleasure. I guess that should've been a sign that something wasn't right.

Still, I wasn't able to stay away from him. It had been dangerous and exciting but ultimately sad, which I'd learned the hard way. He and his prom date, Ally Sue, had kissed and posed for pictures while, across the street from his house, I'd watched in the shadows. The next night we were together, and I'd asked him if they'd had sex.

"Yeah, but it didn't mean anything. I had to show her that I was into her. It woulda looked suspicious otherwise."

A month or so later, Griffin left for college. I'd known we were done. I saw him on social media, dating all these girls, and realized I'd been nothing but a dirty secret. After that, I lost my passion for swimming and concentrated solely on football.

At football camp, I couldn't take my eyes off the thick thighs in skintight pants and went back to my shower-time rub-outs. My coaches told me I had a shot at a football scholarship if I kept up my stats and my grades, so I knew I had to put my sex drive aside and concentrate on the future. My dick could wait. I had plans, and nothing was gonna derail them.

I was gonna be a football star and take care of my momma.

Daddy died in a car crash when I was nine, and Momma remarried Theo McGrath some three years later. My momma had next to nothing—in his teens, Daddy had spent some time in prison for theft, bar fights, and breaking and entering. And despite trying to get his act together, it had been hard for him to get steady work. The only job he'd managed to keep was delivering food, and that was what killed him—one rainy night he took a curve too fast and went over the side and into the ravine. The car and him burned to a crisp.

Momma'd had her job working at Burger Benny's, and for three years it had been her and me. Theo worked on a construction project next door to the burger joint, and they'd started dating. As a kid, I'd resented his attempts at trying to be nice to me and pushed him away, believing that to accept him would be disloyal to my daddy. Once I left for college I'd eased up, but I still never gave him the chance he wanted. It was a problem I needed to work on.

Every penny Momma received from Daddy's insurance went toward my football camp. A full scholarship to college was a dream—one that I had the chance of making a reality. So that was what I focused on.

Now here I was, on the number-one ranked college football team in the country, on the verge of winning the game that would bring us the national championship and glory. NFL scouts were everywhere, and I'd signed with an agent who also represented Devlin and a number of other college players, along with NFL superstars and Hollywood movie stars.

Life was fucking good.

We took the line at 2nd and goal, and I hovered on my toes, electricity surging through every vein in my body. I was ready to put this baby in the W column. If we made this touchdown, we'd be champions. We knew it, and the stadium rocked and rolled on our fever.

"Blue 22, Blue 22, hut, hut," Devil shouted, and we broke. I raced to the five-yard line, shadowed by a defensive end, but as far as I was concerned, I was alone on the field, aside from Devil. The ball sailed straight into my arms, that familiar acceleration pushed my feet into overdrive, and I smashed through the tackle's hold and drove into the end zone.

"Yeah, yeah! Whoo-hoo!" My teammate Dante Williams grabbed me and we hugged; then the rest of the team mobbed me and lifted me up in the air.

"Way to go, Blink. We did it," Devlin yelled and put his hands under me, raising me higher. Ten of my teammates were touching me, yet I could only feel Dev's hands on me. He cupped my ass, and shocked, I gazed into his laughing face and sparkling eyes. I slid down, and he engulfed me in a hug.

"We did it," I mumbled into his shoulder.

"Yeah, we sure as hell did." A teasing grin split his face. "Catch ya later, Blink."

Our national championship assured, the press surrounded us, and Dev and I did interviews together and separately. Spotting Momma in the stands, I ran to her. "Momma, I can't believe it!"

She leaned over and hugged me. "Baby, I always knew you could. Your daddy would be so proud." Those last words were spoken in a whisper. As always, I teared up at any mention of my daddy.

Theo grabbed and hugged me. "Good for you. They robbed you of the Heisman. Now go sign them endorsement deals and make a ton of money."

My smile was thin. "I'm always gonna do right by my momma."

Theo frowned. " 'Course you are. I know I ain't your daddy, but I can still be damn proud of you. And I am. Always have been."

My insides got all twisted up because no matter how hard I tried, I couldn't let Daddy's memory go. But I held out a hand to Theo, and we hugged again. Theo had been there for all the milestones in my life, never wavering in his support.

Sensing the tension, Momma squeezed my hand. "Brody's gonna go celebrate with his friends. We'll see him later. And he's got that fancy New York agent now, like all those famous people. He's smart, and he knows what to do." She gave me another hug. "We'll talk later. You go do what you gotta do and have the best night."

"I will, Momma. Love you."

The following hours were a whirlwind of more interviews and calls with Ezra Green, my agent.

"I'll tell you exactly what I said to Devlin. Never accept the first good deal that comes your way. You came in third for the Heisman. You and Devlin are top picks—first round in the draft for sure. You're gonna have plenty of choices, and I want to make sure you're taken care of. At the moment, the last three teams to win division titles and the Super Bowl are waiting for my callbacks on their offers, plus some teams in their rebuilding phase that are willing to spend the big bucks."

"Thanks, Ezra. I know my major is business, but I'm still confused reading through all of it."

Laughter filled my ears. "That's why you have me. My advice right now? Go out and celebrate with your team. I'm sure you're gonna have a night you'll never forget. There's plenty of time to make the right decision."

I took a shower and lay on the bed in my hotel room, reveling in the silence after all the hours of noise assaulting me from every direction. We'd been told by our coaches that if we won the championship, our lives would change in an instant, and I had a feeling we'd only seen the beginning. My phone was blowing up with texts from influencers, high school kids I hadn't spoken to in years, companies offering endorsements, and tons of sexy DMs from half-naked girls. I checked the group chat with my friends on the team, and read that they'd started to gather at the hotel bar.

Lord, I was primed and ready to let loose for the night. Dressed in jeans and an Orange Bowl championship T-shirt, I took the elevator down to the lobby, where after signing autographs and taking pictures, I finally found my teammates. Dante stood up and pumped his fist, then megaphoned his hands.

"Blink. Sit that butt right here and have a drink."

I squeezed in between Everett Hayes and Lovell Barton, two of the biggest and best tackles in college football. Both were also definitely on their way to the NFL in the first or second round. We bumped fists.

"Bro, you were the *man*. That catch was like threading the needle. How high did you jump? Damn." Lovell—whose nickname was Lover because dude had a way with the ladies—lifted his beer. "Here's to the draft."

Everett—nicknamed Corvette or Vette for his speed—handed me a beer, and I took a long, sweet drink and licked my lips. "Damn, that was good."

"Have another, choirboy."

I peered over my shoulder and met Dev's dancing green eyes. "Very funny. Aren't you tired of teasin' me?"

"Why, when it's so much fun?"

I rolled my eyes and finished my beer.

Ever since Dev found out I went to church services the morning of every game, he'd teased me about it, but I didn't care. I needed a bit of quiet time to get my head together before the ruckus began.

"Lemme in." Dev edged his bulk between Lover and me.

"Dude, get your own seat," Lover sputtered.

Dev put his lips to Lover's ear and whispered something, and a wide grin broke across Lover's face. "Really? Well, if that's the case." He rose and flipped his braids, then rubbed his hands together. "I'll be seein' you, jokers." With a swagger, he walked away, straight to a beautiful woman sitting on a stool, her long legs crossed. He leaned against the bar and ordered a bottle of champagne. They toasted, and I shook my head.

"Leave it to Lover-boy."

Dev sipped his beer and shifted closer. The hairs on my arms rose at his breath on my cheek. "What about you? You must have them lining up." His lips moved closer. "Or are you too good a boy?"

I stared straight ahead, hoping to God Dev didn't feel the shivers running through me. I was grateful I was sitting so no one could see the boner in my pants. "I do okay. Not like you, though."

Devil Summers didn't get his nickname only for giving hell to his opponents on the field. He was a ladies' man who went through cheerleaders and beauty queens like grains of sand slipping through his fingers. I'd never seen him with the same girl twice on campus. And yeah, I looked.

That was why his attention earlier confused the hell out of me. Did he know I'd been crushing on him for the four years we'd played together? I thought I'd been discreet, but it was hard to keep my eyes from straying to that perfect body adorned with all those delicious tattoos. He was so fucking hot, and I would willingly set myself on fire for him.

"Well, stick by me, and I'll give you some pointers."

We spent the next two hours eating wings and drinking beer, which I wisely interspersed with water. Dev had left our table to make his rounds, and from the corner of my eye I saw him tucked into a booth, nuzzling a blond in a tight Blue Waves tank top and tiny Daisy Dukes. Fascinated, I had the vantage point to watch his hand cup her butt and knead it while she wiggled on his lap and kissed his neck. Blazing green eyes met mine, and he winked at me before teasing those long fingers up and down her thigh.

"Jesus." I sucked in a breath but couldn't stop staring. I don't know what shocked me more—the fact that I was watching Devil fondle some girl, or that he never took his eyes off me. My heart pounded, and sweat broke out all over my body.

Finally, he bent to whisper in her ear, and she nodded with excitement and took out her phone. She took a slew of selfies, kissing his cheek and clinging to his neck. Several minutes of the photo fest went on, and then he gave her a slight push off his lap. Giggling, she ran off to her friends. Dev reached for his phone, and I tore my gaze away and gulped the rest of my water. God help me, all I could imagine was Devil's big hands on me.

What the hell was going on? Dev was my teammate. And straight. We were friendly but not close friends, and we'd played together for four years. I'd never gotten a vibe from him.

"You okay?" Vette nudged my shoulder. "You're all red."

"Yeah. Just drinkin' too fast, is all."

Devil stood in the center of the room. About twenty of us from the team remained. "I've got reservations at the Hawk. My treat to the team. Move it or lose it."

The Hawk was a unique restaurant for sure. An elegant steak house in the front with a decadent dance club in the back, it was set on expansive grounds, boasting firepits and several outdoor hot tubs. Guests could stay overnight in luxury cabins.

Vette whistled. "Damn. Guess it pays to have rich parents. The Hawk is *the* place down here."

Dev frowned. "This is from me. It has nothing to do with them." Without another word, he stormed off.

In our years playing together, Dev had rarely mentioned his parents. All we knew about the esteemed professors Summers was that they both taught at Ivy League universities—his father in Connecticut, his mother in New York City. Leonard Summers was a quantum physics professor, and Sandra Roan-Summers taught Medieval History and Classical Literature. Devil never let on if there was any family strife, but their absence from every single game for all four years—even this championship one in our senior year—spoke volumes. Despite his family issues, Dev kept a positive attitude. He wasn't a bragger about his family's money or how much he'd made from endorsements, but tonight it seemed he was willing to show it in a big way.

We all piled into the Sprinter vans waiting outside and took off down the highway. We finished off multiple champagne bottles, and by the time we arrived, all of us were a bit toasted. Dev waited for us outside and threw an arm around my shoulders as we were ushered to a private room with two long tables.

"Blink next to me 'cause he and I scored that winning touchdown. He's my man tonight. Lover, you and Vette over there, and Dante, Trevor, and Purdy sit here." Everyone took their seats while I processed Dev's words that I was his man tonight.

If only.

Shit. How the hell was I supposed to sit for a whole meal with his thick, hairy thigh pressed to mine?

Somehow, I managed to consume enough steak and potatoes to soak up all the alcohol, so by the time we moved to the club, I was steady on my feet.

"Let's hit the club," Dev yelled. "Anyone wants back to the hotel, the Sprinters are waiting. I've rented out cabins for those who wanna stay. Just ask Justine, the hostess."

At least fifteen of us stayed.

The music was banging, and we took to the dance floor. I found myself a tall beauty whose dark skin glistened in the strobe lights. I ground into her, and she leaned in to kiss me. Her lips were soft and sweet, but they did nothing for me. My teammates catcalled us and clapped, but the more I tried, the less I was into it. All of a sudden, Dev joined us and pressed up against her while laying his hands on my hips. Again, those glittering eyes latched on to mine and *voilà*. My dick sprang to life.

"*Mmm*, baby," my dance partner purred. "That feels good. I wouldn't mind taking both of you home." She wiggled her ass into me while kissing Dev.

"Nah, baby. I don't share," Dev said. "I'm gonna get a drink." With one searching gaze aimed at me, he walked away, and my desire vanished.

I gave my partner an apologetic smile. "I'm gonna take a break. It's been a day."

Disappointment marred her pretty eyes. "Okay. Find me later. I'll be waiting." A long red nail trailed under my chin, and she disappeared.

I felt bad but knew I'd be avoiding her the rest of the night. Bottle of beer in hand, I watched as one by one, my teammates hooked up or left, and then I wandered outside to sit by one of the firepits. Staring into the flames, I wondered if I'd ever be able to be myself. The loneliness was so damn crushing, and I wished I had someone to share the thrill of this win with.

Night rolled in, and the sky darkened from lavender to midnight blue. A thousand stars sprinkled above me, and in the forest behind us, an owl hooted. Footsteps sounded, and I looked up. Dev stood in front of me.

"Mind if I join you?"

CHAPTER TWO

Dev

Oh, yeah. There he is.

I waited, anticipation crawling through my veins. I'd decided, win or lose today, I was going to make my move on Brody "Blink" Martin. Four years of desperation. Longing. Wishing I could throw caution to the wind and act on my lust and desire. Knowing it would never happen. Brody was straight. Or so I'd thought.

Until one game I'd been on the bench, resting a strained shoulder and watching him play–and had caught him subtly checking out the asses of opposing players when he thought no one would notice. I'd finally gotten the answer I'd been hoping for.

And if it turned out I was wrong and he wasn't into it, or me, I knew he wouldn't tell anyone. Brody was a team player, and he took that seriously. He'd never threaten or blackmail me. Brody was that sweet, good Southern boy. Loved his mother, went to church, and helped anyone who asked. I swear he'd give a homeless man the shirt off his back or the shoes off his feet. A truly good person.

And hot as fucking hell.

Some of the guys had met ladies and retired to the cabins, while others had decided to split and return to the hotel alone or with their girl of choice. Me? I had a whole other plan. One that involved my sexy-as-fuck teammate, who I hoped would be more than that by the time the night ended.

I stood at the edge of the firepit, waiting for his answer, while my hungry gaze roamed over him. Thick, reddish-brown hair, wide blue eyes, and a smattering of freckles across the bridge of his nose. Broad shoulders, a tight, round ass, and the biggest set of thighs this side of the Mississippi. Those baby blue eyes held mine, firelight playing off his slightly tense but curious face.

"Yeah, sure, Dev. 'Course you can."

Maybe he expected me to sit opposite him, but I chose the seat by his side. He shifted a few inches away to give me room, but I put a hand on his arm.

"Don't."

He froze, and through parted lips, I saw the tip of his pink tongue. I wanted to taste it. Suck on it. The sight of it sent my stomach into a free fall. I'd bet he didn't even know how gorgeous he was.

"Dev," he hissed. "The guys–"

"All gone," I murmured. "They're either in their own cabins, or they returned to the hotel." I licked my lips, and Brody's breath hitched. "It's just you and me out here."

"What the hell's goin' on? What're you doin'?"

That sexy drawl was such a turn-on, and I had to hold off from pouncing on him. I leaned in close. "I want to kiss you."

Brody's jaw dropped. "Wh-what? But you're—"

"Gay." I cupped his cheek, my thumb tracing those full lips I'd had filthy dreams about sucking my dick. "And I think you are too. Am I right?"

Dumbfounded, he nodded, and relief crashed through me as I brushed my mouth to his. A gasp of air escaped him.

"Oh God, Dev," he groaned. The sound went straight to my balls, and I lost it.

We attacked each other like wild beasts, Brody shocking me with the ferocity of his need. His tongue met mine and I sucked it while his hands dug into my hair to hold my head steady. He nipped and sucked at my lips and jaw. My cock was hard as a fucking iron pole, and if I didn't stop, I'd come in my shorts like a horny kid. I pushed him off and gazed into his flushed face.

"That's not your first kiss from a guy, is it?"

His chest rose and fell. "No. Yours?"

His confession surprised me. I'd thought my country boy would be a virgin, and I'd have to teach him. Me? I'd been having sex since I was sixteen. It was easy to find what I needed—go on a few gay message boards, meet up in some out-of-the-way place, and get laid. No strings, merely a way to get my rocks off. But I didn't fuck where I lived because I had no desire to be fodder for New York City gossip. To get what I needed, I went upstate or to Jersey. Connecticut or Long Island. I didn't mind traveling.

"I've been with guys." I kissed Brody again, addicted to his taste, the sounds of his breathing, unable to put into words why this felt different. "You wanna go to the cabin?"

A shy smile ticked up the corner of his mouth. Damn, that was sexy. When he nodded, I took his hand in mine and led him to the largest structure at the edge of the site, which I'd reserved for myself. The door opened to a huge room with a fireplace and a big furry rug in front of it. Wooden beams crisscrossed the ceiling, and glass sliders led to a deck with a Jacuzzi and chaise lounges. The bedroom was in the back. I'd had the staff fill the fridge with champagne, beer, and snacks.

Brody surveyed the space. "This is nice." He swiveled, taking it all in. "Our whole house would fit in here. My momma would freak if she saw this."

I knew we were from two different worlds, but I didn't care about any of that. I had the man I'd craved for years, alone and willing. I took his face between my hands and kissed him. Our tongues played and rubbed, and I tugged at his shirt.

"Off. All of it."

"You too," he croaked out, his voice rough with need, and we stripped out of our clothes in seconds flat. I devoured the sight of his naked body—flat, ridged abs and that heavy, beautiful dick rising between those powerful thighs. I'd seen it plenty of times in the locker room and in my filthy dreams. But now I licked my lips, knowing it was mine for the night. Brody's hungry gaze ate me up as well, and it was almost painful to move, but I had to touch him. I laid my hand on his chest, and the rapid pump of his heart matched my frenzied beat.

"Oh God," Brody groaned as our bodies pressed together. Precome slicked my stomach, and my cock throbbed and ached.

"Fuck, Brody. I want...*ahh*." I lost it when his big hand wrapped around our shafts and began to jack us off. My fingers dug into his shoulders as I rode that rubdown, and my toes curled as my orgasm smashed through me.

"Fuck," I called out, come shooting from my dick in the most mind-blowing climax of my life. Brody shouted out a moment later, and we sank to the large sectional sofa, collapsing in a tangle of arms and legs.

Minutes passed, and I cracked open one eye to see Brody lying by me, his chest heaving. It was a while before I was able to remember how to speak.

"That was incredible."

"*Mmm*." Eyes still closed, Brody smiled. "Sure was."

I eyed his beautiful body, finally available for me to touch and play with. I ran my hands over his sticky abs and tweaked his nipples. Brody opened his eyes and I got on all fours, hovering above his groin. My mouth watered at his musky scent, and I tongued his dick. It twitched and filled.

"Tastes so good." I continued to lick up and down the rapidly stiffening shaft and sucked the fat head.

"Fuck me, Dev," Brody breathed, his hands playing with my hair. "This is so damn hot. I've dreamed about you for years. What you'd feel like." He met my eyes and hesitated for a beat. "Inside me."

Lust slammed into me, and panting, I sat on my heels, my dick stiff and ready for action again.

"I want that."

I scrambled off and pulled him up, but once we were standing, I didn't want to rush anything. I'd planned this evening on a hope and a prayer that Brody would be sharing it with me, that we'd spend the night ripping up the sheets from wild, uncontrollable sex. But now that he was here, I wanted more than the physical. It was disconcerting, and I grew nervous and unsure. Why, I couldn't say.

"Do you want a drink or a snack?" I asked, and Brody's face screwed up in question.

"Huh? Don't you wanna...you know?" A cute blush rose over his face, and he ducked his head. I tipped up his chin and pressed a soft kiss to his lips.

"Oh, yeah. We're gonna do that. Don't you worry." I grabbed a butt cheek and squeezed. "Look how perfectly you fit in my hand."

Brody ran his fingers up the tats on my arms. "These are so gorgeous. What made you get them?"

Would it kill the vibe to say it was a way to get a rise out of my stuffy parents? Their lives were so measured and precise, I tried whatever I could to cause a misstep—getting tattoos was the first, and playing football was another. It might've started out as a joke, but I soon discovered how much I loved the game and how damn good I was—so good that colleges couldn't throw scholarships at me fast enough. I decided it was what I wanted. The one thing in my life I could say was absolutely mine.

Of course Mother and Father had believed I'd be attending one of their illustrious universities. I'd had the grades and the football talent, but at my announcement that I'd picked a school based on their stellar football program and not academic status, they'd been horrified and had expressed their emotions with stern frowns and multisyllabic words of disappointment.

"I just like them. They look badass."

"*Mmm.*" Brody's hands pinched my butt. "This ass is pretty bad." He slid a rough finger down my crack, making my nerves explode and my dick jerk. "I like it."

I kissed his collarbone and sank my teeth into the curve of his neck and shoulder. "I like you." He hissed, and I licked the red mark. "A lot."

"I...I never knew. You're always surrounded by girls."

"And I've never slept with any of them." At his shocked face, I chuckled. "I tell them I don't trust condoms not to break, and God knows I can't risk the chance that they're not on birth control. It's saved the day. But dammit, I hate having to hide it. Don't you?" I brushed aside the thick swath of reddish-brown hair hanging over his brow.

"Yeah. But I get it. I've tried datin' but never got beyond a first or second date. They probably think I'm a jerk."

I shook my head. "No way. You're a nice guy."

I didn't think Brody even listened to what I said. He stared off into the distance. "No way can I ever say nothin', though. I don't think my momma would care—I hope. Not sure about Theo, but it don't really matter if he does or doesn't."

We'd all played ball together for years but knew little of each other's personal lives. Curious to delve deeper into Brody's, I leaned against the big kitchen island. "You and he don't get along? I've seen him at the games, though, cheering you on. He's into it."

"Oh, he's all right, and he loves my momma." Brows pulled together, Brody lifted a shoulder. "But he ain't ever gonna replace my daddy." He pinched his eyes shut. "Silly, huh? I'm twenty-one and still missin' my father who's been dead for more than ten years."

That was a whole lot of hurt resting inside Brody. I put my arms around him and held him. "Hey. It's okay. We all have shit we gotta deal with."

"Like your parents?" I tensed, and Brody arched a brow. "They didn't come today. I see things too. They never come to any of our games. Not even this championship one."

My smile was thin. "They're not football fans."

He ran his knuckles across my cheek in a touch so sweet and gentle, I fucking trembled. "Dev, c'mon."

This was getting more personal than I'd imagined. This was supposed to be about wild, hot sex and lots of it. I raised my face to the ceiling, blew out a breath, and spoke to the rough wooden beams.

"Throwing a ball isn't good enough for the only child of Professors Sandra and Leonard Summers. I disappointed them by not following the path they primed me for since birth—the scholarly route." I mimicked my father's upper-crust accent. "*Devlin Summers. A boy with your illustrious background doesn't play football. This is not what we've planned for you. You have the ability to follow in our footsteps and those of your grandparents and great-grandparents. Instead, you waste it on something that doesn't require your brain, only brute force.*"

"Oh, wow." Brody's entire demeanor changed. He grew stiff and put some distance between us. "So, uh...your mom and dad...they're really smart, huh?"

"You could say so." I didn't like Brody so far away, and reached for him, but he sidestepped me. My heart sank. This response was exactly why I never spoke about my family. My ancestors' names were engrained in the hallowed halls of many institutions, including the Supreme Court.

"Don't. Please, Brody."

"Don't what?" he asked, but his eyes skittered away.

"Look at me differently just because you think my parents are special. They're not. And I'm nothing like them. At all."

His shoulders sagged. "I dunno."

That hurt. "Before I mentioned it, you treated me like everyone else, and I am. I'm just me. Dev. The guy who throws a football well. The guy who's wanted you for four years, and the last thing we should be doing tonight is wasting our time together talking about my parents. I should be kissing you." This time when I reached for him, he let me, and I fell into the hot sweetness of his mouth.

"Dev." He sighed. "I want you so bad, but—"

"No. No buts. Not now. Who knows if we'll get this chance again?"

Speaking those words filled me with sadness, but I knew they were the truth. The rest of the year would be a whirlwind of draft choices, endorsements, and meetings with our agents and NFL teams. Plus graduation. Neither of us could predict where we'd end up, but it was highly unlikely we'd be on the same team.

Brody gripped my hand tighter. "Okay."

"Lemme grab a bottle of champagne."

We kissed all the way to the bedroom, stoking our lust. The cabin's bedrooms were spacious and boasted skylights, allowing the pale moonlight to lay in silvery stripes across the bed. I dropped the bottle on the bed, needing two hands to hold him closer. I'd never wanted anyone with such desperate longing. Brody's hands rested on my shoulders, anchoring me to the floor.

"I can't get enough of you," I whispered.

"You ain't had me yet."

"What're we waiting for, then?" I tugged the pout of his lower lip between my teeth. "Let's make that happen."

He lay under me on the bed and spread his legs, giving me the wide-open sight of his ass. I moved in closer and licked a path across his hole. Brody jumped beneath me.

"Fuck, that's good."

"You like it? I'll do it again." I teased and sucked his rim, fucking him with my tongue until he writhed beneath me, his hole hot and silky against my lips. I watched his face to see what he liked, because giving Brody Martin pleasure was all I wanted.

"Dev, *Dev*, fuck me. Fuck me," he yelled, and I liked hearing him call out my name. One last lick, and I patted his ass.

"On all fours."

Brody rolled onto his stomach, and I smoothed my hands over those beautiful pale cheeks before sticking my fingers into my mouth and slipping one, then two inside him.

"Jesus, you're like fucking fire in there." I played with him for another minute, squeezing his balls lightly and reaching under him to pull his dick.

"Fuck you, do it already," he snarled and peered over his shoulder, that normally sweet face fierce, eyes blazing.

"You're hot when you wanna get fucked, aren't you?" Damn, he was beautiful. And mine. The lube and condoms I'd had delivered earlier were on the bed. I rolled a condom on and lubed up. "Ready for me?" I held his waist, and he reached out to grab the headboard.

"God, yes."

The first push into his ass was like opening the doors of heaven, and I couldn't go slow. My hips snapped, and a strangled sound burst free from Brody.

"Oh God, oh God."

"Dammit. Make that sound again."

Brody groaned. "Dev, please," he implored.

As I thrust, he lifted his ass higher and sucked me in farther. I was lost in the heat and hunger, out of control, needing to bury myself so far in Brody, I'd never leave him. He squeezed me tight, one hand working his dick while the other held on to the headboard as I drove into him.

We were loud in our passion for each other, the walls echoing with our shouts and grunts. My blood boiled, and I knew I was close to the edge. I tried to prolong the pleasure, dragging my dick out of him slowly, then slamming it back, but he grew wise to my game and squeezed his ass around my dick.

"Fuck, Brody. Fuck me. I can't...you're...oh, God." Like before, my climax ripped into me without warning, at the same time as Brody's. My vision faded to black and I saw stars as if I'd been knocked off my feet and sacked. My cock pulsed hard, filling the rubber, and I fell on top of a sweat-soaked Brody, who still twitched and shook in the aftermath of his orgasm.

"Jesus," Brody whispered. "That was fuckin' wild."

"Yeah. It sure as hell was." And so was I. Wild for Brody Martin. But what the hell could I do about it?

CHAPTER THREE

Brody

Five months later – graduation day

I searched the crowd, but I couldn't see Momma. I knew she was there in a bright-pink dress, hair all made up, and beaming a proud smile. Graduation day from college was all she'd ever talked about. The culmination of hers and my daddy's dream for me, but I don't think either of them ever thought my life would turn out like this.

As Ezra had predicted, I'd been a first-round pick—number six, to be exact—and chosen by the Austin Lonestars. A four-year contract worth ten million dollars. I still couldn't wrap my brain around numbers like that, but Ezra sat down with me, Momma, and Theo and explained it all to us, and how to set up my finances to make sure my money was protected.

Dev had been picked number three in the draft by the Brooklyn Kings, and while I was thrilled for him, it hurt to know he was gonna be halfway across the country from me. And we were in different divisions, so we'd hardly ever get to play against each other unless we both got to the Super Bowl.

Yeah, we were still together, and I was fucking crazy about him.

I continued to scan the crowd and squinted. I spotted her in the tenth row and waved both hands above my head, then laughed at my silliness.

Dummy. Text her and tell her to look at the lineup. I sent her a message and watched as she received it and lifted her head. I waved both hands, and she spotted me and waved and blew kisses.

The first thing I'd done with my preseason signing bonus was get Momma out of the tiny house and into a newly built home. I didn't want her working anymore, but she'd pushed back, telling me she couldn't sit all day doing nothing, so she got a job at the library and led the children's story hour. Theo continued to work construction. Momma had given him capital, from the money I'd given her, to set up his own company.

The music started, and the announcements began. Finally, it was time, as the line slowly moved up. I'd gotten my business degree and was determined not to be the country bumpkin people thought. I'd studied my contracts and had made Ezra go over every endorse-ment deal with me.

"Brody Martin."

I walked across the stage, knowing Momma would be recording me, and accepted my diploma from the dean.

"Proud of you, son. Go do great things."

"I'll try, sir."

I held up the rolled paper, and my teammates cheered. I spied Dev near the end of the line, fist-pumping and yelling. I gave them all a holler and left the stage to take my seat with the others. When it was Dev's turn, I stood up and yelled as loudly as I could, then searched every row, hoping for a glimpse of his parents. I didn't see anyone but students clapping and cheering.

Shit. I can't believe nobody came to see him graduate. Dev had told me his parents wouldn't come, but I hadn't believed him.

With the ceremony complete and our caps tossed in the air, the crowds dispersed. I ran and found Momma talking to some of my teammates' parents.

"Momma, I'm here."

"Brody, baby." She held out her arms, and I picked her up and twirled her around.

"I did it, Momma."

"You sure did. Your daddy would be so proud of you."

"Here, look." I handed her the paper, which wasn't the official diploma that would come in the mail, but it was a copy that had my name and all the information. "You keep this."

She carefully put it in her purse. "What a beautiful day. It's perfect."

Theo lounged by her side. "Nice goin', Brody. Congratulations." I accepted a hug from him. "Bet you're hungry from standin' and waitin' so long."

"Yeah. I made a reservation at the Main Cut." Next to the Hawk, it was the nicest steak place in town and where we went for our family celebrations.

All the graduates and their families milled about on the great lawn of the campus, and my teammates and I talked about our summer plans—our group was going to Cancun for a week to hang out and relax before we had to report to our different training camps. I bumped fists and gave and received hugs from everyone's families. All my buddies were there except for the one I wanted to be with most.

"Where's Dev? Aren't his parents here? I'd love to meet them," Momma said, her face concerned.

"No, they're on their yearly European vacation," he spoke over my shoulder. "Why should my graduation stop them from touring the castles?" The brittle voice of my friend and lover made me wince even as he grinned and held out a hand to Theo. "Theo, my man. How's it shaking?"

"Great. Looking forward to being part of the Kings? They look good for the Super Bowl, I figure. They're my bet to win."

"You gambling on the games?" My brow furrowed.

His grin turned to a frown. " 'Course not. Just a figure of speech."

By now I should've resolved my issues with Theo, but I remembered all the days Daddy 'n me had spent swimming in the lake and him teaching me to fish, and I couldn't find a piece of my heart to share. It wasn't fair to Theo, and I vowed to be better.

"Sorry, Theo."

Momma smiled at me, and Theo nodded. "No worries, buddy."

"Hey, Brody. Congratulations."

"You too, Dev." We hugged, a bit awkwardly in front of everyone, but it was so good to be able to put my arms around him without fear. I breathed in his scent, and his eyes, bright with longing, flashed to mine for a second before we let go.

"Sweetheart. Come gimme a hug." Watching Momma hold Dev, pain hit my heart for him, knowing he was alone. "Are you sure your folks won't be here?"

"Absolutely positive."

She frowned and shook her head. Of course she couldn't understand, and neither could I. How did parents miss their child's college graduation? Even if Southern Miami, the football-proud university, wasn't where they'd wanted Dev to go to school, it was one of those milestones engrained in your life forever. "You come out to dinner with us, honey."

Dev's dark brows shot high. "Uh, I don't want to intrude…"

A pang of longing hit me hard, and I wished we could sit together at the table like all the other boyfriends and girlfriends with their parents.

"You're not," I said softly. "You shouldn't be alone tonight."

It was a wonderful meal, and Dev kept everyone laughing with his stories of living in New York City and the wild things he and his friends had done in high school. We'd ordered several bottles of champagne, and Momma had two glasses, which had her giggling like a schoolgirl. She fanned her pink face.

"I think I'd better get myself to the hotel and go to bed. I'm a little tipsy."

Theo finished his piece of graduation cake. "Come on, Faith. I'll get some coffee in ya."

Dev checked his phone. "The guys are all getting together tonight for a farewell. Wanna go? I have my car. I can drive you there and home after."

"Go on, honey," Momma insisted. "Have fun with your friends."

I kissed her cheek. "Thanks, Momma."

Surprising me, Dev kissed her as well. "Thank you for including me in your family celebration."

"Aw, honey. You're Brody's best friend. That makes you family."

Theo held Momma close and led her away. Dev and I walked to his car—a sleek black Porsche. "No back seat to fool around in." He laughed as he started the engine. "We'll have to wait until after."

"I'm sorry your parents aren't here."

His jaw tightened. "It doesn't matter." He took one hand off the wheel and slid it up my thigh. "You're the only person I want to be with. It's been torture with exams and everything. I missed you so damn much."

"Missed you too." Late-night stolen moments out of town weren't enough for me either. "Not like we're gonna be able to be alone tonight, hangin' out at Woody's. Everybody's gonna be there."

"True, but if you get a headache and I have to take you home early, I might wanna swing by the Hawk and visit our cabin again." His green eyes glimmered. "Remember how good it was that first time?"

A throb of lust hit me hard, leaving me breathless with desire. "Yeah. That was an incredible night."

"Let's do it again."

We spent our evening hanging out with our boys and finalizing plans for our trip to Cancun in two days. Lover bought a round of beers, and we raised our bottles. "To the beach."

Vette finished his and wiped his mouth. "Me and Dante are gonna room together."

"Cool. I think Brody and I will too." Dev kicked my foot. "Better not snore, country boy."

"Shut up," I growled, grinning like a fool, thinking of the week we'd spend together. All night. Just the two of us.

"C'mon, my dudes. It's our last time on campus together. Let's find some ladies and party." Dante had his arm around a pretty woman, and they took to the dance floor.

To everyone's surprise, Lover had started dating the woman he'd met the night of our Orange Bowl win, and they slow-danced, kissing and staring into each other's eyes. Vette approached a group of young women, and Dev and I followed him, exchanging glances, knowing the rules of the game.

Make it look real.

For two hours, we danced, bought the ladies drinks, took selfies, and signed whatever was thrust in our faces. After a bathroom break, Dev met me outside the door and caught my arm. He pulled me into the shadows.

"Ready to blow this joint?"

I touched the tip of my tongue to my lips. "I'm ready to blow you."

"Fuck me," Dev breathed. "Let's go."

I put on my most pathetic face and joined the guys at the bar. "I feel sick, guys. Gonna have to leave." My fake groan earned me a glass of water.

"Since I drove us here, I'm gonna take him home, then probably go to my place after and crash," Dev said.

"Aw, man. That sucks." Dante waved his hand. "Better make sure you're a hundred percent for the trip. 'Cause you know it's gonna get wild."

I forced a smile. "Oh, I know."

Dev nudged my shoulder. "Ready? I don't want you heaving in my car."

Nodding, I trudged out of the bar. We walked to Dev's car, and I slid into the passenger seat.

"You could've been a theater major with that performance."

I grinned. "Come on, Dr. Devil. Time for you to give me my exam. I think I need oral and internal."

Dev's gaze grew heated. "You better stop, or else I may jump you in the car, and that would be fucking uncomfortable."

The ride to the Hawk took about ten minutes, but I kept Dev entertained by teasing my hand up and down his bare thigh and over the zipper of his shorts.

"I can't wait to have this. All mine."

Dev panted and, with a strangled sound, pulled into the driveway of the Hawk. We raced to the cabin and made it past the front door, but I stopped and grabbed Dev.

"Brody," he groaned. "I—"

"Shh. I know what you want." I sank to my knees and tugged at his shorts until they fell to the floor. That gorgeous, thick cock sprang free, and I took him in my mouth. Those big hands played in my hair while his hips thrust fast.

"Oh God, oh God. I can't stop it."

I worked my tongue harder and went for the kill, slipping my finger past his sac to tease and play with his rim. The second I nudged inside him, Dev exploded, and I drank every drop he gave me.

Heavy-lidded green eyes met mine, and then Dev joined me on the floor. He made quick work of my zipper and jacked me off fast and dirty while he kissed me, our tongues tangling.

"*Mmm*, my God, what you're doing to me." He squeezed my sac and I threw my head back and hissed.

"Dev, please." He returned to rubbing me, precome coating his hand.

Dev growled in my ear. "Baby, we have a whole week in Mexico. This is just a taste. I can't wait to fuck you to the sound of the ocean. Stuff you full of me. Gonna make you scream 'cause I love to hear you call out my name."

"Dev," I moaned, grabbing his shoulders while I writhed and shook under him.

"Brody, baby. We have to make this last. I'm gonna miss you so fucking bad."

"Me too. I don't wanna think about it." It was the black cloud hanging over us, the only ugliness in the perfect world we'd created.

He kissed me and I came, shouting his name against his lips as my come coated his shirt. I held on to him, breathing his sweat and heat, and he pulled me close. His mouth tasted sweet, our frenzied kisses turned languid and gentle.

"I don't know what I'm gonna do without you when you're gone."

"Me neither, Dev."

The end game was to make it through each day until we had to say good-bye.

CHAPTER FOUR

Dev

Two years later

I unlocked the front door of my parents' town house and wheeled my suitcase behind me. Hugo, their house man, greeted me with a smile.

"Devlin. It's so nice to see you again. Welcome home."

I wouldn't correct him by saying my parents' house had never been home to me. Hugo had worked for my parents for more than thirty years. Never married and devoted to his job, he kept their schedules and the house running.

"Great to see you too, Hugo. Are they here?" To say that receiving a text from my father asking for my presence was a surprise would be the understatement of the year. The fact that they'd instructed me to bring evening attire was puzzling, but I was sure they'd fill me in.

"No. They're at a luncheon benefit for the library."

"Oh."

Seeing the confusion on my face, he held out his hand. "Let me take your luggage to your room. They said to make yourself comfortable. I have a light snack prepared for you, unless you'd like something more substantial."

"Thanks. That's great, but you don't have to wait on me. I'll take it upstairs myself."

"Well..." For the first time, Hugo seemed uncomfortable. "A few things have changed since you were last here. Your father took over your old bedroom as his study."

It shouldn't have upset me as much as it did, but my room had been the only place in this mausoleum of a house where I could be myself. My sanctuary not only from my parents' stifling rules of behavior and expectations but also for my sexuality. I'd spent hours reading up on Stonewall and the history of the gay rights movement and the toll AIDS had taken on the community.

The room at the top of the staircase had been mine, and to now see it co-opted by my father, the built-ins filled with books he'd written or edited, felt like an important part of my life had been erased. I left the office and saw Hugo waiting for me at the far end of the hallway, next to one of the guest rooms.

"Here we are," Hugo said brightly, but his downcast eyes told a different story. He knew what my parents had done to me.

"Thanks. I think I'll pass on the lunch for now."

"Whatever you like. Just press number one on the house phone as always, but you should have what you need."

He left me, and I lay on the bed, staring at the ceiling. For two years I'd been playing for the Kings, just a skip across the river to Brooklyn, yet my parents had never bothered to attend a single home game. Not even for the playoffs. I rolled onto my side.

"Probably a good thing. They would've berated me for losing. A *Summers doesn't come in second,*" I mimicked my mother's patrician voice. God, just half an hour in this house, and the walls were closing in on me.

With it nearing the end of the off-season, I missed Brody terribly, but he had endorsement commercials filming in London, Paris, and Rome. Prior to him leaving, we'd managed to coordinate our busy schedules and spend some uninterrupted time together. I relived our final night together.

"Do you know how much I hate watching you walk out the door?" I played with the ends of Brody's hair as we lay together, snug in bed. My personal assistant, Fallon, had found us a secluded fishing cabin, deep in the 9 Lakes region of Tennessee. We'd heard Vette talk about the area for years, and we'd managed two glorious weeks to ourselves. But now it was time to leave.

"About as much as I do leaving you behind, knowin' when I come home, it's trainin' camp and preseason and another six months of not seein' each other." His sigh gusted in my ear. "But I'd rather have half a year with you than nothin' at all. So I'll take what I can get."

I rolled on top of him. "You can have it all. Everything. You already do. Dammit, Brody, I didn't think it was gonna be so hard."

His fingertip traced my mouth. "I was taught it ain't worth having if it's too easy."

"*And I'd rather have you in my heart than nothing at all. We're gonna make it, Brody. As long as we keep our eyes on the prize. And know our end game is to be together.*"

So I was left to myself, which I hated, and I'd even contemplated flying to Europe to see him, but then my parents sent their cryptic message, and my first thought was, *Are they sick?* I immediately dismissed the idea. No germ would dare enter the bodies of the great Professors Leonard Summers and Sandra Roan-Summers.

I pulled out my phone.

Hi. What're you doing?

My phone pinged.

Night here. Gonna go eat with some of the actors on set.

I sighed.

Don't meet some sexy Italian man who'll whisper sweet nothings in your ear.

Brody responded immediately with a laughing emoji.

Why would I want anyone else when I've got you?

And he did have me. Body and soul. Every single inch. Happiness settled in my chest, and I sent a heart emoji in return.

"God, we were so dumb. Four years we wasted, too afraid to let each other know how we felt and what we wanted."

It was more than simple want, though. I'd never lacked for sex. It was easy enough to find guys like me—unable to come out, afraid because of family or the society they lived in. Fear walked hand in hand with shame. Not shame that I was gay, because I loved who I was. But shame that I didn't have the courage to come out and be that hero some kid might need, all because I wanted to play pro ball.

Being with Brody these past two years, taking our stolen moments where we could find them, I'd realized I craved a real life with him. The going-out-for-breakfast-at-the-diner, walking-hand-in-hand-on-the-street kind of life. Early on we'd decided to keep our relationship secret, knowing if we did come out, our careers would most likely be finished before they'd barely had a chance to begin. It hurt like hell, and we hated lying to our friends, but we didn't know what else to do.

"It sucks," I muttered, folding the pillow under my head. "We shouldn't have to hide. This isn't the Dark Ages."

Voices filtered through my closed door, and I sat up. "Speaking of the Dark Ages." I hopped out of bed and opened my suitcase to change, then decided against it. My parents would have to take me as they found me.

From the top of the stairs, I studied my parents as my mother gave Hugo her wrap. It had been more than a year since I'd seen them—I'd had to play on both Thanksgiving and Christmas. Not that I'd received an invitation to dinner for either holiday. When I'd called to speak with them, Hugo had informed me that they had been invited to a dean's home for Thanksgiving, and they'd spent the Christmas vacation skiing in Gstaad. I'd ordered takeout after I'd returned home from the games.

My mother, elegant as ever, had kept the same upswept blond hairdo which drew attention to her delicate bone structure. The black suit fit her bone-thin frame, and the artfully applied makeup made her appear ten years younger than her fifty-seven years.

As for my father, he stood tall and trim in a handmade charcoal suit, his once thick head of dark hair now salt-and-pepper, which only made him more distinguished. Here I was, the black sheep—hair longer than proper in their eyes, stubbled cheeks, and tattoos adorning my arms and body.

"Hello, Mother, Father." I descended the staircase to greet them. Neither had ever been called Mom or Dad. Certainly not Mommy and Daddy. The idea made my lips twitch. I couldn't imagine the horror on their faces if I ever called them that.

Thinking of Brody's mother and the close relationship they had, I made myself promise to try harder with them. Maybe now that I was older and successful, they would understand how I wanted to live my life.

"Devlin. Hello." My mother gave me her cheek and air-kissed mine. The stark contrast between this greeting and the hugs and sugar-scented kisses I received from Brody's mom couldn't have been more apparent.

"You're looking lovely as always, Mother. And Father, how are you, sir?" No back slaps or hugs. Merely a handshake and a brief nod acknowledging my presence.

"I'm well. You seem...healthy."

I grinned. "My last three away games were in the South, so I managed to grab a little pool time in between training and practices."

He grimaced. "I see."

My mother put a hand on his arm. "Why don't we sit in the living room? Hugo, could you bring some tea, please?"

"Of course."

I followed them into the pristine living room. Ebony wood floors offset the stark white walls and sofa. Oil paintings portraying still life hung on the walls. All as untouched as a museum. As a child, the only time I'd ever entered this room had been to receive a tongue-lashing from my father concerning my failures as a Summers.

"When did you arrive?" my mother asked.

"About an hour ago. Hugo said you were at a charity luncheon."

"Yes, for the library. We're giving a large donation to the science wing. Your father is gifting all his books and papers from the commencement of his career." Her lips curved in a smile. "We're very proud of him, aren't we?"

I realized I was included in that "we" and nodded. "Yes, of course. It's very exciting and a great honor, Father. Congratulations."

"Thank you, Devlin. There's an event being held Saturday night. I'd like you to attend."

Was it silly of me to be hopeful that this could be the start of a reconciliation between us? I was willing to put the hurtful past behind us if they were.

"I'd be happy to. Thank you for inviting me."

I could see my mother eyeing my arms, and I bit my tongue so I wouldn't make a flippant remark.

"It's formal attire. I can assume you have a tuxedo?" she questioned. "We did request for you to bring one."

"Yes, of course. I'm not always in uniform, you know. I've been to many events where a tux is required, including the ESPY awards that took place in Hollywood. Remember? I invited you to come because I was getting an award for the best play in a football game."

"We couldn't make it." Dismissive as always when I brought up my career, she sipped her tea. "But in reference to the dedication, we'd like you to promise that you won't speak to the press about football. Only about how proud you are of your father."

My brow furrowed. "How am I supposed to stop them from asking me? And why does it matter?"

My mother set her cup on the tray and fixed me with that steely gaze she was famous for in her lectures. "Because the night is about your father and his accomplishments. Not about you and football."

I hadn't wanted our discussion to turn acrimonious, but I couldn't resist a clapback. "Don't worry. I know you're not interested in my life. I'll make sure not to mention it at all."

"There's no need to get defensive, Devlin. Your mother is only looking out for me. I'd thought you'd be happy to attend as a family."

I wanted to shout that it wasn't my fault we hadn't been a family in years. I'd tried everything possible to get them to come to my high school and college games, but they were always away lecturing or too busy writing or at speaking engagements. Father's obligations were in Connecticut, and he would only come home on the weekends, while Mother remained in the city but was never available.

There was always an excuse, and when they'd failed to show for my graduation, I'd given up hope. This invitation could be the cornerstone for building a new relationship, one that I wanted, despite how they'd turned their backs on me. I'd seen how it should be, not only with Brody and his mom, but my other teammates and their families—always there. Always supportive and encouraging. And while it was nice to have my friends' families in my corner, even to see them attending my games if I happened to play close enough to where they lived, it wasn't the same as having my own parents cheering me on.

"I am happy that we can attend together," I told them, "and I appreciate the invitation. I promise I won't do anything to take the spotlight off you."

The shadow of a smile played around my father's lips. "Good. We'll leave at six p.m. The car will be waiting."

I nodded, unsure what to say next. They sat, comfortable in their silence, while my restlessness grew. Had I been dismissed? They hadn't asked a single thing about my life—personally or professionally.

"I bought an apartment in Tribeca. It's very nice. One day you should both come visit."

My father frowned. "I hope you're not throwing away money on frivolous things. I recall seeing you on the television in a sports car. Highly unnecessary in the city."

My temper flared, but outwardly I kept my cool. "Well, I hardly think real estate in the city is frivolous. I majored in economics and business management. Knowing I'd be making a lot of money, I wanted to make sure I understood my finances." I thought they'd be impressed and that it would alleviate some of their anger at my choice of career. "I'm fully aware that playing sports is for a limited time, and this way I have a viable degree."

"I still find it hard to understand." My mother sighed, disapproval and disappointment oozing from her every pore.

"What?"

"Why you chose this route when you could've been anything you wanted. You're intelligent, and yet you're wasting your life throwing a ball."

My eyes narrowed. "Football is way beyond a physical game. It's psychological. You have to memorize plays and understand your opponent. We learn people skills and how to work as a team. I do a lot more than simply throwing a ball."

"Most of these players can't even speak proper English. They get arrested for drugs or violent crimes. These aren't the people you should be associating with.

Even though you didn't apply yourself as we'd hoped, with our name, you could've attended any university, and yet you chose some no-name, backwater place."

Their snobbery was astonishing. I thought of Lovell, raised by a single mother who'd worked two jobs to put him and his six brothers and sisters through school—every one of them a success. Dante's parents, both in law enforcement, who made him call home every night so they knew he was safe, and text them that he'd landed safely after every flight. And Brody's mother, who'd barely had two nickels to rub together but was rich in love.

It took all my strength of will to remain calm. "My backwater place has one of the finest football programs in the country. I did the best I could in high school—I'm sorry I didn't live up to your expectations. But I love playing football. It's all I ever wanted. Can't you be happy for me that I'm living my dream?"

My mother didn't answer but rose to her feet, and I stood with her. "I'm going to rest before dinner." She walked away, leaving my father and me alone. Figuring he wasn't going to add anything of value to the conversation, I turned to leave.

"Devlin."

I stopped and faced him. "Yes, sir?"

"Now that your mother's left the room, let's talk, man to man."

Curious and a little amused, I returned to my seat. "What about?"

His green eyes met mine. "I've heard stories of how wild the lives of ball players are. I hope you're taking precautions."

Oh, this was fun. At the age of twenty-three, I was finally getting the lecture from my father about the facts of life. I blinked, pretending innocence. "Precautions? What do you mean? Like security?"

"No," he huffed. "Sex. As in protection. You don't want to get one of those bimbos pregnant. Your mother and I would never accept that. Your name has come up in passing among my colleagues, and it would be highly embarrassing to have to explain how a son of mine could be stupid enough to fall for that old trap." He pointed a finger at me and lowered his voice. "Don't think with your cock. Wrap it up."

Stunned by my father's language, I couldn't help laughing at the irony of the situation. "Don't worry. I promise you, I will never get a woman pregnant. I'm going to my *new* room."

This time when I walked out, he didn't stop me.

Saturday night, the three of us entered the benefit. I, ever the dutiful son, two steps behind my parents, stood aside and watched as they were interviewed and had their pictures taken on the step and repeat. A murmur rose from the crowd, and my heart sank. As anticipated, several press people recognized me.

"That's Devlin Summers, the football player. He's their son."

"Devil, look this way."

"Devil, can we get your picture with your parents?"

"Devil, what're your team's chances for the Super Bowl this year?"

Devil, Devil, Devil.

I could see my mother grow stiff and the storm of anger rise in my father's eyes. I put my hands up. "This night isn't about me. I'm here to support my father's donation of his books and papers, as well as my parents' extremely generous gift to the library. And I'd like to match that amount, in my parents' names. Public libraries are the backbone of our educational system, especially for anyone who's unable to afford to buy books."

The cameras didn't stop clicking and flashing, and I couldn't wait to walk away. I joined my parents, who stood on a receiving line to welcome people. The moment I appeared, the microphones switched to me, and the questions turned to me. I rushed to shut them down.

"Sorry, everyone. I'm not here as a sports figure tonight, and I don't plan to answer any questions. As I said before, I'm here solely to support my parents. Please respect that." I walked away, proud of myself for adhering to my parents' wishes. The thing was, I agreed with them. This night wasn't about me. I escaped to the reception area, heading straight to the bar, where I ordered a Reposado with lime and stood surveying the crowd.

A woman ordered a glass of champagne and stood by my side. "Nice turnout, considering the subject."

I grinned. "What? You're not into quantum physics and theories of relativity? Force equals M A and all that jazz?"

She laughed, eyes sparkling. "I prefer a different type of force and mass."

I didn't miss the double entendre and the interest in her eyes, but I didn't play along. She sipped her drink and tried again.

"I know you didn't want to talk sports with the reporters, but you have a pretty tough schedule this upcoming season."

"You're a fan, I see. I barely know the schedule yet." I chuckled. "And yeah, it's tough, but we've got the talent. The Kings are ready to bring the trophy to New York."

We finished our drinks and got another. She seemed content to stay by my side, and I was in no hurry to leave.

"How do your parents feel about your career choice? I'm sure they were surprised you wanted to play football."

I shrugged. "Yeah, but I had to do what I wanted, whether or not they approved."

"So they didn't? Approve, I mean."

I didn't answer right away, watching my parents work the room, shaking hands and making small talk. They moved in sync, not once looking for me. I'd been nothing but a photo op for them.

"They have their life, and I have mine."

"I'm sure they attend your games. You have that box and everything."

Was she angling for an invitation? My smile was thin as I placed my untouched drink on the bar. The air had become stifling. It was time for me to leave. "We've worked it out to our mutual satisfaction. I'm sorry, I have to leave. It's been nice talking to you."

Without saying good-bye to my parents, I left the library and walked down the block to call for a car, away from the crush. Within minutes, I was speeding up Fifth Avenue toward the park and my parents' brownstone. The car pulled up front, and I asked the driver to wait. I ran upstairs, packed my things, and returned to my ride.

Home in my apartment, I texted Brody.

I miss you so fucking much.

The next morning, I received an angry message from my father.

All we requested was that you not bring attention to yourself for one night, but you couldn't. You just had to speak to a reporter and insinuate we weren't good parents. You've devastated your mother.

"What the fuck are they talking about?" I growled, then saw the notifications from Fallon.

Dev. Call me. This isn't good.

Instead of listening to him, I clicked one of the notifications and groaned. "I can't believe she was a reporter. How the hell was I supposed to know?" Scanning the headline, I let out a vicious curse.

Devil Summers's personal hell. The superstar quarterback reveals the tense relationship between himself and his parents.

She proceeded to build upon what I'd said to her, drawing conclusions from my body language, apparently.

My stomach alternating between free-falling and cramps, I called Fallon, and he picked up before the first ring ended.

"Dev, I—"

"Yeah, I should've known something like this would happen. Just field any requests for comments and say whatever bullshit you think best."

"Of course. I've already started the ball rolling. I've put out this statement: *Devlin Summers unequivocally admires his parents' philanthropic work. They have a relationship built on mutual respect."*

Laughable, but it would get the job done. "Thanks. I knew I could count on you."

"Always."

Fuck my life. I threw my phone aside, wishing Brody were there with me. Only he could make me feel better, because after what happened, I knew my relationship with my parents had gone from bad to worse.

CHAPTER FIVE

Brody

A year and a half later

"You were awesome out there." I trailed my fingers across Dev's stubbled jaw.

He rolled over to face me. "Yeah. Just not awesome enough. Losing the Super Bowl by a field goal hurts like fucking hell." A tiny curve kicked up the corner of his lips before he pouted and fluttered his lashes at me. "I need something to make me feel better. Something only the MVP of the Pro Bowl can give me."

Only two weeks earlier, I'd played in the Pro Bowl and we'd won, 24-10. For my part, I'd caught two touchdowns and rushed for more than a hundred yards. Momma and Theo were in the stands, but I wished Dev could've been there as well. Players in the Super Bowl weren't eligible for the Pro Bowl, so he was with his team, preparing for the big game.

In a flash I jumped him, my knees straddling his hips. "Yeah? What've you got in mind?" I leaned in and kissed him. "How's that?"

A dramatic sigh filled the air, and Dev's lips twitched. "Not bad. But other parts of me need kissing too. They're feeling neglected."

Normally after a game we were too beaten up and hurting to want sex, but we needed each other so badly, it didn't matter. I gripped his stiff cock and took him deep, then lightly scraped my teeth against the hard shaft and tickled the slit. Dev groaned, hips bucking. I licked around the head. Salty precome slipped past my tongue, and I sucked harder, moving swiftly.

"God, Brody, I've missed you so damn much." Dev thrashed back and forth on the pillow, green eyes hazy with lust. "Need you."

"*Mmm*," I moaned, loving those words, and cupped his sac, my fingers reaching past his taint to play along his crease. "Give it all to me."

"Fuck, oh fuck," Dev cried out and came, hips punching quick and fast. He shuddered and lay under me, trembling, chest heaving.

I swallowed the flood of come he pumped down my throat and licked my lips. "Beats the hell out of any champagne."

Dev raised an arm, and I slid into the crook of his neck, tracing the tats with the tip of my tongue. I quivered when he gripped my dick. He expertly stroked me until I gasped and shot all over his hand. With his eyes pinned to mine, he licked each finger clean, then kissed me so I could taste myself in his warm mouth.

"I hate being separated." Dev tugged me closer. "And having to hide this...us."

I snuggled into his neck. "Me too, but there's nothin' we can do about it. At least for now. You just signed that big endorsement deal, and though companies say they're supportive, it's all bullshit talk."

The light in his beautiful eyes dimmed. "I know. And it sucks balls."

For almost four years now, Dev and I had found ways to be together, but it hadn't been easy. Getting alone time had been virtually impossible—we were in separate cities, and life had only gotten more chaotic, more scheduled. Endorsements and required public appearances ate up precious free time when we could've been together. We lived for this, where we could steal quiet moments for only the two of us and be ourselves.

"You know...now that the season's finished, it's still warm by me at home." I kissed Dev's neck. "Why dontcha come and stay for a while? It wouldn't look weird—everyone knows we're friends. You've done it for a week or so other years. Just extend it. You've got a block of free time, and so do I."

He played with my hair, twisting the strands around his fingers. "Yeah? That would be cool."

"Unless you've got other plans..." The less than enthusiastic response got me thinking that maybe he wasn't as all in as I was. No matter how much we texted during the course of a season, things could change. Living in New York, Dev had way more opportunities to meet other people—the bars and clubs could entice even a saint.

It wouldn't be too hard for a devil.

" 'Course not, you're my one and only plan."

Warmth flooded me at Dev's words, and I rubbed my foot on his leg, loving all the scratchy hair against my skin. I ran a hand over his pecs and chest, the hard muscle like a rock beneath my fingers. The man was in peak physical condition, and I was hungry with desire, needing this time to reconnect with him after the months apart. To show him how much I wanted him. In return, his fingertips played along my jaw, tracing my mouth. We were starved for touch, and lying skin to skin was almost as good as having sex. We hadn't left the bed in hours.

Dev sat up, propping himself up on the padded headboard. He'd booked a suite at a hotel, miles outside the game city, where it was less crowded. After giving the required interviews, he'd texted me his room number and left the door ajar. I'd become adept at pulling my cap low and not meeting people's eyes, making it through the lobby unscathed.

"Then what's the problem? We could spend the days fishin' and swimmin' before we gotta go to training camp. Just hangin' out."

"What about your mom and stepfather?"

I'd already thought it out. "Momma loves you, and Theo is a huge fan." My lips twitched. "I think he's a bigger fan of you than he is of me. Bring him a signed jersey or somethin'."

Dev's hand covered mine. "I'd love to spend the off-season with you."

Joy leaped through me. "Awesome."

"But right now..." That wicked grin appeared that never failed to get my blood burning and heart pumping. He reached for me, and I met his kiss in a greedy clash of lips and teeth.

One month later, I waited at the airport for Dev's plane. When I saw him striding out, chatting with fans and stopping to take pictures, my chest swelled with pride. About to go meet him, I felt a tug on my T-shirt and looked down to see a little boy staring up at me.

"Are you Blink Martin?"

"Jimmy, I told you not to bother the man." His apologetic mother gave me a quick, nervous smile. "I'm sorry."

"It's okay. Don't worry about it." I crouched to meet him eye-to-eye. "Yeah, I'm Blink. And your name's Jimmy? How old are you?"

"I'm five."

"No way. I thought at least seven or eight." I winked at his mother. "You a football fan, Jimmy?"

"Uh-huh. Me and my daddy. He's coming home from the war, and he promised we'd go to a game this year. I wish it could be the Lonestars. You're my favorite."

"That's cool." I spotted Dev, and a few yards behind him, a man in uniform in a wheelchair. Dev waved to me, but my focus was on the soldier.

"Daddy, Daddy." Little Jimmy sprinted to his father, and his mother hung back a moment.

"Troy was hurt by an IED. We're lucky all he lost was a leg. Others didn't get to come home. It's been hard workin' and takin' care of Jimmy alone and worryin' about Troy." She brushed away a tear. "I'm sorry to be babblin' on."

"Not to worry. I'm sure you're glad he's home."

"We've been prayin' for this day. I'm Amber, by the way. We're all huge fans of yours. Troy and I watched all your games. Blue Waves forever."

"Hey, Blink. Thanks for picking me up." Dev waited at my side, picking up the signals that something other than a meet and greet was happening. With Jimmy hanging on, the man wheeling Troy pushed the chair over to us, and Amber left me to hug and kiss her husband. Jimmy pulled at his father's arm.

"Daddy, look. It's Blink Martin." Troy's eyes bugged out when Dev waved at him.

"Hey, Troy. Thank you for your service. I'm sure you know my friend Devlin Summers."

Troy's jaw dropped. "Holy shi-moly." He caught himself, and we all laughed. "I never expected such a welcome home. My favorite player and Devil Summers, one of the Super Bowl quarterbacks? Amber, honey, how'd you manage this?"

Before she had a chance to answer, I stepped in. "We can't give away all our secrets, Sergeant. But, since Jimmy here told me you're such huge Lonestars fans, I'm gonna fly you and your family to see our opening game, all expenses paid, including the best suite at the hotel, and all your meals. Plus, you'll sit in my box and get to meet the players."

"Oh, my God," Jimmy yelled, jumping up and down while Amber and Troy gasped.

"Th-that's so generous, Mr. Martin."

"Blink, please. And it's the least I can do for someone who gave so much for our country. Give me your address and phone number, and I'll make all the arrangements."

Amber dug a pen from her purse. "I can't believe this. Thank you so much. You have no idea how much this means to us."

"Here, let me sign your shirt too."

Dev took the pen and signed Jimmy's T-shirt, then handed me the pen. Jimmy couldn't stop staring at his shirt.

Troy held out a hand. "Thank you. I hardly know what to say. Jimmy and I are such huge fans. We saved up to make the trip to your Orange Bowl championship game, and that was a night we'll never forget."

Dev and I shared a smile. "Us neither."

After we took a ton of pictures with not only Troy, Amber, and Jimmy, but all the other people in the airport who recognized us, we retrieved Dev's bag and went on our way.

Dev waited until we were out of the airport grounds and on the road before leaning over to kiss my cheek. "Hi."

I slid my hand on his thigh and squeezed. "Hi, yourself."

"I missed you."

"Missed you more. I've been down here while you and your team were partying it up in the Dominican Republic."

"We had obligations—endorsements and shit like that. Even for the losing team." He laced our fingers together. "But I couldn't wait to leave and be here, with you."

Excited to show off the project I'd worked on for the past year, I took the exit and traveled another ten miles, past large estates behind gates, separated by acres of grass and forest. Another few miles, and I pulled onto a road marked *Private*, driving to a large log cabin. Soaring trees threw shade all around, and the blue sparkle of a lake in the background beckoned.

"I told Momma you'd be stayin' here with me."

A slow grin crept up Dev's face. "Oh, yeah?"

"Yeah. She agreed it didn't make sense to waste money on a hotel when I've got this big new house."

He kissed me hard. "Waste not, want not."

My fingertips skimmed the sharp cut of his cheekbone and jaw. "I want *you*. So damn bad. Shit, Dev. I miss you all the damn time."

Dev's breathing accelerated. "Same, baby. I'm just not myself without you."

Something twisted in my chest, and I couldn't speak for a moment. Instead, I kissed him, sucking his tongue while his big, rough hand caressed my face.

"Let's go."

We didn't bother to take his bag out of my Jeep just yet—we were only gonna get naked. I pulled Dev into the bedroom and fell on him like a starving man. I couldn't get enough of him—that strong neck, those tight brown nipples, the hard-as-granite muscles. His thick cock rested flat on his belly, and my mouth watered, imagining its sharp taste. But Dev didn't lie there passively and let me dominate him.

"Ahh, no fucking way." With a catlike move, he flipped me under him, took my dick and sucked, hard, that wild, wicked tongue dancing on my throbbing length.

"Fuck," I cried out, unable to control my hips, thrusting to the back of his throat. His hum of pleasure vibrated along my shaft, and I twisted the sheets into knots as he worked me over. Dev pulled off me with a juicy *plop*, and sat on his heels. "Need to fuck you," he panted. "So bad. Gotta get inside you."

"Want that too." I opened the nightstand drawer to grab the lube and condoms. Dev tore the packet with his teeth and rolled it down, then lubed himself up. He reached out to slip a finger to me, but I shook my head. "No. Can't wait. Put it in me now."

Dev's eyes widened. "Are you sure—"

"I know it's gonna hurt, but I wanna feel you." My lips kicked up in a grin. "Plus, I got some toys I use when I miss you too much. I'll be okay."

Dev's grin matched my own. "I like it. Dirty boy. You'll have to show me later." He loomed above me and lifted my legs to his shoulders, exposing my hole. "This is mine." He lowered his head and licked my quivering rim, followed by my pulsing erection to my navel. "Every inch of you belongs to me. Only me. Mine. Forever."

"Dev," I whispered. Those possessive words sent a rush of heat through me, and my dick jerked, spilling out precome.

"Yeah. I mean it, baby. There's never gonna be anyone else for me but you. My Brody." His tongue, soft, wet, warm, played inside me, and I couldn't control my whimpers and cries.

"I love you," I called out. "I love you, Dev."

He lifted his flushed face, smiling wide. "I love you too. Always have." He pushed into me, filling up all the emptiness I learned to live with whenever he wasn't with me. "Always will."

It was a homecoming yet new to have Dev make love to me now that we'd said the words out loud. He thrust hard and deep. Sweat dripped from his brow, and his lips drew up in a feral grin. Blood rushed hot through my veins, and my head spun. My skin felt too tight for my body, and I ached as if I suffered from a fever. The mere touch of Dev's hard abs brushing my cock was almost painful in its pleasure.

"Oh, Jesus. Oh, God." The first touch of my hand to my dick sent me hurtling down the precipice, and I came, hitting Dev's abs, chest, and chin. He grabbed my hips, burying himself fully, and came with a harsh sigh. The throb and pulse of his cock sent me reeling again, and I clenched, wanting to hold him with me forever.

"Goddammit, you're so fucking perfect," Dev mumbled in my ear.

I slung a sleep-heavy arm around his neck and pulled him to me. "Perfect for you."

"You know it."

We slept a while, showered, and retrieved his luggage. "Momma's expectin' us for dinner. Family time." I watched him slip on a pair of shorts and a Brooklyn Kings T-shirt. "I did warn you."

"I know, and I don't mind. You know that." Those gorgeous green eyes of his darkened with sadness. "It's nice to be here with you all." From his bag, he took out a cap, jersey, and a T-shirt, plus a football. "Got them for Theo. Signed by all the players." Then a small blue box. "And this is for your mom. I hope she likes it."

Damn, he was sweet, and knowing he hadn't seen his parents in who knows how long, I hurt for him. Without him telling me, I knew he craved love. How could they treat their child like a stranger?

"You know Momma thinks about you. Always talkin' about you." I put my hand to my chest. "*How's Devlin? I don't know why they call him Devil. He's just the nicest.*"

Dev cackled. "She should only know the filthy, naughty dreams I have about her baby boy."

"Oh, yeah?" I kissed him, slow and sweet. "Show me later. In living color. For now, it's time to boogie."

"I'm ready." His arms full, Dev followed me to the Jeep, and we were off.

"Momma lives about five miles down the road." The house I'd built for her had a big vegetable garden and a place for her flowers, plus an indoor spa and a gourmet kitchen with all the bells and whistles. Because she'd asked, I'd given Theo a game room, complete with all the newest video games and high-resolution televisions.

I stopped the car in my usual parking spot, and with Dev on my heels, opened the door. "Momma? We're here."

I heard her footsteps, and a moment later she burst into the center hall. "There he is. Come and give me a hug, sweetheart." She held her arms out to Dev, who handed me the gifts and put his arms around her. The sight of the two people who meant the most to me in the world choked me up. My eyes stung.

"Ms. Faith, you look like a picture." Dev kissed her cheek. "If you weren't my best friend's mother, I'd be knocking on your door for a date."

Her cheeks pinked. "Oh, you silly boy."

"Sorry, but she's still married," Theo drawled with a smile.

"You know I was just kidding. How's it going, Theo?" Dev put out his hand, and Theo shook it.

"Great. Tough luck about the Super Bowl. Fucking ref made some bad calls."

I glared at him. I hated when he cursed in front of Momma.

Dev shrugged. "Is what it is. I brought you some stuff I think you'll like." He took the items from me and gave them to Theo, whose eyes popped wide.

"Daaaaamn. Thanks, man. These are awesome."

"Bet they'll look nice up on the wall, Theo, honey."

"They will at that, sugarplum." He checked out the signatures, his lips moving as he read.

"And for my gorgeous girl..." Dev handed her the box, and we watched as she opened it.

"Oh, my goodness." Her hand covered her mouth. "Devlin, it's so beautiful." She lifted the necklace, the diamonds glittering in the light. "You shouldn't have."

"He can afford it," Theo declared. "Why dontcha give it to me, and I'll put it away for you?"

Dev held out his hand to Momma. "Ms. Faith, I'd love to see it on you. Want me to do the honors?"

Theo and I watched as Dev put the diamond heart necklace on Momma.

"It's beautiful, like you." Dev kissed her cheek.

She touched it and peered in the mirror, admiring it. "Oh, come on now, I bet you say that to all your girls. I've got barbecue waiting, and Devlin's favorite devil's food cake. I know you boys want to go out on the town tonight, so everything's ready when you are."

"Yeah, it's Ladies' Night at the Kitty Kat Club." Theo's eyes lit up. "Y'all won't have trouble finding some sweet young things to dance with. This one"–he tipped his head to me–"hardly never goes out. Time to find yourself a woman, young man. Your mama needs some grandkids to spoil."

"Brody's still young, Devlin too. They're only twenty-five," Momma shushed him.

"Still," Theo insisted. "Kid does nothin' but fish, go to the gym, and hang out with his mother. I bet Devlin can take Brody out and show him a good time."

Dev hooked his arm in Momma's and threw me a wink. His eyes danced.

"I'm gonna try, Theo. I'm gonna do my best."

CHAPTER SIX

Dev

One month later

"I could get very used to this, you know."

Riding me, Brody peered from under the long strands of reddish-brown hair hanging in his face. He'd grown it out in the off-season, and I loved having something to hold on to.

"What? Me on top? Oh fuck, yeah. Right there. Harder."

Pleasure washed over me, and I tabled the discussion as I chased my climax, thrusting up into Brody. I gripped his hips, digging my fingers into his pale skin. I liked seeing my marks on him. We were two big men, and our lovemaking was passionate, loud, and very physical. Each of us bore the evidence of the other's touch.

Brody came a moment after me and rolled off, snuggling into my shoulder. The past month together had only cemented my feelings for him, the depths of which surprised even me. I'd never met a person I wanted more, not only physically, but emotionally. All the emptiness inside me vanished when we were together. I loved simply being with him. Sitting across the table in the morning, eating breakfast, then at the lake, fishing and swimming, watching him with his mother, and seeing all the good things he'd done for people, like showing up at the local day camp to play football with the kids and rebuilding the library after a storm destroyed the roof.

Brody Martin was the best man I'd ever met, and he was mine.

"Now what was it you were sayin'? Could get used to me on top?" His baby-blue eyes twinkled. "It's pretty fuckin' awesome, ain't it?" He bit my earlobe. "I still feel you."

I tightened my arm around him. "I do love that, but I meant just being with you. Living with you." I rubbed our cheeks together. "I wish we could do it all year long."

"Me too." Sadness clouded Brody's expression. "But I don't see that happening unless we're on the same team. Or when we retire." He brushed the hair out of his eyes. "But that's the plan, right? We finish playing, and we'll be together. It's okay."

I wanted to snap, *No, it's not okay. We shouldn't have to hide for a decade. Not anymore.* But it would hurt Brody, and it wasn't his fault. Or mine.

"Yeah. You and me, here or New York. I'd love to take you there and show you everything."

"Not sure I could live in a place with so many people, but I'm dying to see it. Maybe one day when we play there."

"Or..." I sat up, excitement brewing. "We could take a trip there. A few days away, just the two of us. I have to go to the city at some point to meet with my banker and sign stuff for the trusts my grandparents set up for me. Come with me."

"That would be nice."

"Let's do it. I'll have Fallon make all the arrangements. Poor guy's been bored to tears with me down here and no schedule to keep me in line. I have him going through all my fan mail. His cousin Kelsie–they're first cousins, but more like brother and sister–is doing all my social media with him, since I don't have time to figure that stuff out."

Brody nodded. "Yeah. Lizzie's been great as well."

"Have you told her about us?"

He shook his head. "No way. I mean, Ezra had her sign an NDA, but still..." He chewed his lip. "What about you?"

I dipped my head. "Yeah. Fallon is trustworthy. He's like family–actually, better than mine, for sure. And he'd never say anything. His brother and I were close friends and went to school together in the city. I've known him longer than almost anyone."

Fallon's brother, Rory, had died in a car accident. At the funeral, Fallon had cried on my shoulder and told me his parents refused to accept he was gay and told him to leave their house. And because he was eighteen and considered an adult, they'd cut him off, not only emotionally, but financially as well, even going so far as to withdraw their payment for his college tuition. Afraid he might do something drastic, I'd paid all his expenses, and after he graduated, he'd come home from California to work for me. Aside from Brody, he was the only one I'd told about my sexuality.

"Make sure he schedules me in for some Devil time."

I rolled on top of him. "You're twenty-four-seven. Do you not want to go? You don't seem too excited."

"I do. It's just..." Brody shifted away, and I grabbed his wrist.

"What is it? Tell me. No secrets."

"I don't belong there. I'm small town. Country."

I cupped his jaw, forcing his eyes to mine. I hated the self-doubt swimming in those blue depths. "You belong anywhere you want. And where I want you is by my side." I kissed him. "Let it sit for now. We'll go out tonight and get wild."

Brody still looked unsure. "Are you mad? It's silly, but I'm more the quiet type. When I'm in Austin and we're not playin', all I do is spend time at my house there, by the pool, or I find a place to go fishin'."

"I know. It's very pretty there." I'd visited him a few times. "And it was just an idea. I really do love being here with you. And your mother's awesome. I think I gained ten pounds this month." I rubbed my stomach. "Coach Jackson is gonna get on my ass. We should start running and hit the gym." I tangled my fingers in the hair at Brody's nape. "Sex isn't burning enough calories."

"Maybe we ain't giving it enough of the old college try."

Snickering, I kissed him. "Let's get dressed."

It wasn't as if we had a vast choice of drinking establishments, but the one that saw the most action was the Kitty Kat Club. I'd expected a strip club atmosphere, but it was a surprisingly decent spot with a DJ spinning tunes and drinks that weren't too watered down.

We walked in to shouts of welcome—after a month, they knew us and our drink orders. Brody with the bottle of beer he always drank because of his endorsement, and me with my Reposado on the rocks with lime. Within minutes, we had a group surrounding us, some dudes but mostly ladies.

We'd agreed when we were out to put on as good a show as possible—a little kissing and touching allowed but nothing more. So I sat and watched as Brody took to the dance floor with a tall blond who wrapped around him like a python. And I didn't say no to Beth, the curvy redhead who'd been eyeing me since we walked in. We danced across the floor, and she nuzzled me and kissed my neck while I watched Brody's girl rub up on him and kiss his cheek. He smiled down at her.

A possessive growl of annoyance rumbled from my chest. Beth thought it was for her and purred in my ear, "That's so sexy. Wanna get out of here?" She pressed kisses to my chest.

"Sorry, but I gotta stay put." So it wouldn't seem strange that I wasn't giving her what she wanted, I dipped my head and kissed her cheek. She tried every twist and turn to get me excited, but my mind was on Brody. From the corner of my eye, I saw his girl lead him to a dark corner. I trusted him with my life, but I didn't have to like that he could touch a random woman in public but not me, the person who knew him better than anyone in the world.

I threaded my fingers through Beth's silky hair and pecked her on the tip of her nose. "Buy you a drink?"

Hazy-eyed, she fluttered her lashes. "Yeah, sure."

We took a seat at the bar, and she ordered a sea breeze while I homed in on Brody. I watched the blond run a hand up his chest while the other went to his belt buckle. Brody shook his head, and I breathed a sigh of relief when he took her hand and led her back to where we were sitting.

"Hey, you two." I raised a glass. "What're you drinking?"

The girl wrinkled her nose. "I'm out." With a swing of her hips and toss of her hair, she left. Brody shrugged and held up a hand to Janie, who was behind the bar tonight.

"Another one, please."

"You got it." Janie was the owner of the Kitty Kat, and we often spent more time talking to her about football than we did dancing. Her husband was the manager at the local big hotel chain and also worked nights. She handed Brody his beer. "Don't mind that one. She's a star fucker."

Brody's eyes widened while I choked swallowing my drink. "Damn, Janie, warn a guy."

She shrugged. "Sorry. But Desiree was a cheerleader in high school and always went for the athletes. College too, from what I heard." Her grin was sympathetic. "Goes through 'em like Skittles. No offense, but you mighta just been another notch in her bedpost."

"I hope you don't think I'm like that," Beth said to me, pouting as if she'd lost her sure thing.

"Of course not, but I'm just hanging out with my buddy tonight." I figured to get it out in the open.

Disappointment clouded her eyes, and she pouted, but I remained steadfast, and she shrugged. "Okay. Could I, uh, get a picture with y'all?"

"Of course."

Janie took her phone, and Brody and I, plus me alone, took a bunch of pictures with her.

She kissed my cheek. "Thanks. I work morning shift at the Main Street diner if y'all ever wanna come by for waffles."

She drifted off into the crowd. Maybe I was wrong for leading her on, but with Brody around, it was tough keeping up a façade. All I wanted was to be with him.

We sat for a while, signing autographs and taking pictures. At midnight, I leaned into Brody.

"Wanna go?" I whispered in his ear. "I'm ready to be alone with you."

Brody set his bottle on the bar top. "I was ready when we got here."

I grinned and waved Janie over to pay our tab. "Close us out, please. And put Beth's drinks on it as well."

"You got it."

I handed her a wad of twenties. "This is for you."

She stuffed them into the back pocket of her jeans. "Thanks, guys." The bar was emptying out. "Stop by anytime. You're a great draw for business."

"Always happy to help." I winked at her.

"Maybe we could do a fund raiser one night. Charge a cover and donate it to the local homeless shelter. My brother—he's a cop—said we've gotten a lotta young runaways lately."

I checked with Brody and could see the interest in his eyes. "I'm good with that. We'd have to check with our agent to make sure it's okay, but I'm sure he'll say it's not a problem."

"Awesome. Lemme know."

We walked to Brody's Jeep and sat in the car. "I like the idea," Brody stated, starting the engine. The headlights swept across the two-lane road. "It ain't like New York here. We don't get as much help for people as we'd like."

"I'm sure it'll be fine." I waited until we reached his house and he cut the engine. "We can meet Ezra when we take that weekend trip to the city."

Brody nibbled on his bottom lip. "Yeah."

"Why do I feel like you're really not in favor of this?"

"Let's go inside."

Once seated in the living room, Brody kicked off his sneakers and lay with his head in my lap. I stroked his hair.

"Talk to me."

"Dontcha think people will talk? First you're spending all this time with me here; then we go to New York City together? All these eyes on us…"

I frowned. "I hadn't thought of it like that."

"I think you should go alone."

My fingers, which had been stroking his cheek, stopped. "Is that what you want?"

He grabbed my hand. "No. 'Course not. I wish I could be with you every minute of every day. But we agreed when we started seein' each other that we'd have to keep it quiet between us."

Realistically, I knew he was right, but I didn't like it. "I guess it makes sense."

"I know you hate havin' to hide. I do too." Brody kissed my fingers. "How about while you're doin' that, I'll go to that center Janie mentioned and meet the kids and find out more about them."

I bent down and kissed him. "You are such a good person."

Brody's lips curved under mine. "And you're good for me."

I knew I had the better part of the deal. Brody might've grown up with next to nothing, but he'd always known love—how to give and receive it. I'd had everything I could possibly want from birth, except the one thing I'd craved—my parents' time and approval. Meeting Brody, learning how to be a loving partner, had helped me grow forgiveness in my heart. His love gave me hope that as dark as it looked, there might be a light in the future.

"I'll call Ezra in the morning."

Four days later, I sat in Ezra Green's offices in midtown Manhattan. He had a spectacular view of the city, but I was more interested in the pictures on his credenza. He noticed where my attention was directed.

"My family." He reached over and picked up two photos. "This is Roe and me at our wedding. And Roe's grandmother, dancing her heart out."

"You never had any issues about your relationship? From your families, I mean."

Before answering, Ezra set the frames in their places. "Roe's family was never an issue."

"Yours was?"

He sighed and laced his fingers together on the desk. "They had hopes I'd marry a woman and have a family. They went so far as to try and keep Roe and me apart."

The soft smile indicated that the attempt was unsuccessful.

"But you're married."

He held up his finger and wiggled it to show off his ring. "We are. Happier than ever and thinking of starting a family."

It was obvious how deeply in love Ezra was with his husband. "How did you get them to come around?"

Instead of answering, Ezra left his chair and joined me in the second chair in front of his desk.

"You're asking an awful lot of personal questions, Dev. Is there a problem with me being gay and representing you? I've never made a secret of my sexuality, and I didn't expect it to be an issue for you."

A simple question that I only needed to answer *no*. But I didn't want to. Heart pounding, I rubbed my face with my hand and said the words I'd kept under wraps. "I-I'm gay. And it's been hard as hell living in the closet. Aside from my PA, and my boyfriend, you're the only person I've told."

Stunned by my confession, Ezra's green-gold eyes searched my face. He rolled his chair closer to me and took hold of my hands. "Thank you for trusting me. You know you can tell me anything, Dev. I'll always keep your secrets, even if I wish I didn't have to. But in the sports world, especially football, I understand why you're keeping it to yourself."

"It's been so fucking hard," I whispered, almost in tears. I brushed at my lashes. "Some tough-guy image, huh? Who'd think I was the hard-partying Devil Summers if they could see me now?"

"Fuck that shit," Ezra blasted out. "I hate how people equate sports with manliness. Don't fall into that trap."

I sniffled, wiping my eyes with the heel of my hand. "Yeah, I guess so. But I can sure as shit guarantee that the endorsements would dry up. Am I right?"

He nodded. "Yeah, I'm sorry to say. I think a lot of them would. And I'm not telling you to come out publicly. That's a decision you and only you can make." His face cleared, and a slight smile tugged up his lips. "You have a lover...a boyfriend. I'm glad you don't have to go through this alone."

I met his eyes. "I do. But I'm not willing to talk about him. He-he's also private about his personal life."

"Understood. Just know I'll always be your safe space. And regarding the benefit you and Brody want to get involved with, it's a good one. I checked into the shelter—they've taken in many homeless youth and young people who've got no place to live due to losing their jobs, medical bills, or their families turning them out because of their sexuality. Sometimes they assist entire families."

"Great. I'm glad. I'll let Brody know we can go ahead."

Ezra leaned back in his chair. "How's it been, living in the country? Must be a shock to a city boy like you. Nice for you to hang out with your best friend."

Was he fishing for information? I didn't think so, but even if Ezra guessed, I trusted him to keep my secret—mine and Brody's. And thinking of how I'd left Brody, in our bed, sleepy-eyed, hair tangled and my marks all over him, I couldn't wait to go home to him. Being without him these few days only exacerbated my loneliness. I should've been able to visit my parents, but after their last text, I couldn't. So I didn't.

"You know what? It's a whole lot better than I'd have expected." A thought popped into my head, but before I talked to Ezra, I had to speak to Brody. "I have an idea, but I can't talk about it until I check a few things out."

Ezra's eyes crinkled shut with his laughter. "Nothing I like better than a mystery. Call me when you're ready to let me in on the secret."

I gave him a hug. "I will."

I had to get home to Brody and tell him what I was thinking. Hopefully, we'd be on the same page.

CHAPTER SEVEN

Brody

Momma always told me impatience wasn't a good look, but dammit. Four days without Dev, and I missed him. Before he'd come to stay with me, I'd gotten used to the silence of my house and being by myself. Now, I woke up in the middle of the night, and there were no feet tangled up with mine. No big arms holding me close. No kisses or laughter across the table.

It sucked being alone.

Finally, the plane landed, and I waited for Dev to appear. I knew he'd sat in first class and only had a carry-on, so he'd be out first. And there he was, of course talking to people with stars in their eyes. Always there for the fans, he stopped and took pictures with them and signed autographs. He glanced up and spotting me, pointed, and next thing I knew, we were together and surrounded.

"Welcome back," I murmured as we stood and people took out their phones. "You'll have to wait to get home for a proper greeting."

He winked. "I'm counting on it."

After close to ten minutes, Dev hefted the bag on his shoulder. "Okay, guys. Blink and I gotta get goin', but we're in town, getting ready to do a fund raiser for the shelter on Walnut Street. Posters will be going up, so keep an eye out. We'll be doing meet and greets and raffles, so you won't want to miss it."

An excited buzz rose through the crowd, and Dev and I made our getaway. He waited until we'd hit the highway, then leaned over, kissed me, and sighed.

"I missed you."

I took his hand in mine. "Same. I was thinkin' how much I used to like bein' by myself after a full season surrounded by the team, but it ain't true. Not anymore."

Dev played with my fingers. "Yeah. Instead of calling people I know to meet and hang out, I sat in my apartment, staring out the window, wondering what you were doing."

"So you didn't hit the clubs or go out?" I knew I didn't have to worry about Dev stepping out on me, but it was good to hear it from his lips.

"Why bother? The only person I'd want to be with is you. I'm tired of faking it to make everyone else happy. When do we get our chance?"

I didn't have an answer for him, and I squeezed his hand. "I don't know."

Once home and sitting together on the couch, Dev's head in my lap, he reached up to grasp me around the neck and bring my lips to his.

"I told Ezra I'm gay."

"You...did? Why?" Fear shot through me, and it must've revealed itself on my face because Dev shook his head. "No. I didn't mention you at all, if you're worried. That's your story to tell, not mine."

"I'm not worried. I know you wouldn't. But what made you do it?"

Sighing from his whole chest, Dev swung his legs over the couch and sat up to face me, more solemn than I'd ever seen him. "I was in his office and saw the pictures of him and his husband. He's married and happy. They're going to have a family. I-I got so angry that because of what we do, we're forced into this corner, where we can't have that. If anyone could understand, it's him. So I told him."

"He's a good guy."

"He is."

Something changed in Dev's expression. I knew him so well by now that I could tell there was more.

"And what else?"

Nervous wasn't a word in Devlin Summers's vocabulary. He attacked everything with the confidence he'd been born into. But here he was, chewing on his lip. Hesitant. So I waited.

"As I sat in Ezra's office, I got an idea. About how we could be together."

I frowned. "What're you talkin' about?"

Those bright-green eyes flared to life. "It's almost four years that we're playing now. Our rookie contracts are coming up."

"Yeah, I know. Ezra told me he's had offers from other teams, but I don't wanna move farther away."

"How about closer?" Dev cupped my cheek. "What if you came to the Kings?"

I stared at him. "What? Your team?"

Excited, he nodded. "It's the perfect answer. The Lonestars don't need a quarterback—they've got their starter, who's great, and they just signed the top draft pick last year, so it wouldn't make sense for me to go to your team—and Ezra said the Kings are gonna make me a great offer, he's just working out the details. But...what if you could come play on the Kings? We need offense, especially someone big and strong yet quick. You're one of the top tight ends in the country. The Kings like their stars. The fans demand it, and they have the payroll for it."

"I-I dunno. I never thought about it. What did Ezra say?"

"I didn't mention it to him because I wanted to talk to you first. Plus, I'd just come out to him and said I had a boyfriend." He brushed his lips to mine. "I think he'd figure it out pretty easily if I mentioned bringing you to my team."

"Wow, I guess...yeah...that could be amazing. But wouldn't they have already made inquiries if they were interested?"

"Not necessarily. You know how fast these things can happen. Right now they're focusing on defense, but I know one of our tight ends has been talking about retiring lately. You can talk to Ezra about it, and he can put out feelers. The Kings have a solid general management team, always searching for the best. Their owner is gay. If anything damaging ever happened to us, I bet we'd have his support."

"Yeah, that's true. I've seen articles about him." Anticipation rushed through me. "It would be pretty fuckin' awesome to be on the same team again."

Dev grinned. "Yeah. It really fucking would be. And you can get a place in the city—it doesn't even have to be near mine. But we'd be with each other, all the damn time." He kissed me. "I want that so much."

Freshman year, if anyone had told me that the gorgeous quarterback with the wicked smile and the devil in his eyes would be my lover, I would've asked them what they were smoking. But here we were, almost eight years later, and he was the love of my life. I'd do anything to be with him.

"I want it too. Let's do it."

Dev reached for me. "We can call him later."

I met his hungry lips in a burning kiss. "Yeah, later."

Much later, I set up the grill while Dev swam in the lake. It was near dusk, and we'd spent the whole afternoon in bed, rediscovering each other as if we'd been separated for months instead of days. I'd thought it would be hard and fast, but Dev took his time, leaving not a single inch of my body untouched by his lips and tongue. I returned the favor, loving his shouts of passion and how he held me tight as he came. I ached all over, but I couldn't stop grinning.

"I love seeing you like this." Wrapped in a towel, Dev walked up the steps to the deck and joined me. "It makes me happy."

"You're the one who makes me happy." I flipped the burgers and set the spatula on the table. "The only one."

"Same." Dev kissed me. "Have I told you how fucking sexy you are with the longer hair?" He twirled his fingers in the waves. It was past my ears now, and I'd taken to holding it back in a short bun when I exercised.

"Yeah, every chance you get. I figure I'll keep it until the season starts. It'll be too much of a pain to keep up with under the helmet." I laughed at Dev's pout. "Don't get grumpy. I'll grow it out next year."

"Good. I'm gonna run and take a shower before we eat. Then go to the Kitty Kat? We can talk to Janie about the fund raiser."

"Yeah, sounds like a plan."

Hearing the water running and getting the table on the deck set up for dinner, I thought about how nice it would be to be able to do this all the time. Football was great and had already given me so much, but damn, there was somethin' to be said about the simple life of being with the person you loved and sharing the quiet moments.

"You have a very serious look on your face." Dev slipped his arms around me, and I leaned into his broad chest. Droplets from his wet hair slid down my cheek.

"I was thinking about us. And the future."

"Me too. If you can get this trade and we can be together, it'll change everything."

I turned to face him. "Yeah, but there's somethin' I didn't consider."

"What is it?" He searched my face, and his breath caught. "Your mother. You don't wanna leave her here."

I hung my head. "I know it's silly, but—"

"No. It's one of the things I love about you. How much your mother means to you. Why not wait until the offer is made? Maybe she'll want to live in New York."

I made a face. "No way she's gonna leave. She's spent her whole life here. She loves the country."

Dev grinned. "You know, we have grass and trees there too. She can live on Long Island or Westchester. Or farther north, where it's as rural as it is here."

"Yeah, sure."

He patted my cheek. "Oh, ye of little faith. One day I'll take you there, and you'll have to eat your words."

"Right now I want my burger. I'm hungry."

We ate and headed to the Kitty Kat. Janie gave me a hug and kissed Dev.

"I was worried you was gonna leave and not come back."

"Who, me? Nah. You're stuck with me," Dev told her. "I like it here so much, I'm thinking of getting a little place so I don't have to camp out at Blink's all the time and cramp his style."

I rolled my eyes. "Yeah, right. Go on with yourself."

He winked at me and took the drink Janie handed him. "Busy tonight."

She worked as she talked. "Yep. And I ain't complainin' about it. So." She paused and took payment from several customers. "You guys up for the benefit?"

I set my bottle on the bar top. "Yep."

Dev swallowed and nodded. "Yeah. I was thinking raffles—stuff like signed merch and photos, and meet and greets. We might even be able to get some of our buddies from other teams to come if they don't have commitments."

Her eyes lit up. "Awesome. When were you thinkin'?"

I met Dev's eyes. "We'll have to call everyone and let you know tomorrow or the day after. That okay?"

"Yeah, 'course. Thanks, guys. This is really gonna help. They've gotten a lot of newcomers lately and can't handle the overflow."

"They need a new building or another one."

"All it takes is money." She shrugged, and Dev raised his brows.

"We'll let you know," Dev said. We went to grab a table. "Are you thinking what I am?"

I scratched my cheek. "If what you're gonna say is to buy them another building and renovate it, then yeah."

"Not only renovate it, but make it a usable place. Swimming pool, a ball field, swings...a whole rec center. And it'll have the added benefit of creating jobs for the local community."

I wished I could lean across the table and kiss him. Instead, I smiled. "Yeah. I'm loving it." I lowered my voice to a whisper. "And you."

His answering wink was all I needed.

Two months later, Dev and I stood before the construction site of the twenty-thousand square-foot vacant warehouse we'd bought. Renovations had started immediately. Inside, the space would be divided into living quarters, several kitchens, and gathering spaces with televisions, video games and computers, a library and playrooms. Outdoors, the landscapers were laying sod on what was planned to be a baseball field, the pool area had been dug, and our foreman was pointing out to the builder where the playground would be located. Forty acres of land gave us a lot to work with.

"Looking awesome, isn't it?" Dev nudged me and flipped up his sunglasses.

"Incredible how quickly it all came together after the benefit."

Dante and Lovell had jumped on board and made the trip, but Everett was in Europe, doing a promotional tour. He sent a big check and did a Zoom call with fans. The benefit had raised half a million dollars, mainly because we'd convinced our teams and sponsors that it would be amazing press for them to contribute to such a worthy cause.

It had been great hanging out with the old gang, and though Dev and I had to cool our relationship in front of them, when it was time for them all to leave, I missed them like hell.

My phone buzzed, and Ezra's name flashed up on the screen. "It's Ezra. Maybe he's got some news about a new contract."

The day after Dev returned from New York, I'd called Ezra and casually mentioned I'd be interested in fielding offers from East Coast teams, specifically the Brooklyn Kings. He didn't question my change of heart and had been sending me texts of offers from other teams, as well as the Brooklyn Kings.

"Hello? Ezra?"

"It's me. And as my husband's grandmother would say, have I got a deal for you."

With each clause he read to me, my brows rose, until Dev tugged at my arm, hissing, "What? What?"

"Uh…so what do you think, Ezra? It sounds like a win to me."

"I want to see if they'll help your mother relocate."

"That would be great."

"Yeah. I had a few things to counteroffer them. They're pretty minor, but I have to make it look like we're not too eager."

I chuckled. "I hear ya. Well, I'm on board with it, and you know my buddy is all for it."

"I'm sure he is," Ezra murmured. "How is Dev? You two get that shelter fixed up and running?"

"Yeah, and thanks for sending us all that merch from all your other clients. Movie and television star autographs brought in a ton of money. We had the old building updated, and the new one is under construction."

"Excellent. All right. I'll contact the Kings, and I don't expect much pushback. They need you, plus they want to keep their quarterback happy."

My face burned. Ezra had to know Dev and I were together, but I wasn't about to tell him on the phone. Coach had always taught us that face-to-face was the way to handle your business, personal or professional.

"Thanks, Ezra. Appreciate it."

"That's what I'm here for. And when you get to the city, I hope you and Dev will have dinner with my husband and myself."

Dev gave me a thumbs-up.

"Yeah. I'd like that, and I'm sure Dev will too. Take care, Ezra. Talk soon." I ended the call.

"Well?"

I grinned. "Start spreadin' the news."

CHAPTER EIGHT

Dev

It was opening day for the new shelter, and a huge crowd had formed. The town had basically shut down, and Brody and I had hired a band, food vendors, and everything needed to keep children entertained. Everett had returned from his promotional tour and joined us. We'd all taken turns showing the kids—and quite a few parents—how to throw and catch a ball, and now Everett was posing for pictures.

I chomped on a hot dog. "Vette's got an admirer." I tipped my head to the woman who'd been hovering by his side for the past hour, getting him bottles of water and a towel to dry his sweating face. Brody frowned.

"I went to school with Dora Lee. She had it rough. Her father went to jail, and her momma was killed in a car accident. Her grandparents raised her, and they were stricter than a state-prison warden. When she got pregnant by a Black guy, they tossed her out on the street, the racist pigs. She lived in the shelter for years while trying to take care of the baby and working at the local supermarket."

I huffed and shook my head. "I don't understand family who turn their backs on their kids."

"Me neither." Brody kicked at the ground, and I could see something was eating away at him.

"What's wrong?"

He chewed his lip. "I think before I leave, I'm gonna tell Momma."

This wasn't a conversation to have in the middle of a fair. I led him to one of the picnic tables set up under tents. The area was emptying out, as it was getting close to dinnertime and most people were playing games or had already left.

"You sure?" I asked him. "What made you decide now?"

"It's time. Plus, with me leavin' and all, it'll be easier if she's not okay with it."

Under the table, where people couldn't see, I nudged his foot. "Are you still upset she's not coming with you?"

Those big blue eyes reflected the painful talk they'd had. "I guess."

"You never told me about it. Only that she wanted to stay."

"Dev—"

"No. Please, Brody." My eyes expressed what I couldn't show him with actions. "Talk to me."

"She's lived here all her life and it's too late to make a switch. That's all."

I crossed my arms and glared at him. "Bullshit. You're lying."

"The fuck you call me a liar." He scowled at me.

Our first real disagreement. I leaned in closer. "Baby, I love you, but I know there's more." He hung his head, which only solidified what I suspected. "Did it have anything to do with me?"

First he paled, then turned red, and that was all I needed to know. "No, 'course not."

"Please? You won't hurt my feelings. I'll always love you and your mom."

He lifted a shoulder and clasped his hands on the wooden table. "She really did say she wasn't interested in moving because her whole life was here with Theo. So I teased her and said I thought I was her life. I told her we could go to Broadway and have real good pizza. See the tree at Rockefeller Center at Christmas."

It all sounded pretty innocuous to me. "But something happened."

His fingers gripped tighter, the knuckles turning whiter. "You know Momma loves you."

It was as I suspected. My smile was thin. "Yeah. I know."

"Baby—"

"Please." I held his gaze. "Tell me."

Brody gave a sharp nod, then a sigh of defeat. "Okay. I made all the arguments I could, and she didn't say anything. Finally, she looked up at me and asked if I was doing all this because of you."

"Me? You mean because we're together?" The last few words were said in a whisper as I spotted several people walking toward us.

"No. It was more like, am I making this big decision to follow you. That's all."

That was enough. My heart sank. I thought Brody's mom and I got along, certainly better than I ever had with my own mother. For her to think Brody was coming to New York simply to be with me and not doing what was best for his career devastated me. Early on, when my parents had told me over and over how I'd disappointed them, I'd learned to hold that pain inside. But God, it hurt. Badly. Now I knew I had no one completely on my side except Brody, and even then, I was tearing him apart with this decision. I wasn't being fair to him.

"What did you say?" I asked in a low voice.

"Don't look like that," he pleaded. "You know how I feel. Nothin' and nobody could ever make me do anything I didn't wanna. And I told you it was a long shot that she'd wanna move. But that won't change my mind or how I feel about you. Nothing ever could."

Hoping my smile would reassure him, I nodded. "I know. And I do understand. More than you know. I'm not going to insist you stay in the city if you don't want."

"What're you talkin' about? I want this trade, I swear. Momma didn't mean it like that. She loves you."

I dismissed his protests. "Let's do this. We'll both have apartments in the city, but after the season is over, you go home, and after a month or so, I'll follow and hang out. Like we've been doing this time."

"Dev, you don't think the press is gonna think it's odd that two guys hang out only with each other—no women?"

Annoyed that he was right, I crushed the empty cup in my hand. "Dammit. I'm trying to make it work for us, but it's ridiculous. What the hell are we supposed to do? Get married to women and live a lie? I wouldn't do that to a woman or to you."

"I don't know, baby. It sucks balls."

"If you don't want to stay in the city in the off-season then I'll buy a place for myself down here somewhere.

Not in the same town, but close enough that it wouldn't be hard to see each other. All I know is that I'm not going to spend half the year without you. I'm thinking about the end game all the damn time. You and me together." I kicked the dirt under the table. "Love shouldn't be so fucking hard."

Brody sighed. "We'll work it out."

But at what cost?

Vette joined us, his arm around the shoulders of the petite, blond Dora Lee. "What's up, my dudes? Y'all look like you were havin' an intense conversation."

Brody and I rose to our feet, and he gave a wave to the couple. "Nothin'. Just figuring some stuff out. Hey, Dora Lee. How's little Nicky?"

"Not so little anymore. He's almost ten and taller than me. Wants to play football." She gazed up at Vette. "Everett said he'd be happy to show him some special moves after dinner." Her bright-pink nails played against his copper-brown skin, tracing the rose tattoo under her fingers. Over the years, Vette had accumulated numerous tats, and he and I had spent some time comparing.

From the intensity of Vette's dark eyes as he gazed down at her, I'd bet he'd be showin' Dora Lee some special moves as well. "No one better than Vette."

"Hey, baby?" Vette bent to kiss Dora Lee. "Why don't you find Nicky, and we'll go out to dinner. Wherever you'd like. I just need to talk to my boys here for a moment. Wait for me by the car?" He dug out keys from his shorts. "It's the white Escalade."

Her skin flushed pink, and her blue eyes glowed. "Oh, okay. Thanks." She smiled shyly at us. "Bye, Brody. Nice to meet you, Devlin."

"Call me Dev. And same."

Vette watched her walk away. "*Mmm-mmm*. She is so fine."

"Don't fuck with her, Vette," Brody growled, acting like a big brother. "She's had it rough."

Vette's eyes narrowed. "You think I didn't talk to her? I'm not just tryin' to get in her pants. She told me about those supposed grandparents of hers. And the guy who got her pregnant and ran. Bastards. All of 'em."

Brody's shoulders relaxed. "I just don't want to see her hurt again. She's a nice person who deserves good things."

"Maybe that could be me." He ran a hand over his tight braids. "Something about her makes me wanna protect her. She's so sweet, and she has no one to care about her and Nicky."

I grinned and exchanged a look with Brody, but he remained skeptical. "Are you saying you fell for her? In one day?"

He shrugged. "No reason why it can't happen. Guess we'll see how it goes." We stood for a few, and I wondered why he lingered when Dora Lee and Nicky were waiting. Vette shifted nervously from foot to foot. Several people had entered the tent, and Vette pointed over to a spot under a tree, away from the noise. "Got a sec?"

Brody was as confused as I was. "Yeah, sure."

I leaned against the tree, wondering what was going on.

Vette scratched his cheek and bit his lip. "Lemme ask y'all something."

I was checking my phone. "Yeah? What's up?"

"Are you two a couple? Like...together?"

The phone fell out of my hands and I lost my breath. I scrambled to pick it up and sputtered. "Wh-what? Why would you say that?" The unexpected and shocking question rattled me, and I shoved the phone into my pocket, hoping no one could see how my hands trembled.

Brody huffed. "What the hell, Vette?"

"Listen, I swear I'd never say nothing, but I remember that trip to Cancun and how you two shared a room. Y'all were different together than the rest of us. I don't know how to explain it. I noticed, every off-season, y'all spend it together." He lowered his voice to a whisper. "I never seen you with girls or nothin'. Devil, in college...I know you never had a girl stay the night." He placed his hands on our stiff-as-a-board shoulders and squeezed lightly. "Hey. I don't care. Y'all are my best friends, and that ain't never gonna change. Just want you to know that if it's true, I got your backs. And now I'm gonna go find my lady. Talk to you later."

Still frozen, we watched him leave toward the parking lot.

Brody shook his head. "Damn. I thought we were doing so well hidin' it."

"I guess not. Makes me wonder who else might be thinking the same thing."

"You're thinking where there's smoke, there's fire."

Gazing at Brody's dejected face, I wanted to hold him and say it was gonna be all right, but I didn't know if that was true. If rumors started to spread, we'd have to deny it and prove them wrong by rejecting who we were inside. All to keep playing football. And that was a fucked-up way to live.

I toed the dirt with my sneaker, wishing I could kick the damn tree down. "Maybe you're right and I should hold off on coming here to visit." We left the shade of the tree and headed for the playground, where plenty of kids still took advantage of the swings and slide. "Are you still going to come out to your mother?"

Under his tan, Brody paled, but he set his jaw. "Yeah. Training camp begins soon, and I got tons of things to do. Get the stuff from my place in Texas to New York, find an apartment. Do you wanna leave with me? I can drop you off at home."

"No, I'll get a ride from someone." It had never made sense for me to rent a car, as I always used Brody's or we were together.

"We're good, right?"

More serious than I'd ever seen him, he nodded. "Always."

Relieved, I nodded. "Okay. Later."

After he drove away, I wandered to the playground and sat on a bench, watching the kids run around. Janie appeared in front of me.

"Mind if I sit?"

"Be my guest."

She stretched out her long legs. "Where's your other half?"

I jerked my head up. "What?"

She snorted. "C'mon. This is the first time I've seen you by yourself since you came here. You and Brody are attached at the hip. Lemme ask you somethin'."

"Shoot." The kids shrieking made me smile as they soared higher and higher on the swings.

"I know you and Blink are best friends, but you could go anywhere in the world. Why're you here?"

A chill ran through me. Was she fishing for information? Did she know and think she was going to out me? Nonchalantly inspecting my nails, I shrugged. "Exactly for that reason. I've been everywhere–Europe, Asia, the Middle East. Believe it or not, I enjoy the quiet, peaceful life you all have here."

"Bet it's a lot different than New York City. You thinkin' of settling down here? You could have your pick of the ladies."

I chuckled. "I haven't thought about settling down. I'm only twenty-five." I decided to change the subject. "What about you and Tom? You guys travel?"

"Honey, I ain't been outta this town in ten years." She drank from her water bottle. "But I can't complain. I'm happy running the Kitty Kat, and we have our house and dogs—neither of us ever wanted kids. Me 'n Tom are thrilled with how you and Brody have stepped up, and not only renovated the original shelter, but put this all together so quickly. You really made your mark."

Aside from my football prowess, I hadn't received much praise in my life. I almost didn't know what to do with it. "Thanks, but I didn't do it for accolades, and I know Brody didn't either. It's important to give back, and I'm happy to help. I have several favorite charities in the city I donate my time and money to as well."

"Well, we sure appreciate it. What you've done here will make a whole lotta difference. We've already had inquiries from people who need a safe space."

My heart sank. "I don't know why I was hoping it would be empty for a while, but it's here because of necessity." I squinted into the sun.

"Unfortunately not. Like that couple there? He was injured overseas, and they're scrambling to keep their house. He can't work yet, and her income from working at the beauty parlor just don't cut it."

I peered at the man and woman, whose little boy had come running from playing on the swings. "Damn. I know them. That little boy is Jimmy. I met them when Brody picked me up at the airport. That's terrible. You said they might lose their house?" At her nod, I got to my feet. This was fucking unacceptable. "I gotta go. I'll talk to you."

Leaving Janie, I strode away from the grounds, intent on making my way to Main Street. It wasn't yet three o'clock, so I knew the bank should still be open, but I still jogged there. I was panting from my mile-long jog in the warm weather, and quite a few people stared at me as I took a second to enjoy the cool air on my flushed face.

"May I help you?" A customer service rep walked over to me.

"Yes. I need to speak to the manager." His brows rose, and while I never used my fame to push myself into place, I didn't have time for explanations. "Please. I'm Devlin Summers. I'd like to talk to him about some business."

"Oh, of course, I'm sorry. I didn't recognize you."

"It's not a problem. Thank you."

He led me to the bank manager's desk.

An hour later, I shook his hand, my task complete. "Pleasure doing business with you. Please make sure they get the papers as soon as they're filed, so they know the house is theirs."

"I'm sure they'll want to thank you. Can you leave your number, Mr. Summers?"

"I don't want them to know. I'd like it to be anonymous." I gave him a salute. "Have a great rest of your day."

By the time I walked out of the bank, it was past the sun's zenith. I could've called for a car to drive me to Brody's, but I chose to walk and clear my head because despite my paying off Amber and Troy's mortgage, I couldn't get the earlier conversation with Brody out of my head. I hated that his mother thought I'd pushed him to make the change. I didn't think that was the case. It was my suggestion, but it was a business decision as well. The Kings were paying him a lot more than the Lonestars. If I didn't believe it would be a good career move for Brody, I wouldn't have proposed it.

I walked and walked, leaving the town behind me and heading toward Brody's house. Occasionally we'd go jogging, and I knew a path through the wooded area that avoided the main road.

Was I too pushy? Brody wasn't the type to follow what I wanted. He made his own decisions. I might be the leader of my team, but Brody and I were equals in our relationship. I loved him so much, I wanted him with me, and knowing my team could use a player like him, I'd lobbied for him to join me, even though he'd never indicated that he wanted it.

I stopped at an open space where a stream of crystal blue water rushed by, and I splashed my overheated face. A startled deer ran past me, and I smiled.

"Man, you are not on Mercer Street." I took a seat on the leaf-covered ground and sat for a few moments, soaking in the sounds of the forest, listening to the birdsong and breathing. I understood why Brody loved it here.

Dripping with sweat by the time I reached his house, I made a decision. Brody might not be happy about it, but I knew it was for the best if we wanted to be together forever.

That was our end game, and I was damned if I'd let anything screw it up.

CHAPTER NINE

Brody

As I rode around the curve, Momma's car came into view. Theo's wasn't in the driveway, and relief flooded me. Although seeing how he treated her with respect and kept working at his company had shown me he cared for her, that it wasn't about the money, I was still reserved at best. But Momma was happy, so I'd learned to shut up and let her live her life.

"Momma?" I called out when I entered.

"In the kitchen."

Sniffing with appreciation, I followed my nose. "*Mmm.* Whatcha cookin'?"

"Bakin'," she corrected. "Cinnamon buns and peach cobbler. I made extra for you to take home, for you and Dev."

"Thanks. Can we...can you sit for a sec?" That swoop of fear hit my stomach, and it must've shown on my face, as Momma took one look at me and took off her apron.

"What is it? Is something wrong?"

I pulled out a chair and waited until she sat before taking a seat next to her. "No. nothing's wrong. I'm fine. Everything's great."

She put a hand to her heart. "Thank God. And Devlin? He's okay?"

"Yeah, no problems. I just left the opening of the new shelter and rec center. I...I need to talk to you and tell you something."

She folded her hands in front of her. "All right. I'm listening."

Now that the time was here, I was a nervous wreck. On the field I could face the biggest, fiercest tackles, but here, sitting in this sweet-scented kitchen, I was a quivering mess.

"I, uh, I'm gay, Momma. I've known since I was eleven. I'm also...I'm in love with Dev. And he loves me back." I thought my heart would jump out of my chest while I spoke, but now that I'd told her, it all clicked into place, and finally, after years of being stuck underwater, I broke the surface to breathe.

"Oh, my sweet boy." She smiled. "Don't you think I know?"

My jaw dropped. "What...how...I don't understand. You knew? Since when?"

"I guess it was high school when I'd go to the games and see all the cheerleaders and girls all over you and you never paid them no mind. Same in college. You never talked about girls or goin' out and meetin' people. It was always the game and your friends. And then, when you told us you were movin' to New York, where Devlin is, I was hopin' you'd find the right time to share with me."

Shaking my head, I rubbed my face. "I can't believe you knew all along. I was so scared. Maybe not scared, but worried you might change your mind about me."

"Never *ever* think that." Her fist made contact with the tabletop. "You are my life, my son. I would die for you. And I want you to be happy." She wiped her eyes. "And Devlin? You've been together since college, I'm assumin'?"

"We only acknowledged it senior year, the night we won the championship." I didn't even realize the heaviness weighing me down until now. I was light as air. "Since then we've tried all sorts of ways to be together without raising suspicion. But we've been together for years, and it's only gotten better."

"Four years is a long time," she mused, "but you're still young. You both have a whole lotta livin' to do. Are you sure you're really ready?"

"I love him, Momma. And he loves me back. We wanna be together, and me signin' with the Kings is gonna make it possible." Tears burned, and I wiped the heel of my hand against my eyes. "We're tired of bein' apart for half the year."

Her hand rested on mine. "I know. I can't imagine how hard it must be. Just don't lose yourself up there. Remember how you were raised and know you don't have to change."

"I won't. I just want to be happy."

"And being with Dev makes you happy."

I nodded and whispered, "Yeah."

She sniffled and met my gaze. "Then you go to New York and give them everything you got. And I'll come to cheer you in the Super Bowl."

Finally, I could laugh. "You're getting a little ahead of yourself, Momma."

"I don't think so," she said, her eyes soft and filled with so much tenderness, my chest hurt, knowing moments like these were fleeting. "I think if you're content and loved, there's nothin' you can't do."

"I'd better go. Lots of stuff to get together, preparing for the move."

"Don't forget the cobbler and cinnamon buns. Hold on while I make them ready for you."

She bustled about the kitchen, putting them in a bag for me. She gave me the parcel, I took her hand. "Are you happy? Theo's treatin' you okay?"

"I know he's not your daddy and he's rough around the edges, but he's been there for me. In the beginning he tried too hard with you, I think, but he's mellowed. We're good."

"I'm glad. I guess I was wrong about him."

She held me close. "You were, and maybe one day you'll sit down with him and tell him that." She kissed my cheek. "Now go on home to Dev and enjoy yourself. Maybe come by tomorrow, and we'll have dinner. I got a nice rack of ribs."

"*Mmm.* You know you don't have to ask twice." I hugged her again. "Love you, Momma."

"I love you too, Brody."

In a much better mood now that I'd gotten everything out in the open, I couldn't wait to get home to Dev and tell him how well the conversation had gone. I parked, and carrying the desserts, entered the house, calling for him.

"Dev. Momma made us cinnamon buns and cobbler, and if you don't get your butt out here, I might eat the whole thing."

No answering shout and, in fact, the house remained eerily quiet. My footsteps quickened as I walked through the rooms, reaching the bedroom last. Maybe he was in the bathroom.

"Dev?"

That was when I noticed his stuff was gone. I about-faced and went to the dresser. All his drawers were empty. I sank to the bed.

"What the fuck?" My phone buzzed, and it was him. "Dev. What the hell is goin' on? Where are you?"

"At the airport. Waiting for my plane home."

"What? You just left me? Why? What's wrong?"

"I spent a lot of time this afternoon thinking about what your mother said. You know I love you."

"I-I love you too. But it's gonna be okay. I told Momma, and it's all right. She said she knew."

Dev blew out a big sigh. "I'm so glad for you, baby. But I'm not surprised. Ms. Faith is a smart lady. But see, I'm trying not to be selfish. I want you to have these last few weeks with your mother. I didn't tell you because I knew you'd try and make me stay, but in my heart, I know this is right for you. Ms. Faith needs this time with you. And after, I'm gonna have you all to myself up here, and I promise we will find a way to be together."

There was nothing sexier in the world than a possessive, growling Devil Summers. It never failed to set my blood on fire, but now he wasn't here to quench my thirst. Frustrated, I hit the pillow with my fist. Twice.

"I dunno whether to punch you in the face for makin' me think you left for good, or hug you for bein' so thoughtful. Dev," I groaned. "I hate being here without you. It don't seem right anymore."

"I'll never leave you. I miss you too, baby. So damn much. But soon we'll be together. On the field and off."

I lay on the bed, cuddled up to Dev's pillow that still smelled like him.

"Yeah. Together."

I stood in my brand-new apartment overlooking the river. Dev and I had checked out places the real estate agent had sent me, and knowing I wouldn't want to be in a people-filled area like SoHo or Tribeca, she'd suggested West Chelsea. The moment I stepped into the sun-filled apartment, with floor-to-ceiling views of the water, I knew it was the right one. It boasted a huge terrace—for New York City standards—and I could see myself and Dev sitting out there watching the sunset.

Having viewed close to ten apartments, I told my agent to put in an offer on the condo, and it was accepted. I was now an owner of a tiny piece of Manhattan. And I took a slew of pictures and sent them to Momma.

Dev came from behind me and slipped his arms around my waist. "Welcome home."

I set the phone on the kitchen island and cupped his face between my hands. "They're bringin' the bed later today." I kissed him, and his lips curved under mine.

"Yeah? You think not having a bed is gonna stop me from taking what I want?"

That husky rasp always got me, and I sighed when he sank to his knees, taking my shorts and briefs with him. Already aching, my dick sprang up, and Dev sucked me hard and fast, his fingers gripping my thighs. Four years or forty, I'd never get tired of his touch. I gazed down, met his eyes, and he fucking winked at me.

"Fucking hell, Dev." I hissed and his teeth scraped my rock-hard shaft. My hands tightened in his hair, and at his throaty sounds of encouragement, I thrust into his warm mouth. "That's it, that's it." I cried out and came, my head flung back, as pinwheels of color burst in my mind's eye.

Dev hummed as he sucked the last drop, then rested on his heels with a blissful expression. I joined him and kissed his lips, tasting myself. His fingers tangled in my hair, keeping his face to mine.

"I love you, Brody."

"Me too. Now come here and let me love you."

With the same grace he showed on the field, wriggling his way out of tight spots, Dev got naked below the waist in seconds flat. I laid him on the rug, admiring his gorgeous body. Always a vocal lover, Dev groaned loud and long as I pumped his shaft between my lips and played with his balls.

"Fuck me, Brody, oh God." He dug into the rug and hiked his hips up, forcing his thick cock down my throat, and I held him there. After all the years together, I could sense his impending orgasm, but I wanted more from him today. I released him.

"What the hell," he gasped, fixing me with a glare. "Fuck, Brody, I was almost there."

"Yeah, but I want something more from you." I twirled my finger. "Turn over."

A salacious gleam lit his eyes. "*Mmm*. Okay, I'm not mad about it anymore." He rested on his forearms, presenting me with his beautiful ass.

"Everyone else gets to look at this on Sundays, but only I get to touch it." I grabbed each cheek and squeezed hard.

Dev moaned. "Oh yeah, baby. Take what you want. It's yours."

I dove in, sliding my tongue past the rim, and he grunted. "Taste so good, baby. I could eat you all day long." I spread him wide and went in on him like a starving man. Dev's groans and cries rose in the air, and he pushed his ass into my face as I licked and sucked him.

"Oh God, Brody, please," Dev panted and worked his dick. I stopped licking him to wet my fingers and slide them deep inside him. "Fuck," he screamed and came hard, spilling out beneath him. He lay facedown, his body glistening with sweat as tremors rippled underneath his skin. He turned his head to the side and flashed that famous, wicked grin.

"Good thing I had my clothes underneath me and didn't mess up the rug. Someone might've thought you had a puppy that had an accident."

I ruffled his hair and lay beside him. "My very own Devil-dog."

He shook with laughter, then turned to face me. "You're happy?"

"Are you kiddin' me?" I pushed the hair out of his eyes. "You have to ask?"

Dev sat up. "I wouldn't if I didn't want to make sure. And I'm not talking about the sex." His eyes grew soft. "That's always amazing. But it's been a whirlwind these past few weeks with your move and getting the apartment. I just need to check."

I pulled him close so his leg straddled my hips. Our chests touched, and my nose brushed his. I craved that physical contact.

"When you left, I thought it wouldn't be a big deal. Like, I'd been alone all those years during the season, and it was fine–our videos and off-season meet-ups were good enough."

Dev's smile imprinted on my cheek. "Good enough isn't what I'm looking for with you. I'm a greedy bastard."

I chuckled. "So am I. And havin' you with me these past months taught me that. I missed everything about you." I rubbed his cheek with mine. "No one singin' in the shower. Knowin' I didn't need to buy a second pint of ice cream. The empty seat next to me in the car and across the table. You're part of me now, and when you're gone, it's like I'm not whole."

He put his arms around me. "And now here we are. Together. Forever."

"Nothing to keep us apart."

CHAPTER TEN

Dev

"Green 64, Green 64, hut, hut."

I faded back from the line of scrimmage and pivoted, scanning the field. Brody was double-teamed, so I threw to my second favorite receiver, Jonas Armstrong. A perfect spiral into his arms, and with his trademark explosive speed, he took off, evading tackles and making it untouched into the end zone. If this had been an actual game, the crowd would be roaring with approval, but instead we walked to midfield to listen to Coach instruct us on what we had and hadn't done correctly.

It was mandatory minicamp training, and preseason games were beginning the following week. All of us had been in the zone, training hard all day, every day for the past two weeks. As I'd predicted, Brody had fit right in, and there was a sense of anticipation that this year we might be able to bring a Super Bowl win after missing it by a hair the year before. We were hungry, and we wanted it.

Coach Jackson, along with the offensive and defensive coaches, gathered together. "Summers, try and step out of the snap quicker. The Roadrunners have that big moose of a defensive end who can move like a son of a bitch. We know they'll be gunning for you."

I nodded. "Got it, Coach."

"Yeah, Devil. Don't want that pretty face of yours getting knocked up," Marlon Lane, one of my buddies, razzed me, and I grinned and flipped him off.

"Beautiful catch, Armstrong. Just keep doing what you're doing. Martin, keep your eyes on the tackles. They're gonna double-team ya, but I know you've got the moves."

I kept a neutral face.

Coach, you have no idea.

As always, Brody listened carefully, and on our next play, he sidestepped the two-man team covering him and caught my pass to run for thirty yards. Coach clapped his hands.

"That's what I'm talking about. All right. Break for the day. Get your sleep, no partying with the groupies—no matter how cute—and see you here tomorrow."

We tramped off the field and hit the locker rooms. Brody got there first and was already in the shower. I stripped out of my pads and gear and joined him and the others. It felt like heaven to let the hot water soak my aching muscles. My post-game massage was going to feel so damn good. I dried off, and with a towel around my waist, returned to the locker room.

"Dude, we're lookin' sharp out there." Jonas soft-punched me in the shoulder. "You kept it together during the off-season or what?"

"You could say that. Spent lots of days jogging and avoiding ice cream."

"Don't believe him," Brody called out from across the room.

"Hey, you be quiet over there, newbie," I cackled.

"Blink's a great addition. He's big and fast. Knows where to be when you throw the ball." Jonas pulled on his T-shirt. I eyed him. Jonas was a rock—six foot three and two hundred thirty pounds of solid muscle. Hitting him was like running into a wall, and I knew he and Brody would get along.

"Yeah, we spent some time together on the off-season, and as soon as I knew he'd be coming here, I showed him the playbook and we ran some plays."

"Man, you only think about football." Jonas shook his head. "You need to get out more."

"I do just fine, thanks." Thinking of my time with Brody, I knew I wouldn't change a single second. "I take it you did something else?"

"You know it. My wife and I found a house, and we're gonna have a baby." He proudly displayed a picture of them on a gorgeous beach, with his lady showing off a sweet baby bump.

"Congrats. That's awesome." I was genuinely happy for him, even though I had zero interest in children.

"How about you? No one catch your eye? Or is the Devil having too much fun playing the field?"

I winked. "Life is short, my man. Gotta grab all the fun while I can."

Zeke Cunningham, the place kicker, strolled by. "Or maybe you're too busy playing with someone already on the field, huh?"

Jonas's brow furrowed, and fear prickled through me, but I kept my head. "What the hell's that supposed to mean?"

Zeke shrugged. "Just sayin'."

I crossed my arms. "So far I don't hear you saying anything but a lot of shit that doesn't mean anything."

Zeke's locker was across the aisle, near Brody, who was halfway dressed but had stopped to listen. Music was blaring, and most everyone was minding their own business, not paying attention to Zeke. He was a bit of a hothead but always aced his kicks, so people left him alone.

Zeke faced me with a mocking smile and a calculating gleam in his eyes. "Just that you've got this *biiig* rep as Devil, like you're a ladies' man and wild in the sack, but I've never seen you with nobody. Who was the last chick you went out with? Far as I know, you spent your whole summer with your best friend, old Blink here, who you asked to be signed."

"Yeah?" I tightened the towel and advanced on him. "You've been checking up on me? Why's that?"

We were about the same height, but I was so ferociously angry, he took a step back.

Zeke shrugged. "Just stating the obvious."

I glanced around to see Jonas and Marlon watching us. "Which is what? You're flapping your gums now, but I'm not hearing anything."

"I've heard some girls say you're not into them, no matter how hard they try. What's up with that?"

I'd prepared for times like this. With a lazy grin, I leaned on the wall of lockers. "You've been talking to my sloppy seconds, Zeke? What makes you think I need to get it on with every woman I see? I'm not a hound dog. Maybe I have standards."

Zeke snorted. "Yeah, sure. They said you'll do it all except slip it to them. What's the matter? Can't get it up for some pussy?"

With a frown, Jonas intervened. "Man, you need to stop speaking about women like that. I didn't talk about my relationship with Ebony until we were serious. Leave Dev alone."

"Let him talk. He's got a bug up his ass about me, and he's bringing Blink into it for no reason. Guy's only been here a minute."

"I don't got nothing up my ass. Can you say the same?" He snickered, and I lost it and pushed him up against the locker door.

"What the fuck does that mean?"

By now a crowd had gathered, and Zeke's lips curled. "You a pitcher or a catcher? Maybe you and good ole boy Blink here were living it up down South in more ways than one."

I poked him in the chest. "Why, 'cause I don't go waving my dick in front of every woman and get myself into trouble? I'm not the one running to Coach to help get him out of his messes." Two women had already proved that Zeke fathered their children, and he was supposed to be paying a nice chunk of child support. "First thing I learned in college from my coach was wrap it up. Next was football first. Too bad you can't say the same."

"All I'm saying–"

I cupped my ear. "You're still talking? You're even more of a fucking idiot than I thought. Stay out of my way and keep my name and Blink's out of your dumbass mouth."

I walked away but I heard Zeke snipe, "Protecting your boy?"

Red flashed before my eyes, but Jonas held me by the arm.

"Don't," he warned. "Coach will fine you for fighting, and that dude ain't worth it. Besides, Blink can take care of himself. Lookit."

Brody took my place in front of Zeke and, towering over him, pointed a finger in his face.

"I'm nobody's boy, get it? My momma taught me to respect women and not talk about them like you do. Now shut the fuck up and get outta my way, you hear?" Brody knocked Zeke's shoulder on his way past, sending him stumbling a few steps. "See y'all later."

He strode out of the room, and I dropped my towel and got dressed without another word. Everyone else started talking as if nothing happened. Marlon took out his crossbody bag and slung it over his chest.

"Don't listen to that motherfucker. He should be more concerned about kicking the ball than talking some stupid shit. You do you, brother."

"I plan on it. No one is entitled to my private life. Or yours, yours, or yours." I pointed to each of my teammates. "Just because we play ball doesn't mean we have to perpetuate the stereotype of wild men running after women like dogs with their tongues hanging out. I don't know about you, but I respect women. I think of them as more than sexual objects."

Jonas nodded vehemently. "Right on. I got three sisters, and if anyone thinks they're supposed to put out, they'd better tell that to my face."

My teammates crowded around me.

"You're right."

"Damn straight."

"Anyone ever talked about my mama like that, I'll knock their head off."

"You know it. Fuck that shit."

Zeke slammed the door to his locker and stalked out. My wildly galloping pulse steadied, and I pulled my bag over my shoulder. *Crisis averted.* While Brody had to be upset, I needed to remain behind with my team and be the leader I was.

"See you all tomorrow. Only a few more days until preseason. Let's get ready to kick some butt."

A shout rose in the room, and I walked out with Marlon, only to be stopped by Coach Jackson.

"Summers, hold up a sec."

I caught Marlon's eye. "Catch you tomorrow."

"Later."

I waited, unsure what Coach wanted. A quick rundown of my playing form since camp started didn't reveal any glaring problems, aside from the usual need to drop some excess weight and put on the muscle, plus simply get into the groove of playing.

"What's up, Coach? Everything okay?"

"Yeah, yeah. You're looking good out there. Are you having a problem with Zeke?" Serious brown eyes met mine. "I caught some of what was going down in the locker room."

Shame licked through me. "That was my fault. I shouldn't have allowed his stupid mouth to get to me. I'm sorry, Coach. I won't let it happen again."

"Good. You're the leader, Dev. You have to learn to rise above the foolishness, no matter how much it might upset you."

I hung my head. "I know. I have to remember, football first."

"We have a tough but workable schedule this year and a good shot at winning the division and going all the way. I don't want conflict among the team. We have one mission—to win."

Chafing under his criticism, my cheeks grew hot, and I nodded. "I understand, Coach."

"But the management of the Kings as well as the field staff are as concerned about the players' mental states as we are about your physical. And not only you—every member of the team. So if anything is going on you want to talk about, I'm available. No waiting."

Shit. Did Coach think what Zeke was insinuating was true? "I-I'm okay. Everything's great. Really. We've just all gotta get in the same mindset."

Coach's face remained skeptical. "You know, Dev, I've had players get in all kinds of jams—pregnant girlfriends, drugs, gambling...there's very little I haven't seen." He took me by the shoulder, and something in his expression gentled. "I remember you saying you don't have a good relationship with your parents. I hope you know that you can talk to me about anything. And if you don't feel comfortable with that, the Kings have people you can speak with."

"I'm good, Coach. Promise. The way Zeke talked was disrespectful to women, and I didn't like it."

I could see something working behind Coach's eyes and waited. "You know, I think we can make this a teachable moment. I'm going to suggest to the owner that we do a public service message about respecting women—we all know how violence and abuse against women is a problem with athletes. Would you be up for that?"

"Yeah, sure. I think it would be great. And I know the guys would be as well."

A satisfied smile broke across Coach's face. "Excellent. I'll talk to the owner, and we'll come up with something." He gave me a playful shove. "Now go get your massage."

I saluted him. "Yes, sir."

Laughing, I walked away toward the spa, where Enzo, my massage therapist, was waiting for me.

"There he is. I thought you forgot about me." Enzo winked.

Enzo was built like a boxer—big arms and shoulders and a broad, well-muscled chest. At fifty, I had no doubt he was in better shape than some men half his age—maybe because he had a husband fifteen years younger than him—they'd been together for years.

"Not on your life. I've been looking forward to this all day."

I left my bag on the chair and followed him into the room, decorated in soothing tones of pale green and beige. My body ached from the strenuous activity, and I couldn't wait for Enzo's rubdown.

While I stripped, he prepared his magic potion of oils and creams, and I lay face down. The second he touched my shoulders, he protested.

"What the hell, man? You're so tense. Relax."

"I'm trying."

Enzo kneaded and pressed hard, digging into the tight knots, and I groaned, then sighed. "Damn, that feels good."

"I see you like it. You sound like my husband and me when we're doing the deed." He snickered, and I grinned.

"You're ridiculous."

I'd had him as my massage therapist since I was drafted, and we talked about everything—neither of us had good relationships with our families, and we'd bonded over that sad fact. Regardless, I knew some of the guys didn't like having a gay man do their massages. Another reason why I knew I had to keep quiet about who I was. My mind drifted while he worked on me, and I thought about Brody and how great it had been having him with me all the time. Each week we'd switch between staying at my place and his, and so far it worked out perfectly.

He spun his fingers, in a circle. "Turn over. I need to get the oils into your arms and chest."

I did as he asked and closed my eyes. Training camp and the season would make our social lives pretty much nonexistent, so we had plenty of time to spend with each other. And I was fine with that. There was no one else I'd rather be with. It had been so damn lonely all these years without him, and going to sleep and waking up with him every night and day was exactly how I'd pictured it. Our sex life had only gotten better, which I hadn't thought possible, and I knew it was because we were finally together where we belonged.

"You must be thinking about some really beautiful lady," Enzo murmured, and my eyes flew open. The tent in the sheet covering my hips was impossible to miss. My fault for thinking about Brody. My cheeks burned, but all I could do was shrug and laugh it off.

"You know how it is." Damn, did that sound as lame as I thought?

Enzo took it in stride. "Better make sure it's packed away before you go outside. That's a deadly weapon. You might get arrested."

I rolled my eyes. "Knock it off."

"I'm serious. Or maybe go find a pretty lady to help you with that." One last rub, and he was finished. He wiped off the excess oil and handed me my shirt.

"Enough," I snapped, having reached my limit with people talking about my sex life, but then was instantly contrite. "Sorry. I apologize. I'm just tired."

"It's okay. Everything all right? Like I said, you're very tense."

I managed a smile. "I'm okay. Preseason nerves, I guess."

"You're the best. I think this is the year."

This time my laughter was genuine. "You say that at the start of every season."

"But now I see you happy for the first time. You have your best friend with you. That makes all the difference, I think."

I hopped off the table to put my briefs and shorts on. "Yeah, it does."

As we walked to the door, he slung an arm around my shoulders. "It's good to have someone you know will always have your back. Maybe you might think about talking to your parents?"

Startled by the out-of-the-blue remark, I stopped. "What brought this on? Why would I want to talk to them?"

Lines of sorrow etched deep in his face. "Over the summer my mother died. I hadn't seen nor heard from her in almost twenty years. I tried, but she refused. I didn't even get a chance to go to her funeral—I found out when someone who didn't know the extent of our estrangement offered me condolences." Wetness glimmered in his eyes. "Don't wait until it's too late. Death doesn't give second chances." He patted me on the shoulder and left.

On my ride home, I thought about that, but I didn't make plans to change things anytime soon. The main difference was that Enzo's mother had shown him love before he came out. Mine never did.

And that certainly wouldn't change if I ever came out to them. I had enough in my life trying to make sure Brody was comfortable up here and keeping the team together. People needed me, and I wasn't about to jeopardize that for the two people who should love me no matter what but didn't.

I took out my phone and sent a text.

Coming home. Be ready for me.

I received an immediate answer.
I'm always ready.
That right there was all I needed.

CHAPTER ELEVEN

Brody

A week later—first preseason game

"Blue 82, Blue 82, hut, hut."

I sped to the edge of the line of scrimmage and danced on my feet, waiting. As practiced, I took off for center field, surprising the defensive ends double-teaming me. Or trying to.

"Dev," I screamed, knowing he couldn't hear me but hoping he might have that sixth sense we had with each other. And like that Orange Bowl game, he slipped like a runny egg in a nonstick pan, sidestepped, and faded back to throw. The ball soared like an arc in the blue, blue sky and fell in my arms. "Come to Papa."

With the fans cheering, I motored to the end zone and scored. My teammates mobbed me, and we left the field slowly so the special teams could come out. Zeke made the kick, and we'd won our first preseason game, 31-10.

We streamed into the locker room, laughing and reliving the better plays in the game. Coach Jackson and his staff came in, and we all grew quiet.

"Nice work, everyone. Always good to start off the preseason with a win. We had some good moves and a couple of missteps. Take your time to recover, relax, and show up on Wednesday ready to go. We have some films of the Pilots to watch."

I'd gotten a bruise on my knee that the team physician looked at and said wasn't anything to worry about. I couldn't wait to get into the whirlpool, and after my knee was iced, I soaked in the churning water, and then in some Epsom salts. I ached all over and after my stretch with the trainer, was ready to go home and relax. Dev and I had a night planned of takeout and watching a movie.

I glanced around for Dev and saw him with ice on his shoulder, getting a rubdown from Enzo. I figured it would be a while before they finished assessing him, and decided to head home, so I sent him a text to come whenever he wanted. I'd be waiting.

At my apartment, I stripped down to my boxers, lay on the sectional, and called Momma.

"Hey, honey. I see you won today. You played great with your new team. Everybody nice there?"

I managed a smile. Lord, she was cute. "It's all good. And yeah, it was a good win. I'm home and just conked out on the couch, staring at the river."

"Sounds pretty. You make sure you rest, you hear me?"

It might hurt my ribs, but her scolding had me chuckling. "Yes, Momma. I know. Like I said, I'm relaxing. Might take a nap."

"Good idea. And you're enjoying it up there?"

"I am. Surprised even me 'cause I didn't think I'd like bein' in crowds of people. But Dev's taken me to Central Park, and we drove out to some beaches, then upstate to the mountains, where we went fishin'. That was pretty cool. It's like they've got everything within a hundred miles."

"That makes me feel better about you bein' in New York."

Something bugged me. "Momma, I lived in Texas when I was with the Lonestars. That was far away too. Why're you so worried now?"

"But you weren't living in the city. And it's different. Lots more people, crime...and I'm still not sure."

"Not sure about what?"

"Oh, honey, I know you and Devlin love each other, but you've never been with anyone else. Maybe you're rushing all this."

I pinched my eyes shut. Now was not the time to tell her that wasn't true.

"Momma, I know the difference. And I know what I have with Dev is real. You just have to trust me."

"I do. I'll let you go rest now. Talk to you soon."

"Bye."

I flipped on the television, turning it to ESPN, where they were doing a rundown of the day's games. I grinned as they showed my catch and Dev jumping up and down and fist-pumping. I stretched and closed my eyes.

Just gonna take a lil snooze.

My eyelids fluttered open to Dev pressing kisses to my face. "Hello, Sleeping Beauty."

I yawned. "What time is it?"

"Almost eight."

Shocked, I struggled up to sitting. "What? I slept for over two hours? Damn."

"I had a nice time watching you." He lay beside me. "You're cute when you sleep. Then again, you're always cute."

Still achy, I rolled my neck a few times. "Cute and hungry. What do you want for dinner?"

"I'm thinking Pad Thai or pizza?"

"*Mmm.* Or both?"

Dev made a face. "That's not happening as long as I'm here." He slid his foot up my leg. "You were so good out there today. I knew you'd be an asset to the team."

"Thanks. I think we're really comin' together. This is the first time I'm playin' for a contender, and the vibe is so different. The fans, they're like on steroids."

Dev snorted with laughter. "Ow, don't make me laugh. I'm still so fucking sore, even after a whirlpool and massage. But yeah. Just wait until the regular season."

"It gets wild, huh?"

Those green eyes sparkled as he nuzzled into my neck. "Let's just say there are two kinds of fandoms. One is the die-hards who love us no matter what. They have season tickets, know every stat of every player, and stay with us through the hard times."

"Yeah. Those are the best. But I get it when fans are frustrated. They pay a lotta money for their tickets and think we're slackers if we keep losin'. I heard a lotta that. When I was with the Lonestars, they'd been rebuilding for a few years, but it just wasn't clicking."

He nodded against my chest. "Uh-huh. Then there's the other kind. The ones who take it a little too far. And I know, everyone loves a winner, and these people expect New York teams to win. So we've got that pressure. Now add on the fact that we came so damn close last year, and we're one of the favorites to go all the way this year. If we suck and lose, they'll get on us like you've never seen."

"Yeah. That's how it was with the Lonestars fans. They'd boo us if we sucked."

"Here, they'll boo, yell at us, call us names, and tell the teams who should be traded."

Now that I'd cut my hair for the season—something Dev vociferously protested and whined about for over a week—he played with my chest hair and swirled it around his fingers.

"They have no problem telling us we suck." His lips kicked up. "In multiple languages."

"I can deal with it."

"I know. You're tough."

Not really. He should only know all those nights I'd spent missing him when he wasn't with me. Phone calls and stolen weekends weren't enough. This off-season together had proved it.

"It was like old times, playing on the same team. I never thought I'd get the chance again. Thank you for suggesting it and lightin' a fire under my ass to make the move."

"Having a team that works together instead of a bunch of egos on the field makes all the difference."

Laughing, I nudged his cheek with my nose. "No ego where you're concerned, am I right? I saw you working the crowd."

He snickered. "What can I say? I get off on hearing the roar. But seriously? Nothing gets me more pumped than being on the field, driving for the goal line, momentum on our side and the fans giving it their all."

Under my fingers I could feel his heart beat faster, and I nuzzled his neck. "Nothin', huh? Guess I'm slippin'."

"Silly. If I didn't have you, I don't think I'd be able to do this at all."

He kissed me, gentle and sweet, not a prelude to sex because our bodies were way too beaten up to think about it, but reaffirming our deep connection.

We sat in silence for a few minutes, before Dev slowly sat up. "Are you happy you're living here now? You don't have any regrets, do you?"

"Who're you, my momma?" As soon as I said it, I wanted to take the words back. Dev's face fell, and his lips twisted in a fake-as-hell attempt at a smile.

"She's still not convinced it was the right move for you, is she?" His head tipped down, hiding his eyes, but I caught the hurt in their green depths. "It's okay. I'm not mad at her. She loves you and wants to make sure you're okay. Like a real mother."

"It's not that. She worries about you too."

"Yeah?" He raised his head and brushed the dark hair out of his sad eyes. "Like how?"

My heart hurt, knowing that he'd never received a mother's love. Outwardly, Dev put on the face of a fun, easygoing man, someone always up for a good time, but only I knew his sensitive side. How fiercely he loved me. How lonely he was. Too many times we'd be together and I'd catch him staring into space. I knew he was thinking about his parents, wondering why they deserted him simply because he wanted to follow his dreams and not theirs.

At my hesitation, he pulled away from me. "Please don't lie to me. You won't hurt my feelings, I promise." He left the couch and began to pace.

"I'll never lie to you. She's concerned, thinkin' that you were my first and I never gave myself a chance to be with anyone else. Please stop. You're makin' me dizzy."

"But that's not true. You told me about the guy from the swim team and a couple of others. I knew you weren't a virgin." He managed a grin. "Not with the way you kissed me by the firepit."

I'd never wanted to have this conversation with Dev because our first time had happened so fast, and I hadn't wanted to break the magic between us. And afterward, we'd both fallen so hard and fast, it had no longer mattered, but I couldn't lie.

"I mean, yeah. We fooled around, got each other off, blowjobs and toys...but full-on sex? You were my first."

Shocked didn't come close to describing Dev's reaction. Pain, hurt, and love all mixed together in his eyes, and he returned to sit by my side.

"Baby, why didn't you ever tell me?"

I couldn't meet his gaze. "I didn't want you to stop that night and have to give you explanations. I'd been thinking about you for so long, and when you showed up and kissed me, all I could think of was how much I wanted you."

Dev cupped my face in his big, rough hands. "I would've been gentler, but I wouldn't have stopped. Taking the chance to kiss you that night was scarier than anything I've ever done. Even going to the Super Bowl."

"Come on, now." I shook my head, but he remained deadly serious.

"This is our lives we're talking about. I could give up football tomorrow, but I could never give you up."

More soft kisses, and we lay cuddled together, watching the lights twinkling across the river. I was glad the conversation about Momma's concerns hadn't taken a bad turn. However she felt, my life was here now with

Dev. Our phones buzzed at almost the same time. Dev pulled his out first.

"It's Ezra. He wants to know if we're interested in meeting him and his husband for dinner tomorrow night."

"I'm down for it. I only met Ezra in person when I signed with him. Everything else has been virtual."

"Great." Dev tapped on his screen. "I'll let him know."

"This place is packed for a Monday night." I gazed around the 2nd Avenue Deli, a no-frills restaurant that smelled like french fries, garlic, and smoked meat. In other words, heaven on a plate.

Ezra's eyes twinkled. "It's packed every night. People think Katz's is the best, but that's not the real thing." At the approach of the waiter with a pile of pickles and bowl of coleslaw, he rubbed his hands together. "Ahh, come to Papa."

"Excuse my husband. He's just finished another fad diet, and this is his first meal since his escape." Monroe—or Roe, as he told us to call him—cast a loving yet long-suffering glance at Ezra, and his dry wit set us all laughing. Even Ezra. When we heard their story, how they'd been separated as childhood sweethearts but found each other years later, it made me realize that none of us had easy lives, and we all had to work for a happiness that shouldn't be so difficult.

I'd never been to a Jewish deli, but if the towering sandwiches and delicious smells were any indication, this wouldn't be my last time. A bunch of people had recognized us, and after some autographs and picture-taking, they left us alone. New Yorkers were cool for the most part and gave celebrities their peace, but even still, Ezra had asked for a booth at the far end of the restaurant, away from the center of the crowd, which the management had accommodated.

Crunching noisily through a pickle, Ezra dismissed Roe's comment about his diet. "Listen. One of my clients wrote this bestseller, and in order to properly market her, I felt it was the right thing to do." He rolled his eyes. "But after one day, I thought I'd die. Only green juice and veggies and salads with the tiniest bit of protein. It was torture." He spooned some coleslaw on his plate.

"You're a meat-and-potatoes guy?" I took some coleslaw, and though it wasn't like Momma's, it was pretty damn good.

"I eat healthy, but it was ridiculous. Forget about that. Can I just say how much I'm loving having the two of you in the same town on the same team? Aside from making it easier for me, I can see you two are enjoying it as well."

While dressing for dinner, Dev and I had discussed it and decided to tell Ezra. It only made sense.

Dev put a hand on my thigh, giving me a comforting squeeze, and that gave me courage to say my truth. "We are. And I think you can already guess the reason." Even though we were separated from the main part of the restaurant, I was still uneasy and leaned forward, lowering my voice. "Dev and I...we're together. Have been since college. And it's been hell hidin' it, but we trust you because..." My gaze shifted to Roe, whose gentle, encouraging smile gave me strength. "Because you're living the life me 'n Dev wish we could. And it gives me hope."

Roe sighed. "Normally I'd say don't wish for anyone else's life, but in this case, I understand. You've picked a profession built on brute force and power and which hasn't yet caught up with recognizing that gay men are just as capable of playing the game as anyone else."

Serious for the moment, Ezra wiped his mouth. "You're both big, strong, alpha males playing an all-American sport. One day, in the not-so-distant future, I'm hoping it might be commonplace to see gay football players living out and proud, but I'm afraid that day hasn't arrived yet."

Roe took Ezra's hand. "You know I'm a psychologist. Please know I'm always available for you if you ever need help or just to talk."

Watching the waiter approach the table with our food, I held off answering until our sandwiches had been placed in front of us.

"Thank you. I hope you'll understand if I say I hope we never have to."

"I do."

We ate and agreed to meet once a month to catch up. On the way home, Dev and I decided to walk a bit. We received some side-eyes, and I caught a few people taking videos.

"I thought that was fun," Dev said, strolling with his hands in his pockets. "They're really the perfect couple."

At the corner of First and 70th, we stopped, and Dev called for a car. In the darkness of the back seat, I felt safe enough to take his hand.

"Is that something you might want one day?" I asked him. "To have what they have?"

Dev laced our fingers together. "It's all I think about. Their life is goals for me."

CHAPTER TWELVE

Dev

Three years later

"Hey, Brody?" I was at the dining-room table, going over our finances. Through the years, I'd kept up with the ins and outs and ups and downs of Wall Street, and I was our designated investment adviser. I enjoyed a little day trading, and keeping an eye on fluctuations in the stock market had enabled our savings to grow exponentially with bonds, treasury bills, and real estate. I wouldn't risk the bulk of our money, though, and had it in stable income funds. I was careful as it wasn't only my future, but Brody's and his mother's as well.

Long ago I'd learned never to trust anyone with my money—I'd heard too many stories of players blindly entrusting their wealth to someone and regretting it.

Every year, I made Brody sit with me, and we'd discuss where and in what to invest. Once a month I crunched the numbers. My parents might think I was wasting my life playing football, but I had to think about what happened when I retired. I didn't want to be one of those players who waited too long and limped away. I wanted to go out on top and needed a plan for when my glory days were done.

"Yeah? What's up?"

"Wanna review your mom's statement with me? I think it's time to move some of her money. She's got a lot of cash from the life insurance after Theo's death, and I think she should invest in tax-free munis or maybe mutual funds. Take a look."

The year before, Theo had been killed in a construction accident. Brody had stayed with her the week after he died, helping her work through her grief. With me, Brody had cried, admitting he'd been wrong in never giving Theo the chance he deserved to be a father to him, and now it was too late.

Instead of answering me, Brody stared off into space, and I knew he wasn't thinking about bank balances. I set the money talk aside for the moment. "It still bothers you, doesn't it?"

"Yeah. You know..." Wetness glimmered in his blue eyes when they met mine. "I never had the chance to say I was sorry for how I treated him. I couldn't even stay past the funeral, since we were in the playoffs, and Momma insisted I needed to be with the team."

"Baby, you'll find the right time to talk to her." I squeezed his hand. "But you softened a lot toward him these past few years. I saw it, and I'm sure they did too."

He lifted a shoulder. "Maybe. Now that she's alone, I just wish she wasn't so far away."

With the payment from the insurance company, Brody had set up a trust for his mother and an investment account that I managed for her. He'd again made his argument for her to move up by us, but she refused. She'd come to the city plenty of times, and enjoyed herself, as far as I could tell, but she wouldn't stay longer than a week.

"Visiting is enough for me. I have my life to live, and you boys have yours."

"You're the money man. I trust you to do what's right. After all, you made her a ton of money on that IPO, and we're all raking it in on that real estate investment trust and the shopping centers. I think we're doing pretty good."

I lazed back in the chair and rolled my neck. "Damn right we are. Let's not forget the two Super Bowl wins in three years that dumped a huge chunk of change in our pockets. Plus, think of all the good stuff we've done–giving to teen shelters and food banks at the cities we play in. You've taught me to take care of those who aren't as fortunate as us. So, pretty good? Fucking awesome is more like it." I spun around in my chair and scanned the pictures on the wall. Me, throwing a forty-yard TD in the last minute in our first Super Bowl win. Brody making a catch and the absolute joy on his face with the ball in his arms in the second Super Bowl victory. Our team accepting the trophy. Brody hugging his mom. The whole team celebrating on the field and at the theme park. Meeting the President at the White House.

Scenes of our life together.

And absolutely nothing from my parents. I'd done the right thing and invited them to all the divisional playoff games, offering to fly them out and put them up at hotels every step of the way. I received a "Thank you, but no thanks." Always the optimist, Brody pointed out that at least they answered and didn't ignore me.

It hurt, but I had Brody by my side, and that was all that mattered.

"I was thinking that even though your mom doesn't want to live here, we should buy an apartment in your building for her. Maybe one day she'll change her mind."

Brody's lips twitched. "Excuse me, you've known Momma for close to ten years. How many times has she changed her mind?"

I huffed out a frustrated breath. Ms. Faith was the sweetest person but stubborn as the day was long. "I know, but real estate is always a good idea." My phone buzzed and vibrated across the table. "It's Ezra. Hey. How's it going?"

"Good. You have a minute? Is Brody with you?"

There was restrained excitement in his voice, and while Ezra was always a little hyper, this time it was different. My curiosity piqued, I closed my laptop so I could focus on Ezra.

"Yeah, Brody's with me. What's going on?"

"Okay. You know after this year's Super Bowl win, you're the hottest commodity. Your contract is up, and I've got an incredible offer. The Cocoa Beach Rockets are looking for a quarterback, and they're willing to pay you. A *lot*."

My gaze darted to Brody, who raised a brow.

"I'm gonna put you on speaker so Brody can hear." I hit the screen. "So the Rockets approached you?"

"Yeah, and the contract is awesome," Ezra said with barely restrained glee that promised a smashing deal. "Fifty million per year, five years. Two hundred fifty million, guaranteed."

"Holy Mother of God," Brody croaked, growing pale.

Even I, who didn't care much about salary, to Ezra's despair, had a hard time wrapping my head around those astronomical figures. I had trusts from my grandparents on both sides that paid me stupid money to live on, so I didn't need to choose a team based on how much I'd make. It wasn't anywhere close to this ridiculous amount the Rockets were offering, but more than enough for me, so I didn't have to worry about anything and could buy whatever I wanted.

Unlike me, Brody still watched every penny he spent and didn't believe in frivolous purchases. He didn't own a car because he thought the price for parking in the city was a sin. One of the reasons I fell for him was his innate goodness and levelheadedness, which he'd carried with him from home to here. He made me a better man.

"Damn, Ezra. That's some serious money."

"Ya think?" He chuckled. "This last Super Bowl shot your star to the moon."

"Yeah, well, it's still a team effort. I'm not out there playing on my own." While in college I could be a bit of a hot dog, once I hit the pros, I knew there was no way to win if I didn't have the respect of all the players, and I worked damn hard to get it.

"You see? That's why you're a natural leader and such an asset to your team. You never take full credit. And I know it's a team effort because I have an offer for Brody as well."

"From the Rockets? I wouldn't mind another team if we go together."

Ezra cleared his throat. "Uh, well, no. For the Spokane Stars. Twelve million a year, three-year contract. I know it's a lot less, but tight ends never get as much as quarterbacks."

Cocoa Beach and Spokane? That didn't bear thinking about. Not even waiting for Brody to answer, I said, "Count me out, Ezra," shaking my head as if he could see me.

"But, Dev. That's a ton of money to walk away from," Ezra argued. "And it's only five years."

Struggling to control my temper, I rubbed my face and took a deep breath. "Only? Brody and I have been sneaking around for almost double that now. We're finally in the same city, and I refuse to go back to seeing him only on the off-season or on the slim chance the leagues have us playing against each other. I'm tired of a piecemeal love affair, when we deserve a seat at the whole damn dinner table, like everyone else."

"Yeah, Ezra," Brody added. "I understand it's a good opportunity, but I'd rather stay where I am."

Ezra's long-suffering sigh filled the room. "I hear you, and I figured you'd both feel this way, but I had to bring you the offers. And Dev? You know that's not the only one. I'm getting calls from other teams as well."

Over the years, I'd become more and more dissatisfied with having to hide our relationship, and it sometimes made me angry at the game for stealing my other joy.

"And you can give them the same answer. Unless Brody and I go together, I wouldn't be interested, and I know you can't say that without the rumor mill exploding, so please, let's just keep the status quo. See what the Kings offer me, make it a little better for Brody too, and we'll stay."

Ezra hummed his disappointment. "Well, be prepared to have an answer for the press. They'll come calling as to why you're rejecting such a lucrative contract."

"Maybe I should just tell them I got married, and I'm keeping it private, and that we don't want to leave New York," I mused.

"Talk about setting off a shit storm. You'd have every gossip rag coming after you to find out who, and don't think they won't speculate about your relationship with Brody, being as close as you are."

"What do you mean? We're discreet. We go out separately plenty of times." I grimaced. "Including plenty of dates with women. It's something we're aware we need to do."

"Hey, I'm not lecturing you guys. Listen, I feel for you. I can't imagine how hard it must be to have to hide your love, and I know how deeply invested you are in your relationship. But you know the personal lives of athletes and celebrities have always been fodder for the gossip mills. Just be careful, is all I'm saying."

It wasn't Ezra's fault the world sucked. "We are. And I didn't mean to take it out on you. I'm not planning on playing football forever, and if it gets to the point where it becomes too much, I'll retire. I've already accomplished my professional dream. I have no problem giving way to someone else to achieve theirs."

"You're a pretty special guy, Dev," Ezra remarked.

I winked at Brody. "I know. Talk to you soon."

Brody stared hard at me after I ended the call.

"What? You disagree with my decision?"

"No, of course not, but like Ezra said, that's a hell of a lot of money to give up."

I put my arms around him. "You're worth more to me than a fat bank account. After a while, it all becomes obscene. You've seen our financials. We're set for life. Neither of us wants for anything material. And the one thing we want, we can't have until we give up the game."

Brody's hands massaged my back, and it felt so damn good, I arched into his touch. "I'm not ready to do that, Dev. I'm not even thirty. Is that gonna be a problem for you? I know we've got a couple of Super Bowls, but I wanna keep playin'."

"Not a problem at all." I kissed his neck, loving that he'd kept the tradition of growing his hair out in the off-season. The silky waves tickled my cheek. "I know you're not ready to retire. Me neither." Something Ezra had mentioned niggled on the edge of my brain. "It might be a wild idea…"

"Gee, when have I heard that before?" Brody chuckled, and I nipped his ear.

"I'm serious. Brody, let's do it." Excitement mounting, I rested my hands on his shoulders and gazed into his beautiful blue eyes.

His brow puckered. "Do what? Take the trades?"

I shoved him. "No." Heart pumping madly, I hesitated, then blurted out, "Let's get married."

His lips kicked up in a grin. "Very funny."

I dug my fingers into his shoulders, holding him steady. "Do you see me laughing?" I held his startled blue eyes with mine. "I'm serious. Marry me. I love you, and I want to finally know we're together. Legally."

Brody's lips parted, his breaths coming in short puffs. "Dev…how…what…what're you thinkin'? How the hell do you think we can get away with this and no one's gonna find out?"

"We make everyone sign an NDA, and if necessary, pay them a ton of money to keep their mouths shut."

"Bribe them?"

I couldn't help smiling at Brody's shock and kissed him.

"Don't think of it as a bribe. It's more like a payment for services rendered. Or, in this case, not speaking." The more I thought about it, the more I liked the idea. "We can get a license and ask Ezra to handle the arrangements for us. It'll be Ezra and Roe, and we'll fly your mother in. We don't need anyone else."

"I—I don't know what to say."

The confusion in his face hurt, and I had to take a step back, gather my thoughts and not snap. "You don't want to marry me?"

"Of course I do." He grabbed my arm. "Just not in a way that we have to sneak around about it."

Frustrated, I shook him off and walked away. "Don't you think we'll always have to? If we wait until we retire, then come out, we'll still be hounded by the press, both good and bad. We won't have a moment's peace. If we do it this way, it's a chance to have it quiet and keep it to ourselves as long as possible."

Brody crossed the room and cupped my face in his hands. "You're serious."

"I am. But you're not sure." And it killed me.

He crushed his mouth to mine, kissing me until I lost my breath. "I'm sure I love you. I just need some time to think about the way we're gonna do it."

I brushed my lips to his. "Time is something we have plenty of."

Instead of returning to our bank statements, I began to research marriage licenses. "I bet we can get married without having to file the certificate. That would solve all our problems." I clicked on some links.

Brody peered over my shoulder and grunted, pointing at the screen. "Nope. Says here that in New York, if you don't file the license, your marriage isn't valid."

"Well, gay marriage is legal in every state. Let's look. One of the fifty has to work for us."

The sun had inched toward the horizon by the time I finished. Brody set a beer in front of me, and I blew him a kiss and took a long grateful drink. He stretched his legs out.

"Find anything useful?" He put the bottle to his lips.

"Yeah. That it isn't as easy as I thought it would be."

He grinned. "Nothing worthwhile ever is."

I arched a brow, still a little hurt by his earlier negativity. "So you're on board with this now?"

Brody set his bottle on the table and took mine from me. "Baby, I was always on board. There's nothing I want more than to spend the rest of my life with you as your husband." His raspy cheek rubbed mine, and I breathed deep of his familiar scent that was as much a part of me as my own. "I love you, Dev."

"I love you too." My excitement rising, I pulled the laptop closer. "Feel like taking a trip to California?"

CHAPTER THIRTEEN

Brody

Two months later

"So I fly out to LA tonight with Ezra," Dev said, "and we go to his parents' house in Beverly Hills. Good thing there're no storms coming. April can be a killer month here for that." As he spoke, he packed shorts, T-shirts, and a dark suit with a white linen shirt. I had a matching one ready to pack. "Tomorrow you pick up your mother from the airport and spend the day with her, and the day after, the two of you meet Roe and take a plane to San Diego. Ezra and I will join you there."

"I feel like we're on a clandestine mission." I sat on the edge of the bed, already missing him. "Ezra thinks this is going to work, right?"

Dev shut the carry-on, zipped it up, and put it on the floor. "Of course it will. The judge is a gay man who regularly performs same-sex weddings, and Ezra is positive he knows all about confidential marriages—we wouldn't be his first. We've signed the affidavits, and once you get there, we'll get the license." He put his arms round me. "In three days we'll be *married*. You'll be stuck with me forever."

"*Hmmm*." I cast my gaze to the ceiling and pretend-sighed. "I guess I have no choice, huh? I mean, we've spent all this money and—*oof*."

Dev pounced on me. His eyes sparkled, and he took my mouth in a bruising kiss. "All these years. I still remember the first time I saw you in the locker room freshman year and thought to myself, *Goddamn, that is one gorgeous man. I wish he was gay and I had the nerve to make a move.* Now here we are, ten years later, and I'm still so fucking lucky you love me. I can't wait to say I do."

I smoothed his hair off his face. "You know I'm never goin' anywhere. And I don't need a piece of paper to prove it."

More solemn than I've ever seen him, Dev's eyes latched on to mine. "I know. But I want it. So many people fought so hard for this right. I want to show everyone that we deserve everything that straight people do."

I had a hunch and ran with it. "Everyone? Or your parents?" More than anything I wished Dev could have a relationship with his mother and father. Not that I believed they'd ever be close, but at least they could acknowledge each other's existence. All these years and barely a word from them left me so angry at them and helpless at what to do about it.

Dev blinked and looked away. "They don't give a damn about me."

"C'mon, now," I protested. "I can't believe that. They might be disappointed in you, but I refuse to believe they don't care at all."

Nothing I could say would sway Dev's feelings. "That's because you were raised by someone who valued their child's emotional well-being and happiness. My parents probably only had me to keep their precious lineage going." His laughter was bitter. "Surprised them, didn't I? It ends with me. They don't know I'm gay. I never told them because they don't deserve to know the best part of me." His fingers teased at the waistband of my sweats. "And that's you. The very best of me."

The complicated relationship between Dev and his parents couldn't be solved in the short time we had. But I hoped one day his parents would see what an incredible human being their son was. And if they never did, it was their loss, and I'd be at his side forever.

Right now, he was driving me wild with his touch, and I couldn't think of anything except how much I needed him. He tugged down my pants and briefs and stripped out of his. Staring at him, I reached out, and we laced our fingers together.

"The next time we sleep together in this bed, we'll be married." I rubbed our joined hands on my face.

"*Mmm.* Husband. That sounds nice."

I kissed him, my lips lingering on his. "You in me sounds even nicer."

"I have three hours before the car comes to pick me up."

I ran my hands over his arms, my fingertips tracing the football tats. He'd only grown more beautiful to me throughout the years. "Better get moving."

He left no inch of me untouched and unloved, starting with my forehead, my fluttering lashes, and the shell of my ear. That warm tongue licked a path down my neck, tickling the tips of my achy nipples, and into the dip of my navel. My dick thrust up, and I ached to feel Dev's lips, but he skirted it to mouth the jut of my hip bone, tease along the inside of my thigh, and kiss the skin behind my knees.

"I'm so glad you've avoided injury. No one better hurt this beautiful body."

"Dev." I sighed. "Is this really happenin'?"

"It is. It finally is." His soothing voice and gentle hands left me weak and trembling. With a gentleness no one who saw his ferocious tenacity on the field would believe, he pushed his fingers in me, and I lit up like a Christmas tree. No matter how many years we'd had together, the countless times we made love, it was always like the first time when Dev touched me—wild, exciting, freeing. Devlin was the only man who made me come alive.

The slick wide head of his dick teased my rim, his blazing green eyes intent and filled with desire. I raised my knees to my shoulders. "In me. Now."

He covered my mouth with his as he thrust deep, and I gasped.

"So fucking perfect," he grunted as he flexed his hips, dragging his shaft out of me, then with a swift punch, driving home. He kept moving, and I grabbed my rigid cock, already wet and sticky from the precome sliding down its length.

"Harder, come on." My hand flashed on my shaft, and Dev increased his pace. Soon the bed was banging against the wall, creaking alarmingly, but I was too lost to care. My balls grew tight, and fire raced up my legs to explode in my belly. "Dev," I shouted as I came, spilling through my fingers, creating a sticky mess between us.

Sweat poured from Dev's face, and his lips thinned in an almost feral snarl of lust as he pounded into me. I was a puddle of post-orgasmic bliss, limp and drained and could only lie and watch as Dev's eyes rolled back in his head as his thick cock pumped me full of his come. We'd stopped using condoms a few years ago, and there was nothing I loved more than feeling all that hot wetness trickle out of me.

We lay locked together, Dev's lips pressed to the rapid pulse at my neck. I wrapped my arms around him. "Everything's gonna be okay."

Two days later, Momma and I stepped off the plane in San Diego to bright sunshine and warm sun. I stretched my arms out. "Now this is what I'm talkin' about. Do you know it's below freezing in the city? It's supposed to be spring. Why do I live in New York?"

Roe laughed. "I say that to Ezra all the time. In addition to their homes in La Jolla and Beverly Hills, his parents have a house in Newport Beach they never use. All I want to know is, why am I in the snow and ice instead of lounging on the beach?"

I couldn't agree more. And the few times a year we'd travel to the West Coast to play, we didn't have time to visit the beach.

Dev had texted me that Ezra would be picking us up, and entering the baggage area, I spotted his blond head. He greeted Roe with a kiss, then hugged me. "Good flight?"

"I slept most of the way, even with the cramped seats."

His eyes danced. "Sorry, but even first class is a tight squeeze for big lugs like you. Ms. Faith, how are you? I'm so glad to see you again."

"You too, honey."

They hugged, and I couldn't help smiling. Over the years, Ezra had met my mother when she'd visit the city, and she loved his jokes. Ezra took her suitcase, and we were off to the garage...where Dev sat, with a grin as wide as the Pacific, waiting in the back seat of the giant Land Cruiser.

"Hello, husband-to-be."

Overjoyed to see him, I gave him a quick kiss, knowing our reunion would be saved for later. He hugged Momma next, and my heart twisted. He still believed she wasn't one hundred percent in his corner.

"Ms. Faith, I'm so happy to see you."

"I am too, honey. All ready for the big day?"

Dev met my eyes. "I've been ready for years."

The drive from the airport to La Jolla was pretty short, but still, I was relieved to finally get there. Ezra and Roe showed us to our rooms, but after dropping off our luggage, Dev, Momma, and I gravitated to the spacious backyard, where fragrant rose bushes dominated the landscape. A table was set with glasses, a pitcher of iced tea, and a bucket of ice filled with water bottles. Dev poured us our drinks, and we sat under the umbrella, the sun shimmering in the blue sky overhead.

"Tell me again why you came out here to get married and couldn't do it at home or in New York," Momma said and took a sip of lemonade.

Dev opened his mouth, but I jumped in first. "Mainly, we want to keep it secret. In every other state, a license must be filed after the commitment ceremony or marriage, and it's public. California has a confidential license. It's sealed, and no one but us can request a copy."

Her face screwed up in thought. "But it's legal in other states?"

Here came the tricky part. "Yes and no. It's recognized, but it can get messy. Court orders are needed for proof of the license, and lawyers worry that because there's no public record, it can be harder to prove ownership of assets in case of divorce."

"Which isn't going to happen," Dev interjected. "We did all the research, and this was the best solution for now. Once we're no longer playing and out of the public eye, we'll do a big, more public celebration and get married in New York."

"That makes sense. Did you invite your parents, honey?"

Joy drained from Dev's face, and he turned away to gaze at the glittering water of the pool. "No. My parents don't know I'm gay, and I don't think they'd come anyway."

"Oh, Devlin. I'm sorry. Maybe one day you'll be able to work it out."

Dev hung his head. "I don't think so. Every major event in my life, I've always made sure to invite them, and they've refused every single one. It's pretty obvious they want nothing to do with me."

She reached out and squeezed his arm. "I love you, honey. In the beginnin' I was hesitant, thinkin' because you're a big-city guy, you might be too strong an influence on Brody and lead him away from the values he grew up with. I was a little overprotective, but that was before I really got to know you."

"I'd never do anything to hurt him," Dev responded, his voice thick with emotion.

"I'll admit it took me a while to realize that."

"I'm sorry, Momma. I shoulda told you sooner."

She shook her head. "No, baby. You had to come out when you felt right, not because of me." Momma held out a hand to Dev, and he took it gently. "I'm sorry I made you feel badly. I was wrong. It's taken me too long to tell you that I think you're a wonderful man and the perfect partner for Brody. And I think of you as my own."

His lips trembled, and I knew Dev was overwhelmed by Momma's words.

"Please...don't apologize to me," he whispered.

"You love Brody, and I was a mama bear. Theo used to tell me to lay off, but I ignored him." She sniffled and shifted her gaze to me for a moment. "I know you and he had a difficult relationship, but he truly did love me. And he cared about you. I wish you could've made your peace before he was taken away from me."

The tears came, and I hung my head. It was a weight I would always carry with me.

Dev leaned over and kissed her cheek. "I'm very sorry he isn't here. But I'm so glad you are and that you're going to be my mother." Wetness shone in his eyes, and I was stunned to see a tear roll down his cheek. "I'll admit, I've always been jealous of Brody for having the best mom in the world, and now I get to have you too."

Holding hands, the three of us sat for a few minutes as a warm breeze blew past. Clouds painted white streaks in the sky, and birds chirped. Butterflies flitted in and out of the rose bushes.

"It's so lovely here," Momma said. "A beautiful place for a wedding. I think I'm gonna go rest for a bit. It's been a while since I traveled across the country."

We stood, and she kissed us and left. Dev sighed and kicked off his sneakers. "Wanna sit by the pool?"

I followed his lead, and the two of us played footsie in the water for a while. I massaged his shoulders. "I'm glad you and Momma had that talk. Do you feel better now?"

He leaned his head on my shoulder. "I feel better when you're with me."

I always marveled at the two sides of Dev—the charismatic, risk-taking firecracker on the field, who played every single game as if it were the Super Bowl, contrasted with the soft and loving man who'd stolen my heart the very first time he kissed me.

"You know, none of your competitors would believe that the big bad Devil Summers on the field is such a pussycat in real life."

"Meow," he purred and rubbed his cheek to mine. "Your mother had a good idea. Let's go to our bedroom and I'll show you how big and bad I really am."

"Just make sure I'm able to walk tomorrow."

With a twinkle in his eye, he pushed me into the pool and took off running toward the house. I scrambled out, and dripping wet, caught up to him right before he got to the glass sliders.

"You're in so much trouble," I growled, pressing up against him.

Still laughing, he slung an arm around my neck. "Promise?"

I smacked his ass. "You're gonna be the one who's limpin'. Now get upstairs, unless you want me to throw you over my shoulder."

"*Pfft.*" He snorted and slid open the door. "I'd like to see you try."

Oh, it was on. I crept up behind him and tackled him at the knees, then hoisted him over my shoulder.

"Never double-dog dare a country boy."

CHAPTER FOURTEEN

Dev

The following day

"By the power vested in me by the State of California, I now pronounce you married and husbands to each other. Go ahead, guys. Seal it with a kiss." Judge Barry Graves stepped aside, and I took Brody's face between my hands.

"I love you, husband," I murmured for his ears only and brushed his lips with mine, then placed a kiss on his forehead. "Forever and for always."

Tears swam in those big blue eyes, but Brody smiled and ran his nose down my cheek, settling his mouth on mine for a brief moment. "I love you too, husband."

Hands clasped together, we turned and raised them above our heads. Our small audience clapped, cheered, and whistled. Ms. Faith, stunning in a blue dress to match her eyes, was the first one to greet us.

"You both look so handsome. I love you so much." I watched as she kissed and hugged Brody, her small frame dwarfed by his bulk. Afterward, she turned to me. "Come give me a hug."

She put her arms around me, and I bent to kiss her. She stopped me and put a hand to my cheek. "I know how much you love Brody and how hard he loves you in return. Always be honest with each other. And don't be afraid to lean on him. I love you like my own, but my greatest wish is to see you try and find your way back home again."

"I love you too. And I promise to keep loving Brody with everything I have."

Next, I hugged Roe, followed by Ezra. "I know I've made it difficult by not taking the big deals, but some things are more important than money." Sunlight gleamed on my thin gold band. We'd decided not to get matching rings and to wear them on different hands so as not to call attention, in case people noticed.

"I get it. And I admire you, even if I could've made a nice juicy percentage off it." His laughter was infectious, and I joined him, so damn happy, my heart hurt.

"Thank you for giving us this wedding and doing all you have for us. You're way beyond merely my agent. You're a good friend, and I appreciate everything."

"You and Brody are a wonderful couple, and I know you're going to be happy together. Maybe you'll even bring home another Lombardi trophy."

"That's the plan, my man." I hugged him again.

"Not so fast with that trophy, my dude. I might have somethin' to say about that."

A bright smile greeted me when I faced Vette, and we jumped each other. "Aw, man, it's so damn good to see you." I hugged Dora Lee. "And you're still as pretty as ever. How's the baby?"

She accepted my kiss on her cheek. "He's great. Just started walking, and of course his first word was *Daddy*." She gazed up at Vette with adoring eyes. "Vette's already got him a football and tiny cleats."

"Never too young." He took out his phone and showed me a picture of the four of them. Nicky held EJ's hand, and Vette had his arm around Dora Lee. They'd gotten married two years earlier, and Brody and I, along with about half the team, had gone to the wedding. We'd decided to tell them because we wanted one friend to share the day with us, and since Vette had pretty much guessed on his own.

"Proud papa."

"You know it." He squeezed Dora Lee. "We want a houseful. Working on number three."

Bright red, Dora Lee gasped. "Vette, stop." She put her hands to her cheeks, and he swooped in and gave her a kiss.

"Aw, baby, this is Devil we're talkin' to. He knows what's up." He winked at me. "Even if he is playing for the other team."

I groaned and shook my head. "Oh God, that was bad. But I'm really thrilled you could come and support us. I know family time is precious in the off-season."

Dora Lee said, "Brody was always nice to me in high school and didn't treat me bad like the other kids. And Ms. Faith was like a mother to me. I don't forget." She twirled the huge diamond on her hand. "I'm so grateful."

"I love you, baby." Vette hugged her tight. "You don't ever have to worry about stuff like that. Not anymore. You're my lady, and you deserve the best."

"I've got that. You."

It was bittersweet to see them so in love. On the one hand, I was happy for them and I knew how much they cared for each other. But it also made me recognize the big divide and how Brody and I had to create a sham life to be together. I sighed, knowing it was unfair, but that I couldn't change things.

"What was that sound?" Brody slid his big arms around me, and my dark thoughts vanished. I leaned into his muscled chest.

"Nothing. Just thinking."

He chuckled. "No thinkin' today. Only feeling. And I feel like giving my husband a kiss."

I faced him and held onto his big, broad shoulders. "I like the sound of that. Husband. Even though I've always belonged to you, hearing those words makes it all so real."

Brody kissed me, and Vette whooped it up in the background. I laughed, wishing it could always be like this—surrounded by friends, with the sun in our faces. The only person missing for me was Fallon, who'd gotten the flu and stayed home. His cousin Kelsie had stayed to take care of him. Brody's PA, Lizzie, stood to the side, having flown in late last night. She was leaving early in the morning—she had exams she couldn't miss—and Brody and I would have a small dinner for all three of them when we got back.

"What's real is I'm starving." Still holding on to Brody with one hand, I pointed at the long tables set up in the expansive patio area. "Let's eat."

Ezra and Roe had really outdone themselves with the wedding feast. Not because it was so elaborate, but because of the love and attention I could see had been put into every detail. One table held fresh seafood—crab legs, shrimp, poached salmon, and trays of caviar with all the accompaniments. Ezra's housekeeper attended to the platters of prime rib and filet mignon, and the people who ran his West Coast office, Sunny and his wife, Angie, were there too, passing platters of mini hot dogs, meatballs, and assorted finger food. There was a gorgeous display of fresh fruit and cheeses, and a round table for the three-tiered wedding cake, along with another setup with every kind of cake, cookie, and pastry imaginable.

In order to keep the number of outsiders down, Ezra had used his own staff and had made them sign confidentiality agreements, plus Brody and I had given each person a substantial payment for working that day. Was it a bribe to keep quiet? Maybe so, but I put my faith in people's innate goodness, as well as the money we gave them, to do the right thing.

We trusted our guests to take candid photos and videos, and there were plenty of cameras out when Brody and I smashed the cake in each other's faces, then kissed off the buttercream. It was a perfect day, and at one point I pulled Brody aside for a moment to ourselves. Music had started playing from the backyard speakers, and Vette slow-danced with Dora Lee. I was anticipating our honeymoon. Ezra had loaned us the house in Newport Beach. It was private and had a view of the water, which was all that mattered to us. We planned to drive up tomorrow after brunch—and after making sure Ms. Faith got off okay—and stay there for the week. Ezra had reassured us that he'd lent the home to other high-profile clients who needed anonymity. All I wanted was sun, sleep, and Brody, not necessarily in that order.

"How're you doing?" I asked Brody.

"I'm good. Just thinkin' about my daddy and what he woulda thought of me."

This was new. Brody rarely talked about his father. "I'm sure he would've loved you no matter what."

Brody leaned against the wall, pensive, and figuring he was working out something in his head, I waited, giving him the time he needed.

"And I can't stop thinkin' about Theo. I was so wrong, Dev. All those years Momma and Theo were married. I shoulda given him a chance. He wasn't a bad guy—I woulda resented anyone who came in and tried so hard to be my daddy. I thought I'd have time to talk to him, but it just slipped away. And now he's gone, and I never got a chance to tell him I was glad he was there to make Momma happy."

Guilt was a crushing weight to bear, especially for someone who possessed such a soft and loving heart, like Brody. While it was true that he'd never given Theo a chance, I couldn't imagine how hard it must've been for a little boy to lose the father he loved, only to have another man try and take his place.

"Maybe now's the time to tell your mother that. She always wanted the two of you to get along. It would probably bring her some peace. But don't beat yourself up over things that can't be changed."

Brody listened, but being the stubborn man he was, I knew he'd gotten that perception of himself ingrained in his head, and it was hard to change his mind. Only one person could do that. When it was apparent he wasn't going to respond, I decided to change the topic and nudged him.

"Look at Vette and Dora Lee. He sure is crazy about her. Reminds me of the first time I saw you." That day in the Waves' locker room, at our first team meeting, I was so damn nervous, knowing I was the backup quarterback to the number one college player in the country. Then I saw Brody, and a different kind of nerves blossomed in my stomach. "I couldn't believe I'd have to play with a guy on my team and worry about getting a hard-on every time I'd step out on the field." I ran my knuckles along Brody's jaw. "I took way too many cold showers all those years, thinking of you and that gorgeous body under me. But the connection was instantaneous. So many times I wanted to say something, but I held back."

"Instead, you teased me. Callin' me choirboy." A dimple popped out on his cheek. "And I remember checking you out in the showers. Wishing I could run my fingers over those tats. Feel your skin." His eyes grew heated. "Now they're mine."

"You're still my choirboy. So good and honest." Unable to resist him, I kissed his lips, feeling them soften beneath mine. "You've made me see God plenty of times."

"You better stop 'cause it's about to get X-rated if you keep it up."

"Oh, I'm gonna keep it up. All night long." I winked and patted his cheek just as Ezra came by and grabbed Brody's hand.

"Come on, big guy. Let's boogie."

Roe leaned against the wall and held up his hands. "I've had enough. He and my ninety-five-year-old grandmother can wear me out. Please take him."

We watched as Ezra and Brody danced alongside Momma and Vette while Dora Lee took a video. Roe accepted a glass of champagne from a passing waiter.

"How do you feel being a married man?"

I thought about it for a moment. "Not much different than before. I know Brody didn't really understand why I wanted to do this so badly, but it means a lot to me, someone who didn't grow up with a sense of family like he did, to have us legally formalized."

"I'm very sorry your parents aren't here. They're missing out on seeing your happiness, and it's a shame."

I gazed at Brody laughing as he, Ezra, and Vette now took control of the floor. Ms. Faith had given up and stood with Dora Lee, watching Brody.

"I think it's shameful on their part, but there's nothing I can do to change their minds. They've never tried to understand me, and I've given up trying." The waiter passed by again with flutes of champagne, and this time I took one.

"I understand how frustrating it can be. Ezra's parents were similar—they didn't think I was good enough and wanted him to marry a girl, have kids, and run the family business. They did everything they possibly could to keep us apart. In the end, they came around because they saw how badly Ezra and I wanted to be together and how much we loved each other. I'm hoping the same will be true for your parents."

The bubbles from the champagne tickled my nose as I drank it, mulling over how to put my emotions into words. I knew Roe was trying to make me feel better.

"There's a difference. Ezra's parents loved him. In their heartless way, they thought they were doing what was best for him. My parents simply don't give a damn. They don't care if I'm happy. They don't care at all." I gulped the rest of my bubbly. "If they did, they wouldn't have spurned every single invitation I've ever sent them, including my college graduation." My smile was paper thin. "I know what you're trying to say, but the only way my parents would ever accept me is if I followed in their footsteps."

"And they don't know you're gay."

A bitter laugh burst from me. "Not a chance. I'm sure that would be another failure on my part. Another rejection from them. I've had enough already, thank you.

They don't get to diminish me or my love for Brody with their snobbery and arrogance." I blinked to clear the tears from my eyes. "That's enough serious talk for the night. I have to say it again, thank you so much for putting this all together for us. You have no idea how much we appreciate it."

Roe hugged me. "Yeah, I do. It's one of the most important days of your life, and you want to spend it with people who care about you."

Which should include my parents, but that wasn't going to happen. "Come on. Let's get some food."

When I checked, Brody had left the dance floor and was sitting at one of the small round tables with his mother. I hoped he was planning on talking to her about Theo. At least one of us deserved to heal.

CHAPTER FIFTEEN

Brody

"Momma, can we talk?"

I mopped my forehead with a bunch of napkins. The sun had set, but Ezra was a maniac on the dance floor, and after two songs, I'd begged off. I spotted Dev in an intense conversation with Roe, and I hoped he would open up about his non-relationship with his parents. It hurt my heart that all these years had passed without so much as a *hello, how're you doing* phone call from them. How Dev had turned out to be such a loving, caring man was one of life's mysteries.

"Sure, honey. Everything okay?" She set her lemonade on the bar. "You're lookin' kinda flushed."

Chuckling, I took her elbow to steer her to one of the small tables near the pool. "I'm good, although I'm out of practice with my dance moves. Ezra is unstoppable."

Momma's wise blue eyes met mine. "I don't think you want to talk about Ezra's dancin'. What's on your mind?"

I fidgeted, trying to figure out the right way to say it. "I'm sorry about Theo."

Her brow puckered. "I know. You came to the funeral and made a nice speech. I appreciated it."

"No, that's not what I meant. I'm sorry for the way I acted toward him from the beginnin'. When you married him, I missed Daddy so much, I resented him comin' in and tryin' to be my father. I never gave him a chance, and lookin' back now, I guess I can't blame him for givin' up tryin'." I rubbed my eyes. "I didn't make it easy for him, and I never got the chance to tell him he was a good man."

Tears streaked down Momma's face. "It was hard. I shoulda put the two of you together and let you talk it out, but Theo kept sayin' to give it time. He didn't wanna push you and force you to like him. Those months turned into years, and you were away so much with football. You know that Theo never hated you, and I know you didn't hate him. But after so many years, he kinda just gave up, like you said." She picked up a napkin and blotted her cheeks. "I do wish you'd had the chance to talk it out face-to-face."

I hung my head, never having felt as low as I did at that moment. "I'm sorry."

"But it's all right now. Hearing you say the words brings peace to my heart. Because your bein' able to admit it out loud means that he knows." She took my hand and squeezed it hard. " 'Cause I believe he's with me and can hear you. So I don't want you to beat yourself up about it. It's your weddin' day. You should only know joy."

I sniffled. "Thanks, Momma. And I am happy."

"I can see that. Never forget this feelin'. I hope it follows you the rest of your life."

My gaze found Dev, who, having finished talking to Roe, now made his way to the dessert table. "I believe it will. I can't imagine my life without Dev in it."

"I know. If there ever were two people meant to be together, it's you and Dev."

Vette and Dora Lee joined Dev, and Vette peered around and asked him a question. Dev glanced in my direction, a beautiful smile breaking out over his face.

"I think your husband wants you," Momma said, releasing my hand. "It's gettin' late anyway, and I need to pack. My flight is in the afternoon, but I don't want to wait and have to rush through brunch."

I rose to my feet and gave her a hug and a kiss. Together we crossed the lawn to the patio. Vette and Dora Lee were saying good-bye to Dev.

"Are you leavin'? You can't stay for brunch tomorrow?"

Vette made a face. "Nah, we got an early flight to get home to the baby and Nicky. Next week we're all goin' to Hawaii for a charity golf tournament. Dora Lee and the kids are comin' along."

Her face brightened. "It's my first time in Hawaii. I can't wait."

"You have fun." I kissed her cheek and hugged Vette. "We'll catch up with you soon."

"Come by and visit the new place. We've finally finished the construction. Dora Lee's been talkin' 'bout having a big housewarming." They'd bought a sprawling home outside Memphis, and I couldn't have been more thrilled for her. Sometimes good things did happen to good people.

"We will."

"Safe flight."

Dev and I watched as they made the rounds to say good-bye, and we looked at each other.

"Momma went inside to finish packin' for tomorrow. We'll see her at brunch."

Dev massaged my back. "*Mmm.* Looks like things are winding down." He stretched his arms over his head and yawned noisily. "I'm a little tired myself."

"*Mmhmm.* You're not foolin' nobody, baby, with that act."

As if overhearing us, Ezra called out, "Don't give up the day job, Devil. Go start the honeymoon already."

To cheers and whistles, I grabbed Dev's hand, and we waved and hustled across the lawn to the far end, where a separate house—or *casita*, as Ezra informed us they called them out here—awaited us for our wedding night. I didn't know what to expect, but when we entered the stucco structure and turned on the light, we both stopped and stared.

"Damn," I whispered. "This is somethin' else, even for Southern California."

"Yeah. And they say Texas is go big or go home," Dev concurred. "They haven't seen La Jolla."

Bouquets of flowers covered almost every available countertop and table. Another wedding cake—two tiers instead of three, and chocolate—sat in the middle of the dining table, along with a bucket of champagne on ice and two crystal flutes.

The room had to be at least thirty feet long and twenty feet wide, with an extra-large sectional sofa facing the wide windows. Large modern art pieces were placed around the room. The floor was cream marble with beautiful inlay work. A large fireplace took up one wall, and the gleaming white kitchen ran the length of the other.

Hand in hand, we kicked off our shoes and walked through the space. I peeked in the refrigerator and found it stocked with champagne, juices, water, and beer, along with caviar, shrimp cocktail, oysters, and smoked salmon, with cheeses on a platter. The freezer held at least five flavors of ice cream.

"I'm kinda full from dinner. We can save all this for a midnight snack," Dev mused but wandered over to the dining table and couldn't resist swiping his finger through a blob of icing from the cake. "*Mmm,* buttercream." He kissed me, and I licked his lips and tongue.

"Delicious. Both the chocolate and you. Let's grab this bottle and get to the bedroom. We don't need the glasses."

The bedroom was almost as spectacular as the living area, with a huge, oversized bed, another fireplace, and fluffy rugs on the pale wooden floor. Glass sliders led to a small deck, where a Jacuzzi waited. Dev unbuttoned his shirt and pulled the curtains shut, then took off his pants. He tossed the clothes to the chair in the corner.

"Ezra had them bring our suitcases here, I see." He sat on the bed, and I crawled across it to be near him.

"We're not gonna need any clothes for the rest of the night."

Dev leaned into my chest, and I kissed his neck, moving down to the collarbone while teasing his nipples. He hummed his approval and reached out to the nightstand. "I wonder if Ezra provided us with—" He cackled. "That crazy idiot. Look at this."

He scooped out a handful of colored dildos in multiple widths and lengths, candy-flavored lube, and edible underwear. Dev waggled his brows. "I do love me some edible undies."

I could feel my face burning. "I can't believe him," I muttered as Dev crawled across the bed to the other nightstand and opened it, whooping with more laughter.

"You're not gonna believe this."

I raised my eyes to the ceiling. "Why do I doubt that, knowing Ezra?" When I faced Dev, he held a jar of chocolate syrup and a canister of whipped cream. "Oh, for God's sake," I groaned. "What is wrong with that man?"

Dev uncapped the whipped cream, pointed the spout to his mouth, and squirted. I watched as his tongue swept over his lips, and my cock stirred. Maybe Ezra wasn't so ridiculous after all. Lust slammed through me, and without giving Dev any warning, I pounced on him and yanked off his briefs.

Beneath me, Dev lay spread-eagled and grinning. "Give it to me, baby." He handed me the canister. I copied him, but I took it further and swallowed his cock, sucking the hard, heavy length as the sweetness filled my throat.

"Oh, damn, that's good. All creamy and foamy, *mmm*." Dev moaned deep in his throat, and I licked the lingering drips of whipped cream from his shaft. I dove in again, taking him in fully. "Brody," he cried out. "Fuck." His avid gaze was pinned to me sliding up and down his dick. "That's so damn hot."

I released him, not wanting him to come too soon. "Not ready," I panted and coated one of the dildos—neon pink with ridges—in cherry-flavored lube. I handed it to Dev and got on all fours. Dev teased the flared head on my hole, then licked it in long, wet laps of his tongue, before pushing it in to the hilt. "Goddamn," I grunted, working my raging hard-on, while Dev dragged the slippery toy in and out of my passage, lighting me up as he drove in faster and faster. I lost control and came, spilling hot and heavy onto the sheets.

"That's it, you're ready now." Dev tossed aside the dildo and sank inside me, his thick cock huge and heavy.

"So good, so fucking good," I panted, still in the throes of my climax. Strong hands dug into my hips, and Dev thrust hard until he groaned and came, filling me with his come. Sweaty and panting, we lay curled around each other.

"You're even hotter now that you're my husband." He kissed my shoulder and up my neck, his lips curving upward. "I've never fucked a married man."

"Your married man. Forever."

Dev slid out of me, and we took a shower together, then opened the bottle of champagne and relaxed in the hot tub, passing it between us. Dev ran his foot over mine.

"I saw you and your mom had an intense-looking conversation."

I swallowed some more of the champagne. "Yeah. I needed to tell her how I felt about Theo and that I was sorry I treated him like I did." The water's frothy bubbles mesmerized me.

Dev inched toward me and put a hand on my arm. "Was it cathartic? Do you feel better now that you've gotten it out in the open?"

I had to think for a moment. "I'm not sure. Yeah, I'm glad I got to tell Momma how I felt, but it doesn't make it better. I definitely coulda been a nicer person to Theo. And I'll never get the chance to do that." My sigh resonated, and I drank more of the champagne.

Dev plucked the bottle from my hand and set it outside the hot tub. "Getting drunk isn't going to help. The memories are still there, like scars you can't get rid of, no matter how hard you try."

"And you know because you tried it?" I challenged him.

Maybe it was a night of confessions. Dev loathed talking about his parents and the past, and I'd always let it slide because I hated upsetting him. Plus, he was a master at avoidance and changing the subject. But if we were going to share our lives, it had to include the good along with the bad.

He slid fully into the tub, allowing only his head and neck to remain above water. "Yeah. I couldn't wait to leave home and go far away to college. I thought it would be so freeing—away from home, no worrying about my parents' disapproval." He stared into the water. "Instead, it was like a prison. Everywhere I'd go on campus, people recognized me from being on the team—it meant I couldn't hook up with anyone. All I did was practice and go to class. I couldn't believe it, but I missed home so damn bad, even my parents' disapproval. I just felt so out of place." He raked a hand through his wet hair. "One night I got invited to a frat party."

That surprised me. "Coach told us those were off-limits."

His smile was heartbreaking. "I know. I did it anyway. And I got shitfaced and called my parents. They didn't care that I said I missed being home. They didn't care about how I felt at all."

The whole story was fascinating. All this had happened while I'd still been learning my way around campus and figuring out who I was as a gay kid, knowing I had my own secrets to hide. Like Dev, I'd struggled, only I'd had a loving mother I could talk to. And, as Dev always teased me, I was that choirboy who sought peace in the faith I'd grown up with.

"Did Coach ever find out?"

He snorted. "Sure as hell did. He fucking laid into me, benched me for two games, and said if I wanted to stay on the team, I'd better never pull a stunt like that again."

That I could believe. "I remember you sitting out and wondered why. I'll bet he was pissed. Coach didn't play."

"Yeah. But he also gave me a wake-up call that I was part of something bigger than my ego. Also, that I was replaceable. I didn't like that. I was used to being number one, the hotshot. There, I was just another number on a jersey. And someone was always waiting in the wings to see me fall." He blinked and sat up, splashing water over the edge. "How did this conversation become about me? We were talking about you and Theo. I think you did all you can do. Your mother understands, and really, what else could you do?"

Dev was right, but I couldn't help feeling bad. However, it was our wedding night, and I didn't want either one of us to spend it thinking of past mistakes. We had our whole lives to look forward to.

I got to my feet. "I'm beginnin' to feel like a prune. Wanna rinse off and have a snack? Then maybe...?" I raised a brow, and Dev grinned and jumped up with a splash.

"Maybe? Hell, no. Definitely."

CHAPTER SIXTEEN

Dev

Six months later

Away games were never my favorite. Of course I preferred my own stadium and the fans cheering us on, but the real reason was purely selfish. It meant time away from Brody. We couldn't risk being together, and with these long stretches, it was now more than two weeks since we'd been able to see each other alone. We'd started on the West Coast, in Portland, this week was San Diego, and the next was down to Texas.

"Second and seven. Let's do this," I urged in the huddle. I positioned myself to take the snap and waited before calling out the play. "Blue 80, Blue 80. Set. Hit."

With the football in my hand, I scrambled to the left, took a few steps back to orient myself, and saw Marlon wide open. The ball sailed into his hands, and he ducked one tackle and broke free of another to spin and gain twenty yards.

"All right. Let's do this again," I called out. Coach Jackson gave me the signals, and we lined up for the first and ten. "White 80, White 80. Set. Hit." I took the snap and faded away from the line. Nathan Woods, the Mountaineers' giant tackle, came barreling through. I only had a second to get rid of the ball, and I sent it sailing toward Brody. I saw him catch it; then stars exploded as I was knocked off my feet by the mountain of a man.

"Ooof. Ow, shit." I lay still for a moment to stop my head from ringing and get my bearings. Jonas Armstrong and Derion Wallace, our biggest wide receivers, helped me get to my feet, and I undid the straps of my helmet and pulled it off. The team medics ran onto the field to check me out.

"Devlin, you okay?" Mike Hatchett appraised me with a sweeping glance. "Anything hurt?"

"I'm fine. Just lost my breath for a sec."

"Let's go," he said with a wave of his hand.

Brow furrowed, I stood my ground. "Go where? It's first and ten. We're almost close enough for Zeke to kick a field goal."

"Dev. There are only two minutes to go, and we're already ahead. Let Fontaine come in."

Luke Fontaine was the backup quarterback and a good kid. I knew he was anxious to get some playing time, and I didn't blame him. Thing was, I didn't like walking off and leaving my team.

"But–"

"No buts. You need to be checked out. Come on." His frown brooked no dissent, and I sighed.

To the jeers and cheers of the crowd, I trudged off the field, my teammates patting me on the back, shoulder, or swatting my ass. No one liked to be taken out of the game. Before I headed down to medical, I turned to see Fontaine hand off the ball, and we gained another three yards.

"Let's go, Dev." Mike led me to the infirmary, where I was poked, prodded, and had a light shined in my eyes. I was made to track fingers, recite the alphabet, and walk a straight line.

"I'm not drunk, you know. Just got knocked off my feet," I joked.

"You know the drill." Dr. Fletcher, our team physician, knew I hated medical attention and always brushed off help. "Don't fight me, and you'll be in the locker room to celebrate the win."

After half an hour, I was free to go. Fletcher put a hand on my arm. "Take care. It gets a little harder when you're closing in on thirty."

"I'm an old man now, huh?" I teased. "I'm good." And left to join my team.

I opened the door to the music blasting and everyone celebrating the win. The press interviewing us had already left, which I was extremely thrilled about. I had zero desire to answer question after question as to whether I was injured.

"Devil, you good?" Marlon shouted above the din. I gave him the thumbs-up and danced my way over to him, Jonas, and Brody.

"Four straight wins, baby!"

I fist-bumped Brody, then the others.

"I love the sound of undefeated on a Sunday evening," I cackled as I took off the rest of the clothing and gear I hadn't removed for the doctors. And because I remembered how it felt playing in my first game, taking the place of a veteran, I walked over to Fontaine.

"Hey, Luke."

The rookie's eyes met mine. "Hi, Dev. You're okay, I hope?"

"Yeah, I'm good. Nice work out there to bring the game home."

Color rose in Luke's face. "It wasn't much. Just running the time out."

"Hey, that's not true and you know it. Games are won and lost in the last few minutes, and they were breathing down our necks. You made sure we played it smart and didn't hotdog it to prove anything."

I held out my fist, and he bumped it, a smile brightening his face. "Thanks. That means a lot."

I soft-punched his shoulder and returned to my locker. "God, I need my massage." I rolled my neck and grunted. "I swear I've discovered parts of my body I never knew existed, and that shit hurts." Brody snickered and I glared. "What're you laughing at?"

"Nothing, *old man*," he teased. "Guess some of us are in better shape than others." He flexed his biceps. "I'm feelin' just fine."

I grinned to myself.

I bet you are. You feel pretty damn good to me.

Marlon slung a towel around his neck. "Lemme ask you something."

"Yeah?" I turned to face the big wide receiver. "What's up?" A frisson of fear shot through me. No matter how well Brody and I hid our relationship, it could all crash and burn at any moment.

"I heard you nixed signing with the Rockets, even though the money was mad sick. What's up with that?"

Relieved that was all, I shrugged. "I don't need all that. I love being on the Kings, and I wanted to stay. Simple. They made me a decent counteroffer, so I'm staying. There's something to be said for loyalty."

"Is that all?" Zeke tossed out his two cents from across the room. "I heard it might be 'cause you got a lil somethin' somethin' stashed away in the city you don't wanna leave." He smirked. "Or maybe a big someone someone."

My hand balled into a fist, and I'd have liked nothing more than to take a swing at his stupid face. However, fighting never solved anything, especially if it would lead to possible injury, bad press, and definite suspension. I chilled the fuck out and raised his dumbass smirk with a sneer of my own.

"Damn, Cunningham, you are awfully interested in my personal life. Maybe you should put all that effort into training harder and figuring out how to make longer kicks. We might not've had such a close game if you'd made those field goals earlier." My lip curled. "Just sayin'."

"You bastard," he spat and jumped in my face, but I didn't flinch, and the team gathered around.

"Go ahead," I said, quiet but deadly. "Do it, and I will have your sorry ass in jail for assault and make sure you never play on this or any team again." I slammed my locker door and glared at him, but he didn't back off.

"You don't think we all notice? You never hanging out with the same girl twice? Hell, you're never seen with any chick."

I rolled my eyes and laughed. "That all you got? Lemme tell you something. I let my playing do the talking to get me in the press, not my personal life. I don't like to talk bad about my teammates, but from what I heard, you're damn lucky your baby mamas don't press charges for child support."

Scowling, he spit on the floor. "Those bitches? They think I'm a fucking ATM. I pay what I want." His sneer disgusted me. "They trapped me with those damn brats. I never wanted them."

Jonas, who had pictures of his daughter hung in his locker and a tattoo of her name over his heart, shook his head. "A man who don't wanna take care of his kids ain't no man at all."

Zeke's face grew red. "They know better than to make me mad." He flexed his fists, and shock hit me like a tidal wave.

"Are you saying you've put your hands on them?"

Zeke shrugged with a grin. "They like it rough."

"You pig. Keep your hands off women." I poked him in the chest. "Haven't you learned anything from those public service messages we do every year? Violence against women isn't being a man. It's being a coward. Stay out of my business and concentrate on your own life. You're lucky your ass isn't in jail." Ignoring his glare, I went to take a shower.

Upon my return, I saw that most of my teammates had left, including Jonas, Marlon, and surprisingly, Zeke. I'd prepared to defend myself further and breathed a sigh of relief.

"I'll catch you later," Brody murmured, sitting on the bench. "I've gotta get in the whirlpool and get a rubdown and stretch. I'm gonna go to the hotel and relax."

I wished I could go with him. "I've got all that, plus my shoulder stuff. The doctors checked me out and said I'm fine. No long-lasting effects."

Big blue eyes traveled over my body, returning to linger on my face. "I'll see you when I see you." Brody hefted his duffel and walked away.

I followed his retreat, longing for him. Much as I loved playing the game, I missed the off-season and our time together.

Two hours later I left the stadium and headed back to the hotel. I texted Brody.

Where are you? I'm starving.

He messaged me immediately.

We're all by the pool, having chicken. Zeke's running his mouth.

My answer was short and succinct.

Fuck him.

The car pulled up and dropped me off. First, I stopped by my room to drop my bag off and change, and I made my way to the outdoor area. A big crowd had gathered, and I ducked in, hoping to slide by, but no luck.

"It's Devil Summers. Look."

"Can I have your autograph?"

"Can we have a picture?"

"Were you hurt? Is that why you were taken out of the game?"

A hand groped my ass, and I whirled to face a blond in a tiny bikini, who gave me a brazen once-over. "You were amazing out there. You're my favorite player."

My smile was thin. I had little use for people who thought it was appropriate to touch others without permission. "Thanks. But we're just hanging out together as a team tonight. No visitors."

"Is that why my friends are there?" She pointed a long, pink-tipped fingernail, then surprised me by wrapping her slim arms around my neck and pressing her lips to mine. "*Mmm*, come on, show me some of those Devil moves."

Her sinuous body rubbed up on mine, and I could see the cameras taking pictures and videos. What I wanted was to pick her up and drop her in the pool, but instead, I undid her clinging hands and tried to keep the anger from my voice.

"I'm sorry, but we're not allowed during the season. Coach's rules." I could barely speak through my tightly clenched jaw and pulled her over to a quieter place.

She pouted, thinking that would sway me. "Zeke doesn't care. He's the one who invited me."

Alarm bells rang. "He did?"

She nodded. "Yeah. He said you'd wanna party."

"And you know Zeke?"

"Oh, yeah. We get together every time he's out here. But he told us you'd be up for it. Maybe the three of us?" She arched a brow and adjusted the strap of her tiny bikini. Through the flimsy fabric, I could see hard nipples poking out.

Unfortunately for her, that was the only thing hard between us.

"Sorry. Team rules." I brushed her cheek with my lips.

Coach was insistent that players not have sex the night before a game and definitely not if we were in the playoffs. And the evening after? I had zero desire and wanted nothing more than to lie down and rest.

"Guess it's your loss, Devil. See ya."

She walked away, her thong giving me a view of a tanned, firm ass. I made a beeline for the pool and an empty chaise by Jonas. Several tables were set up with platters of chicken, coleslaw, and salads. The grill was going with burgers and steaks, and my stomach growled.

"Sure you don't want what she's serving, Dev?" Jonas cracked.

"Bet she wanted something else eaten. *Mmm.*" Marlon shook his head. "She sure was hot and wanted you."

"You guys are acting stupid. Hand me some chicken, please." I tore into a leg. "You think I'm gonna break the rules for some groupie? Besides, she's one of Zeke's regulars. That was enough to make her a big no. I just gave her a kiss to make her feel better for wasting her time."

Brody, who'd remained silent until then, chuckled and tipped his head toward the opposite side of the pool. "Looks to me like she feels okay."

I followed Brody's gaze to see her snuggling with Zeke and another woman.

"He's free to be a fool if he wants. He seems to make a habit of it. The gossip sites all say he's way behind on his child support payments. I hope these women don't think he's going to be a loving father."

This was so damn stupid. Here I was with my husband, and I couldn't even acknowledge him, but some random girl could maul me, and everyone thought that was fine. Sooner or later, something was going to have to give.

CHAPTER SEVENTEEN

Brody

Two months later

I loved a bye week. Having extra days to rest and recharge gave me life. Ezra's friend Ross and his husband owned a cabin upstate, but they were away in Europe, and Ezra said they were happy to lend it to Dev and me. I'd rented a car, and following the GPS, I prepared for a drive upstate.

Dev called as I hit the Thruway. "I just got here. It's gorgeous, but it's already chilly."

I changed lanes. "Guess you'll have to keep my feet warm. And don't hog the blankets."

"Just get up here," Dev growled in that husky voice that set my heart racing. "I'm gonna start a fire and get my surprise ready for you."

"I should be there in about two hours. What's my surprise?"

Dev laughed. "If I told you, it wouldn't be one. See ya."

Without giving me a chance to respond, he ended the call. Knowing Dev, it could be anything from a couples massage to a puppy. I took a swig from my cup of coffee and hit the accelerator. Three days alone with Dev. I couldn't wait.

Less than two hours later, I pulled in front of the large wood-shingled cabin. It reminded me of the house I'd built but, as Dev had said, it was a damn sight colder up here. Tall pines shot to the sky, and evergreen bushes surrounded the area. The lights were on, and Dev's Porsche was in the driveway. Anticipation rushed through my veins, and I pulled my duffel from the back seat and slammed the door shut.

Dev opened the door and waited. I took the steps two at a time and settled my mouth over his. He held me at my hips but didn't grind his pelvis into me as he always did when we'd been apart for a while.

"God, you taste good." I nuzzled into his neck. "Can't wait to lick you all over."

He shook with laughter. "Might wanna table that for a little while, studmuffin." With a twinkle in his eye, he stepped aside. "Surprise."

"Momma, what're you doin' here?" I picked her up and swung her in a circle. "How...when...?" I hugged her tighter.

"Dev flew me in and picked me up this morning. We drove straight from the airport." She threw him a fond look. "Your husband is a speed demon."

I glared at him. "You're not supposed to drive recklessly with my mother in the car."

He put up his hands. "I was never reckless. Just fast. Ms. Faith and I spent a lovely day stocking the fridge, then enjoyed a little picnic by the lake."

"I can't wait to see it."

Momma let go of me. "I'll bet it's beautiful by moonlight. Why don't you go show Brody? I think I'm gonna take a hot bath and get ready for dinner."

Amusement danced in Dev's eyes. "I always listen to your mother."

I slid my arm over Dev's shoulders. "Me too. Let's go."

Hand in hand, we walked outside and down the flat rock steps leading to the lake. The fiery rays of the setting sun reflected off the glittering surface of the water.

"Wow," I breathed. "This is gorgeous. What a view."

Dev kissed my cheek, his gaze as heated as the orange sky. "It sure is." He tugged my hand. "This way." We walked halfway around the lake to where another cabin sat concealed in the trees. He opened the door.

"What's goin' on?" I peered into the space, which was completely furnished. "Who owns this place, and why are you just walking inside?"

He flicked on a light. "Come in."

It was a beautiful cabin, not as grand as the one we were staying in, but comfortable and homey, with a huge fireplace, a large open kitchen, and beams crisscrossing the soaring ceiling.

Dev leaned against the fireplace while I tried to figure out what was going on. "Why are we here?"

"Do you like it?"

"Well, yeah. What's not to like?"

He pulled me near. "I rented it for us this weekend. After we have dinner with your mother, I have security coming to watch over that cabin, but we're going to spend the night here."

"Why?"

He nuzzled into my neck and I shivered, a groan slipping past my lips. "That's why. I need to hear you scream my name, and much as I love your mother, I can't have sex with her in the house."

Laughter bubbled up from my chest. "Fair enough. And yeah, this place is really nice."

"You're really nice." He kissed me, deep and searching. "And really beautiful. It's gotten so crazy with the buildup to the playoffs that we haven't been alone in weeks."

Aside from his gorgeous face and ripped body, what initially attracted me to Dev was his fierceness, on and off the field. That total dedication allowed him to rise to the top. And as intense as he was about football, he was even more committed to showing his love for me in so many ways. This was one of them, and I loved him so much, it was almost painful.

"How do you always know the right thing to do?" I slid my fingers through his hair to anchor him close. My cheek rasped against his ever-present stubble. "I've missed you too, but I never would've thought to do this." I kissed the side of his smiling mouth. "And thank you for bringing up Momma. I haven't seen her since the wedding."

"I know you. And I know what and who you love. It's not a contest." His lips were soft and warm as they moved over mine. "We're both winners."

Seven years later, and his kisses still excited me as much as that first time he'd surprised me by the firepit after our national championship. "Once the season ends, we should go down to the house and lock ourselves away from everyone." He didn't answer me, and I took a step away. "What's wrong?"

"Don't you ever get tired of hiding?"

"Of course. But what can we do? Are you willin' to come out?"

He chewed his lip. "N-no. Not right before the playoffs. It would be too much of a distraction. But I gotta admit, it's something that has been on my mind."

I crossed my arms. "Yeah?" Hearing that wasn't surprising. Over the years, it had always been Dev who'd spoken of his dissatisfaction with needing to hide his sexuality.

"I don't know, Brody. I've won enough Super Bowls already. I don't care about the money or shit like that. We're almost thirty. I'm getting really tired of hiding us."

"I am too," I spoke softly. "I just don't know what to say. I'm not ready to retire. I haven't thought about what I can do with the rest of my life. I can't sit and fish and play golf for the next fifty years or so."

His green eyes blazed. "You can do anything you want." He paced the room, and I let him walk it out, understanding this was his way of thinking things out in his head. Finally, he came to a stop in front of me. "Change of plans. With the bye week, we can take a trip home with your mother and check in and see how the shelter and center are working out. Stay a few days."

We didn't need to return until later in the week to start watching films and learning the playbook. The way my heart jumped at the thought, I knew Dev was right.

"You wouldn't mind?"

A beautiful smile broke across his face. "Baby, as long as I'm with you, I don't care where I am."

Every time he said those words to me, he made the impossible happen—I fell even more in love with him.

"Guess we better tell Momma not to unpack yet."

With a twinkle in his eyes, he popped the top of my jeans and unzipped me. "We have some time. I haven't greeted you properly yet."

Two days later, Dev and I walked into the shelter with armfuls of Kings signed merchandise to give away. We were greeted with hugs by all the staff. Leah, Janie's sister, who worked there full-time, took us around to show us how much better the living conditions were now.

"And all the proper clothing for the adults to wear for job interviews has helped immeasurably. That and the school supplies for the kids..." Tears welled in her eyes. "You two have been incredible."

"It's not only us," I explained. "The Kings organization is behind it as well, and there's more help on the way. They're planning on setting up a satellite office down here to make it easier for scouting and offer jobs to people who want to work for them here or who might be willing to relocate up north."

As I spoke, Leah's hand covered her mouth. "Oh, my goodness. That would change so many lives. Thank you."

"We wanted something permanent we could help with, after our football days are over."

"That's not happening soon, I hope." Troy wheeled himself over to us. "You guys are the best in the league."

"Nah, 'course not," I answered. "How the heck are you? How's Amber and little Jimmy?"

"Amber's working at the hair salon and doin' great. Jimmy comes here after school, and I pick him up after I get off my shift."

"Where're you working now?" Dev asked.

"McPherson's electrical supply. With my degree in electrical engineering and experience in the Army, I help with HVAC systems and industrial installations."

"Great."

"I was wondering about something, Dev. You got a minute?" Troy wheeled a little closer.

"Sure."

I wondered what the exchange was about, but a tiny smile played along Dev's lips.

"I haven't had the chance to see you in a long time. Would you know anything about the mortgage on our house bein' paid off?"

"Now why would I know that?" Dev adjusted the Kings cap on his head, but he didn't fool me. The fact that he hadn't mentioned doing something out of the goodness of his heart was typical Devlin Summers.

"Oh, I don't know." Troy chuckled. "Maybe we received a letter from the bank, stating our mortgage was paid in full and they had our free and clear title."

"I'm sure a lot of people would want to help a hero veteran like yourself." Dev continued his nonchalant approach.

Troy cocked his head. "While that may be true, a little birdie who was at the bank the afternoon of the rec center opening told me she saw you meeting with the bank manager, and magically, my mortgage was gone. *Poof.* Just like that."

Dev grinned. "Ain't it funny how things like that can happen?"

Troy covered his eyes for a second before speaking, his voice thick with emotion. "I can't thank you enough. You have no idea how much it's meant to us. You've changed our lives for the better."

"Just take care of yourselves and Jimmy." Dev extended his hand, and Troy shook his and mine. "That's all we care about."

We distributed the signed T-shirts, footballs, and pictures, then headed home for lunch. I put burgers on the grill, took out two beers, and joined Dev on the couch on the deck.

"That was a real nice thing you did for them. How come you never told me?"

"I don't know. It just happened so quickly, like one minute I saw him and Amber at the center, talking about what they could and couldn't afford, Troy still so worried about being home and in a wheelchair, and the next I was at the bank, paying off the mortgage. It seemed like the right thing to do."

"You always tell me what a good person I am, but do you know how special you are?" I took the bottle from his hand and kissed him.

"I'm not. Anyone would've done it."

Dev hated direct praise and would always push his good deed on someone else. I guessed it had to do with never receiving any positive reinforcement from his parents. He simply didn't enjoy people telling him what a great person he was, or understand how to accept a compliment, but I was here to change that.

"But you were the one who did it. And I love you for it."

"I love you too. I was thinking..."

"Uh-oh," I joked, and he elbowed me.

"Very funny. I'm serious. What would you say about buying a house upstate where we stayed? I'd love to have something the two of us own together."

I hadn't thought about it, but I did love the area. "I'd like that. Especially after the season's finished, it might be a nice place to escape to and hunker down for the winter." I ran my bare foot over his. "Snowed-in in a cabin with you, a fire, and a heap of blankets? I could think of worse things."

Dev's face brightened. "Fantastic. If we call Ezra, he can contact a real estate agent and find us something, I'm sure."

A thought struck me. "But how could we...both our names? Wouldn't that raise red flags? People are bound to find out."

He shrugged and took back his beer. "I mean, friends work together all the time. So to be sure, we'll form a business together and let the corporation buy it." He reached into his pocket and pulled out his phone. "I'll tell Ezra."

Dev's spontaneity was another thing I loved about him, but this was a large purchase, and I wasn't used to spending money like that. When you grew up poor, it was hard to change that habit.

"You're sure about this? You don't think we should think about it?"

He set the phone on the deck railing. "I don't need to think when it feels so right. I know." He leaned in, cupped my cheek, and brushed his lips to mine. "Like kissing you in front of that fire. Best decision I've ever made."

CHAPTER EIGHTEEN

Dev

Six months later

"How's the shoulder?" Brody asked when I came through the door, having taken a car upstate after my PT session in the city.

I grunted.

"That doesn't tell me anything," Brody pressed, and I huffed out a sigh.

"It's the same as it was last week after I came home. It's fine." I kicked my sneakers across the room. "And I don't want to talk about it."

I stormed across the living room to the bar, picked up the bottle of tequila, and splashed at least two shots in the glass. It exploded in my mouth, burned my throat, but warmed my stomach. Brody's scent surrounded me, and he put his arms around my waist. I leaned into his naked chest. My support and rock. I couldn't have gone through this without him to come home to.

"Even to me? We always talk about everything. But ever since the Super Bowl, you've shut me out."

I closed my eyes, pain crashing into my heart. "I'm sorry," I whispered. "I just hate that I disappointed everyone—the fans, the team, myself...I can't stop thinking about it."

Brody kissed my neck. "Dev. You were injured. It happens. You didn't let anyone down."

Brody meant well, but his words didn't register. "In the first quarter? I sure as hell did. I screwed up. It never should've happened. I keep going over the play in my head, and I saw Marlon wide open. I was setting up to throw, and then the next thing I knew, I was lying on a stretcher in an ambulance."

The diagnosis was a concussion and a strained shoulder. Thank God no ligament damage or torn muscle occurred, but I was taken out of the game. My state of mind was another thing as I'd watched the Kings lose the Super Bowl, 35-17.

"I know. And it sucks. But we're ready for training camp next month. The doctors cleared you, right?"

I gulped the rest of the tequila. "Yeah. My email is blowing up with requests for interviews about my 'readiness.' " Did I sound bitter? Maybe because I was. "One major injury in all the years I've been playing, and they're on me like a pack of wolves. Bastards."

"Let Fallon or Ezra handle it." Brody took my hand. "Come sit with me."

I allowed him to walk me to the couch, and I lay with my head in his lap. We'd spent the entire winter and spring up here, hidden away from everyone while I did PT and saw a shrink.

"I'm really okay, baby. I'm anxious to get to camp and show all these assholes how ready I am. My arm is good, the MRI on my head is totally normal, and I just want to get on the field and stop all the rumors."

"What rumors?" Brody's hesitancy had me sitting up.

"Come on. Don't lie to me. You never have before. I've seen the articles. *Is this the Devil's last year as a King? Are the Kings going to trade the Devil and use the rookie?*"

"Since when do you pay attention to sports gossip?"

"Since it's negative about me." I laughed without humor.

"Well, I'm positive you're the sexiest man alive, and I love you." Brody's lips hit mine.

I closed my eyes and let Brody's mouth work its magic. He licked my neck, bit my ear, and nibbled at my collarbone. With a tug to my shirt, I pulled it over my head and wriggled out of my shorts, my cock already hard and throbbing.

"I'm sorry I've been such a pain in the ass." I played with his hair, winding it around my fingers as he sucked and licked my dick. His reddish-brown head bobbed, his tongue licking my shaft. My hips rolled, and Brody hummed as he took me to the back of his throat, the vibration sparking bursts of fire through me.

"Brody, God," I moaned, the tension rising, my orgasm beginning to break through, my body twitching and shivering.

The bastard released me and sat up. His reddened lips smiled, and his flushed face brightened. "I need you in me."

It took me a moment to catch my breath and get my brain cells working. "Get naked," I ordered, pointing at his shorts. I licked my lips as his thick cock was revealed, and couldn't resist running my hand along the hefty length. "So gorgeous. So mine."

I grabbed for the lube on the coffee table and spread some on my fingers, then pushed them into his ass. Brody's groan split the air, but I couldn't play with him for more than a minute—I was bursting with need and had to have him. Now.

Brody climbed on top of me, lined himself up, and sank so slowly, pleasure mixed with the pain of holding myself off from thrusting hard. I clutched his hips, watching the play of emotions across Brody's face, his mouth panting and gasping, his Adam's apple moving as he gulped air. Despite the air conditioning, sweat rolled down his face, the thick strands of all that glorious hair sticking to his face.

He was the sexiest, most beautiful thing I'd ever seen.

"Dev." He sighed when I dug my heels in and drove in deep. He grabbed his swollen cock, and the sight of that fat head moving through Brody's big fist, coupled with the slick sounds of his precome, sent me tumbling over the edge. My nails dug into his hairy thighs as I came, his muscles gripping me tight.

"Brody, oh God." My gaze was fixated on his heavy dick pumping out streams of come, dripping through his grasp, hitting my chest. His lashes fluttered, and with a lust-drunk smile, he leaned in close and kissed me.

"I love you. I always will."

I wrapped my arms around Brody and held him close, our hearts banging in rhythm.

"I love you too. Always and forever."

Final regular season game

"Blue 84, Blue 84. Ready. Set."

I scrambled to my left and handed off the ball, watching our leading rusher gain one yard. At this point, so late in the game, we were merely running out the clock. We had the game in the W column.

We were playing the Cocoa Beach Rockets on their home turf, so the stadium was rocking, but plenty of fans in the stands remembered both Brody and myself winning the national championship in the state, and there were cheers for us as well. Brody's mom had made the trip to see us play, and we'd also flown out Troy, Amber, and Jimmy and put them in a suite. After the game we were all going to have dinner.

The Kings were comfortably ahead, 28-3 with a minute and a half left. We were on the Rockets' forty-yard line and knew the offense was gunning for us. Bad blood simmered from an earlier call in the second quarter that the Rockets thought was in error. It resulted in the Kings scoring a touchdown, which led to some shit-talking and shoulder-knocking between our teams. The refs had needed to separate some of the players, but Coach Jackson had a warning for us: start a fight and end up on the bench.

"White 80, White 80, hut, hut."

The play was the same as before. Hand off the ball to the running back and let the clock tick away. With the game out of reach, I wasn't planning on the defense making a quarterback rush, so I stayed closer to the line of scrimmage than usual.

Big fucking mistake.

Three massive tackles came barreling through and hit me center mass. I ended up beneath close to seven hundred pounds of weight. Pain sliced through me, and I saw stars. Everything in front of my eyes went hazy, then dark. Whistles blew and screams echoed from the crowd. As I passed out from the pain, I muttered, "Fuck."

My eyelids weighed a hundred pounds, so I gave up trying to open them. My ears worked and were the only part of my body that wasn't hurting. I heard beeping and voices murmuring. Time to make a full-body assessment. My left arm moved, and I could make a fist, so that was good. My right arm? Stiff but I could lift it without pain. I wiggled my toes and bent my knees. Again, achy and sore. I could feel bandages wrapped around my knees, but they moved. I breathed a sigh of relief.

"Devlin?"

I froze. It took a minute, but I forced my eyes open to the sight of my mother sitting, not quite at my bedside, but in a chair several feet away. She clutched the handbag in her lap. As always, she was dressed immaculately, her hair freshly done, makeup and nails perfect.

"M-mother?" My voice cracked, and I licked my lips. They were parched and dry to the tip of my tongue. "What're you doing here?"

She blinked. "Do you know where you are?"

I tried to move my head to the side, and a bolt of white-hot pain seared through me. But from the medicinal smell and the machines and IVs, I had a good guess. "Not the Ritz, for sure. Did you redecorate my old room at home again?"

"Really, Devlin? You think this a joking matter?"

I wasn't expecting the warm and fuzzies, but a simple smile and maybe a touch of her hand would've been nice. "No, Mother. I'm assuming I'm in the hospital. But I've been injured other times, and you haven't come."

She blinked. "You've been unconscious for a day."

"Wh-what? It's Monday?"

"Yes. Monday afternoon." She checked her Cartier Panthère watch. "One twelve, to be exact."

"Don't you have class?"

She bowed her head for a moment. "I suppose I deserve that. We received a call from someone on your team that you'd been injured. You put me as your emergency contact."

My lips twitched. "You sound surprised." It had been when I first joined the Kings and filled out all the paperwork. I'd put my mother's name as emergency contact, almost in defiance, and had never changed it, though I'd meant to.

Pink blossomed on her cheeks, but she ignored my response. "We decided since your father had a full day of lectures and I only had a class in the afternoon, I would travel here to speak to the doctor, assess your condition, and move you to New York." Her icy gaze flicked around the room. "I'm sure the care you'll receive at home will be miles ahead of what they can do for you here."

Her obvious discomfort gave me a perverse sense of pleasure. "I don't know, Mother. I hear they make a mean opossum stew here."

Her eyes widened, and she grimaced until she realized I was teasing her. "I don't understand your sense of humor, Devlin. This situation is not funny."

I shifted in the bed, wincing as various aches and pains revealed themselves. "Ouch. What did happen, aside from me being squashed by three giants? It was like having three refrigerators fall on me."

A furrow marred her smooth brow, but instead of answering me, she got to her feet. "I'll let the doctor know you're awake." And left me wondering what the hell was going on.

A nurse appeared. "Mr. Summers, you're awake. So glad to see you're back with us."

I smiled. "Thanks. And please call me Dev."

She blushed. "Okay. How are you feeling? You gave everyone a huge scare. Lots of your team have been waitin' all night." She checked my chart, and my IV, and replaced the bag hanging from the pole.

My heart jumped, then sank. Fuck. Brody must be going insane. "Can someone go out and tell them I'm awake and okay?"

"Oh, don't worry. They will eventually. Now, the doctor will be here in a minute, so you just rest."

Without another word, she left me. Frustrated and annoyed at the nonanswers, I decided to see if I could get out of bed. I lowered the railing, slid my feet to the edge and swung my legs over the side. It took me a few minutes before I could push up on the mattress with my hands. The world turned upside down, everything going hazy. Pain throbbed at my temples, and my stomach heaved.

"Okay, maybe that's not the best move," I whispered and gingerly reversed everything I'd done, but not before wincing at the multitudes of black and blue marks littering my calves and thighs. *Damn, those guys did a number on me.*

A ruddy-faced, dark-haired man in a white coat strode into the room. "Mr. Summers, I hope you weren't thinking of running away from us so soon. I'm Dr. Albright." His blue eyes twinkled. "I was hoping to get some tips on how to throw a perfect spiral to my fifteen-year-old so he'd think I'm a cool dad."

I laughed. "I guess it's up to you to tell me if I can." Upon lifting my arm, there were a few twinges, but nothing that seemed too serious to me. "Frankly, it feels no different than the usual aches and pains after a game."

"That's good to hear. Let's have a look."

For the next hour I was poked and prodded, had my reflexes tested and my eyes checked. He unwrapped the bandages on my knees, which I saw were to protect the abrasions I'd received from the AstroTurf.

"I always did like playing on natural grass," I told him. "Sliding along the fake grass, it burns like hell and takes the skin off."

"Yeah," he said, bending my legs. "It would've been less damage on your knees for sure." He rewrapped the bandages and moved on to my arm. "We've spoken to your team physician and followed your usual post-game procedure with taking care of your shoulder, so you don't have to worry about that."

"Good because I wouldn't want to be out of commission for the next playoff game. I'm thinking that a little rest will do, and I'll be ready."

Dr. Albright set my left arm down and lifted the railing. "I'm not going to lie to you, Mr. Summers. You suffered a concussion, and we need to keep you and run more tests to see how severe it is. I doubt you'll be ready for the next game."

About to contradict him, I refrained. "Can I try and sit up and see how my head feels?"

"I have a feeling you'll make the attempt whether I'm here or not, so I'd rather see it for myself and keep you safe."

Once again, he lowered the railing but hovered at the side of the bed. With caution, now that I already knew what might happen, I slid one foot, then the other over the side as I slowly raised to a seated position.

And promptly threw up. My vision doubled, and I fell back.

"Can we get some help in here, please?" Dr. Albright yelled out, and several people ran in and began to clean up the mess I made.

I lay in bed, head pounding, my heart beating madly. I knew my season was officially finished.

When I could string two words together, I mumbled, "I'm sorry. I didn't mean to cause such a problem."

Dr. Albright frowned. "I'm not going to sugarcoat this. I hope you see now that this isn't merely a little headache. We have you scheduled for an MRI, and once we get the results we can see if there's anything we need to be concerned about."

"Like?" I whispered.

"Brain swelling or a fractured skull. You need to rest and take this seriously." He scribbled some notes. "I'll see you after the tests, and we'll discuss the findings. In the meantime, rest. That's the best medicine."

I suffered through the cleanup of my hospital gown, and smiled weakly at the nurses' aide. "Thank you for everything. I'm sorry to be such trouble."

"Aren't you sweet. That's okay. You just make sure you get yourself better and listen to the doctor. We need you healthy to play." Her genuine warmth reassured me, but I still hated that someone had to be responsible for my pigheadedness.

"I'm thinking that won't be till next year."

"Whatever it takes. We'll take good care of you, don't worry." After dumping the dirty gown, she stopped by my bed. "You know, I remember watching you play in the Orange Bowl. That was the most exciting game I've ever seen—even better than the Super Bowl 'cause we were there in person. When you threw that touchdown to Blink Martin and he caught it, the whole stadium exploded." She poured me a fresh cup of water and moved the rolling table over. "He hasn't left since you were brought in, you know."

"Who?"

"Blink Martin. He's been sitting out there since yesterday after the game. The rest of the team came and went, along with some other people, but he's stayed." Her expression softened. "It's so nice that y'all are still such good friends and care about each other so much."

"Thanks. Can you send him in? I should thank him."

"Sure thing. I'll do that right now."

Brody didn't come. Instead, I was whisked away for an MRI and X-rays. They probably told him I was about to have tests and he could come in after. But he didn't show later either, and the time ticked away.

What the hell was going on?

CHAPTER NINETEEN

Brody

"Brody, you should go back to the hotel." Momma put a hand on my arm, but I couldn't stand being touched.

"I'm not goin' anywhere until I speak to a doctor and hear Dev's okay." My voice quavered, and I was so damn glad the rest of the team and Troy and his family had left. We were alone. "I swear, Momma. When I saw him lyin' there...not movin'...I got so scared." Tears burned in my eyes. "I thought he was dead."

"Oh, dear God, but you know he's goin' to be okay. Not even a broken bone. He's a strong man."

A woman entered the waiting area, and I immediately recognized her from the pictures Dev had shown me. I leaned close to Momma to whisper in her ear.

"That's Dev's mom. I'm surprised she came." A terrible thought struck panic through me. "What if they called her because he's worse than we think? They haven't told us anything."

Momma grabbed my arm. "Don't think like that. We woulda heard somethin'." She smoothed her shirt and stood. "I'm gonna introduce myself."

Now it was my turn to hold on to her. "Momma...you can't. She—she doesn't know about me 'n Dev. She doesn't even know he's gay," I murmured.

"Still," she insisted. "You're teammates and friends and her son is hurt. It's the right thing to do."

Knowing it was useless to argue, I watched her cross the room and listened in.

"Excuse me, are you Mrs. Summers?"

Dev's mother, who'd been writing in a notebook, looked up. "Yes? May I help you?"

"I'm Faith McGrath. Brody's mother? He and Dev are very good friends. I just want you to know that we're prayin' for Dev."

She inclined her head. "Thank you." Nothing further. No giving her name or asking Momma to sit by her side. But Momma wasn't about to give up.

"We were wonderin' if there was any news on Dev's condition. How is he? We're very worried. Dev is such a wonderful man—we've spent a lotta time together in the off-season."

With a sigh, Dev's mother closed her notebook. "That's very kind of you to say. I haven't been given any information. I'm sure they're waiting until after the test results come in. Now, if you'll excuse me, I have a call to make."

She left, and Momma returned to me, shaking her head. "That woman." She shivered. "I swear the temperature is below zero the closer you stand to her."

"She doesn't know anything, I gather." My main concern was Dev's health. Not her personality. From what Dev told me, I knew she was a bitch.

"No. I can't imagine poor Dev growin' up in a house like that. Now I understand why he left and never returned."

The waiting was driving me up the wall. I couldn't sit there any longer and got to my feet. "Do you want a coffee? I gotta get out of here."

"Sure, honey. I'll wait here."

I took the elevator to the cafeteria and got two coffees and a bag of cookies and muffins. A bunch of people recognized me, and as much as I wanted to yell at them to leave me alone, I forced a smile and signed autographs and took pictures. It was close to half an hour before I made it back upstairs. By that time, Jonas and Marlon had arrived and were sitting with Momma.

"Here you go." I handed her the coffee. "I got some stuff to eat too."

"You need to eat something, honey. You barely touched your dinner last night."

I chewed some of a muffin, having no idea what it tasted like. Jonas took the chair next to mine. "Still no news?"

I shook my head.

"Man, that was a nasty hit. Coach said the team is filing a protest. Devil had released the ball. No way three of them should've taken him down."

The food tasted like mud, and I tossed it into the wastebasket. "It doesn't matter. All I want is for him to be okay."

Jonas squeezed my shoulder. "I know, man. We all do. Bunch of us got a prayer circle going."

I heard voices outside the waiting room and thought I recognized Dev's mother's voice. " 'Scuse me. I'll be right back." I exited the waiting room area and found Dev's mother talking to a man, presumably his doctor. "Excuse me, Doctor, how is he?"

The serious-faced doctor stopped speaking to Dev's mother. "I'm sorry, but you're not related to Mr. Summers, are you? You're Blink Martin, correct?"

"Yes, but—"

Dev's mother huffed out her impatience. "I'm sorry, but will you please leave us? I'm discussing my son's condition with his doctor."

I met her green eyes, and unlike Dev's warmth and humor, I saw only ice. I tried to appeal to her. "Please, Mrs. Summers. Dev and I have been best friends since college. He's like my...brother."

God, those words tasted sour on my tongue. If we'd had the guts to come out, if we could've guaranteed the profession we'd both chosen and loved would stand by us, I'd be the one speaking to the doctor and making decisions as his husband, not the woman who barely acknowledged his existence.

Nothing I said melted that frosty facade. "Doctor, can we speak somewhere more privately? Where we won't be disturbed?"

"This way, Mrs. Summers. I'm sure you'll be happy to hear the positive results." The two of them left me standing, but it didn't matter. I'd heard the doctor say positive results, and a wave of relief crashed over me. Even if I couldn't see Dev, hearing he was going to be all right chased away all the darkness.

Still, I ached to see him, so I decided to take a chance and found the nurses' station. Leaning on the desk, I smiled at the women sitting behind their computers. Several men were also present, checking charts, and I knew the moment they recognized me when they elbowed each other, their eyes growing wide with excitement.

"I'm sorry to interrupt, but I was hopin' one of you could help me?"

"What can I do for you?" One of the men stepped forward. "You're Blink Martin, right?"

"Yes, sir."

"Terrible what happened to Devil Summers. I was happy to see he woke up this afternoon."

"That's great news. He had some tests done too, I know."

One of the nurses frowned. "I'm sorry, but we can't discuss that with you."

Not wanting to get on her bad side, I attempted to look contrite. "Oh, I know. I don't mean to get you in trouble. We're all just worried about our friend. Thanks, anyway." I walked away.

Footsteps sounded behind me.

"Hey, Mr. Martin?"

I stopped and turned to see the man who'd spoken to me. When he got close enough for me to see his ID tag, I learned he was a doctor.

"Yes, Dr. Robinson? Call me Blink."

"I can't give you any medical information, but Mr. Summers is in Room 528 if you want to peek in to say hello."

I fist-bumped him. "Thank you, man. I owe you one."

I hurried to the room, hoping Dev was alone. My heart hurt, seeing him lying in the bed, so pale and banged up. I entered and closed the door behind me.

"If you've come to take more blood, I don't have any left."

"How about if I give you a kiss instead?" I walked to his bedside and watched as his eyes flew open, and the biggest smile I'd seen on his face since he won his first Super Bowl curved his lips.

"Brody...baby. Oh God, I missed you."

"I love you." I leaned over and touched my lips to his. Tears fell from my eyes and mixed with the ones on Dev's cheeks. "I was so scared."

His hand touched my face. "I'm okay. No breaks or tears. Just this stupid concussion. I can't sit up yet without getting sick and having pain in my head. But the doctors say I'll make a full recovery." His face fell. "Just not for this season. Which sucks balls."

"Listen to the doctors, and if you behave, I'll suck *your* balls. How's that?" I was so damn happy to see and touch him, I didn't care how bad my joke was.

"Now I know I'll get better." His eyes searched mine. "You're exhausted. You stayed here all night, didn't you?"

"Yeah. Me and Momma. A bunch of the guys are outside now, too. I couldn't leave until I found out what happened to you. Dammit, Dev, I was so worried, sitting out there with no news." I didn't want to upset him, but I wanted to know what happened. "I saw your mother."

Dev's jaw tightened. "Yeah. She scheduled me in."

Despite her barely acknowledging my existence, I didn't want to badmouth her. "C'mon, Dev. She's here. That counts for something."

"I don't want to talk about her." His eyes twinkled. "Are you gonna dress up in a nurse outfit and take care of me?"

My lips twitched, but I sighed. "I wish I could, but we're on the road for the next game. You should hire someone—"

The door burst open, and in walked Dev's mother. Her brows flew up, and her eyes hardened to chips of emerald ice. "Excuse me, but what are you doing here?"

"He came to see me, Mother."

"Well, he can leave now. You're being transferred to New York, and our doctors will look over your case to see if they concur with the diagnosis." She pinned me with a glare. "My son and I have things to discuss, so if you'd please give us some privacy?"

"That's very rude of you, Mother. Brody is very concerned about my health."

One thing about the Summerses. They didn't back off. "That's nice of him, but it has no bearing on me. Now, I've arranged for a plane with medical attention for you. We'll arrive in New York tonight, and you'll be home with us for the duration of your recuperation. The doctor said you don't need to stay in the hospital."

"What? No. Absolutely not." A stunned expression crossed Dev's face, and he struggled to sit up, but paled and sank down on the pillows. My stomach lurched at the sight of him, so weak and hurting.

"You're injured and in no position to argue. Did you expect to return to your home with no one to look after you? I have Hugo with me. He'll come to help you." She met my eyes. "You may leave now. We have this under control. There's nothing for you to do here."

On top of the sheets, Dev's hands curled into fists. "Please don't speak to Brody like that."

"All I'm saying is that you have your family here now. You don't need strangers or anyone else."

"Brody is no stranger." Dev reached out a hand to me, but I hesitated. "It's okay, Brody. I'm not doing this anymore. Maybe a near-death experience changed me, but at least where my family is concerned, no more hiding."

"Devlin, what're you talking about? Does your head hurt?" His mother checked her phone. "I left Hugo waiting at the airport to rent a car. I'll have him go to your hotel room, pack your things, and then we'll return home." She pursed her lips. "The sooner we leave here, the better."

"My head doesn't hurt, Mother. It's just time you knew the truth."

"The truth?" Her eyes narrowed. "Truth about what?"

Dev wiggled his fingers to me, and with my heart pounding, I put my hand in his and watched his mother's eyes blow wide open and her lips part in shock. "I'm gay, Mother. Brody and I have been together for years." His grip on my hand tightened, and I could feel him trembling despite the bravery of his words. "Matter of fact, we're married."

"You're lying," she whispered, her gaze darting between the two of us, landing on our entwined hands.

"No. I'm not. We've hidden it from the public for reasons that should be obvious, but as my *mother*, I'm sure you'd want to know that I'm happy and in a loving relationship."

She licked her lips. "I had no idea...you never...you don't...but you play football," she finally burst out.

"Yeah," Dev joked. "Imagine that." His tone became serious. "I only told you this because Brody deserves full access to my personal life, health records included. Whatever the doctors tell you, you're to tell Brody."

She clasped her hands and directed the full force of those laser sharp eyes on me. *Damn.* Momma was right. Not cold. Arctic. "I'd like to speak with my son. In private, please."

"No. Don't go." Dev lifted his chin. "I told you, Mother. Whatever you can say to me, you can say to the two of us."

At the knock on the door, I dropped his hand and moved away. The doctor poked his head in. "Mrs. Summers, I have the paperwork for your son's discharge."

His brows drew together when he spotted me. "How did you get in here?"

I remained silent and looked to Dev. He nodded to me before he closed his eyes. "I'm tired. I'd like to rest, please."

"I'll talk to you soon. Get better, Dev." I left the room and returned to the waiting area.

The others had gone, but Momma remained. She sat with her head bowed and only raised it as I came near.

"Brody, I was worried. You just walked away and didn't say anything. I had no idea where you were or...anyway." She drew in a deep breath. "Did you find out anything new about Dev?"

"I think we should go to the hotel and talk."

I called for a car, and we returned to the hotel. My phone was blowing up with texts from teammates, other players, the media. I sent a message to my PA, Lizzie, to please handle everything, making sure any statements came through official Kings public relations, then shut it all off.

"Dev told his mother. About us."

Momma's eyes popped wide, and her hand covered her mouth. "Oh, my. Why...what did she say?"

"Typical nonsense at first. Like how could he be gay, he plays football." I rolled my eyes before getting serious again. "But Dev wanted to make sure she gives me any information she receives about his health. And she was not happy about it."

Momma sat and listened but surprised me with her response. "You're not gonna let her stop you, are you? Because it isn't up to her. It's Dev's life, and you're part of it."

"I know. It's just that she's gonna make it real difficult, with Dev staying there."

"And?" Momma raised a brow. "You've been in other, real difficult situations. You spend your training time studying and learning the opposing team. Think of it like that."

I grinned. "Momma, you devil." She was right. This was a playbook for my life, and I didn't plan on losing.

CHAPTER TWENTY

Dev

I folded my arms and glared at my mother. "That was rude and uncalled for."

Unperturbed, she pulled out her phone. "What was?"

"The way you spoke to Brody." When she continued to study her phone and not answer, I snapped. "Mother. Put the damn phone down and listen to me."

She managed to drag her attention away from the screen. "Yes, Devlin. What is it?"

"I said you acted rude toward Brody for no reason."

"He's a stranger."

Astonished at her utter lack of capacity to understand, I managed to keep my anger under control. "Did you hear what I said? Brody is my husband. We've been together since college. We're married."

"Married?" Her gaze met mine. "How did two men so in the public eye manage to keep that a secret?"

"That's not your concern." No way in hell would I tell my mother any of the details. "The fact remains that Brody is the most important person in my life. And you will not shut him out. Is that understood?"

"I'm certainly not going to have such a personal discussion about a family issue here." With disdain, she surveyed my room. "Now Hugo has packed up your things and will meet us at the airport. I'm going to get someone to help you dress and have you discharged so we can leave."

With that pronouncement, she left, and I closed my eyes. How had this become my life? One minute on the road to glory, and the next stuck lying here, dependent on someone else to help me. I rolled my shoulders to get the creaks and aches out, then decided to attempt to sit up again. With that major feat accomplished, I lowered the bed rail and swung my legs over the side. I slowly levered upward and released a sigh of relief that the nausea and pain hadn't returned. The door opened, and a nurse entered.

"Mr. Summers, you shouldn't be getting out of bed by yourself. You need to call us to help you."

I hung my head. "I'm so sorry. I needed to use the bathroom and didn't want to bother you. Could you help me?" I flashed her a smile.

She blushed. "Of course." She slid an arm around my waist, and breathing deeply, I waited a moment before taking a step and was relieved that I felt steady on my feet. The nurse walked me to the bathroom, and she was waiting for me when I came out.

"Thank you. I feel so silly asking someone to come with me."

"You had a head injury, so you have to be careful. Make sure you always have someone there with you."

"He will." My mother reappeared. "I've signed all the necessary papers. As soon as Hugo arrives with your clothes, we can leave."

Ignoring her, I addressed the nurse. "Thank you for your help. I really appreciate everything you and the staff did while I was here."

"It's our job, Mr. Summers. And we're so sorry about what happened. We all hope you recover real quick." She assisted me to the chair by my bedside, and I sank into it. Amazing how I could be on the field playing one of the roughest sports out there, but today I was tired from walking across the room.

"Thank you." After she left, I pointed at my mother. "I need to make sure Hugo has my phone. There are people I have to contact."

"The doctor said you have to rest."

Her audacity was breathtaking. "Listen, Mother. It's nice that you popped up and remembered I existed. I put you down mainly as a joke to myself, figuring if anything ever did happen to me, you'd remember you had a son. I should've changed that emergency contact years ago. The one thing you won't do is keep me from the people in my life who mean something to me. First thing is, I'm not coming to stay at the house with you."

Her jaw set tight. "You're being foolish. The doctor said—"

"Screw the doctors. I'm going home to rest there. In case you don't realize it, I've been on my own since I left for college, and you basically ignored my existence unless it was to trot me out at an event or two. That means I made my own life."

"And that life includes sleeping with a man who barely speaks proper English," she sneered.

I wished I were shocked by her ugly prejudice, but I wasn't. "If you're talking about Brody, he's the best man I've ever met, with the biggest, kindest heart."

"That's sweet. But it doesn't mean anything to me."

My patience, always thin when it came to my parents, had reached the breaking point. "But it does to me. He is the man I love and whom I'm going to be with. Whether or not you approve or care doesn't matter to me. I'm just telling you how it is and how it's going to be."

"Maybe."

"Maybe? What the hell does that mean?" My head started to pound.

"I've had you scheduled for a psychiatric exam. You had a severe knock to your head, and I'm not sure you're in the best state of mind to make the right decisions."

"You have got to be fucking kidding me." I'd always tried to hold my tongue around my parents, but this was beyond the pale. "You think I'm incapable now? This is outrageous. I need my phone right now."

She glanced at her watch. "I was told you might experience sudden outbursts of rage."

No way in hell I would fall into her trap. I steadied my breathing and clasped my hands in my lap. "I'm not raging. I'm annoyed. I do see a therapist." At her startled expression, I smiled. "It must've been the loving childhood I had. But I insist on being able to call my assistant and agent. This is my business, Mother. I have people who work for me and contracts I need to honor."

She eyed me with suspicion, but I remained calm. "Very well," she replied, and inside I cheered. "When we get home. But you're keeping the appointments I made with the psychiatrist and the neurologist."

I'd already won. "Fine with me." All I needed was to get to New York. I already had a plan in mind.

Hugo settled me into the bed. "I have some water here and the medicine your doctor prescribed for pain. Plus your phone and the charger."

I had nothing against poor Hugo. He was only following orders. "Thank you, Hugo. I appreciate it." I pretended to yawn. "I think I'll take a nap. I'm tired."

"Very well. If you need anything, just let me know." He paused. "Your parents had a dinner engagement this evening. They'll be home later."

Of course. Far be it for them to change their plans and stay with me. "No worries. I'm sure I'll go to bed early as it is. Thanks."

He withdrew, and I plugged in my phone. While my head still hurt and I had several bouts of dizziness, I refused to sit still. "Ezra?"

"Jesus, Dev, I've been going wild with worry. How are you? Where the hell are you? I haven't been able to find out a damn thing, and Brody's traveling—"

Simply hearing Ezra's voice made me happy, and I laughed. "I'm here. In New York."

"Oh, thank God. Dammit, Dev, I'm so sorry about what happened. That was a cheap shot by those bastards."

My smile was grim. "Yeah, well, their season has ended, so let them spend the whole off-season thinking about it."

"How're you feeling? I only got a quick text from Brody before the team left, saying you had a bad concussion but thank God no broken bones or muscle damage."

"Yeah. Only damage is to my ego. Dammit, Ezra, I can't believe I'm not gonna be there on the field."

"They're playing for you. They know you're still their leader. Your main objective now is to get strong and healthy again. And you're at your parents'?" The curiosity in his voice couldn't be disguised.

I laughed. "Yeah, I couldn't believe my mother came to see me either. I don't get it."

"Maybe she feels remorse?"

I snorted. "Yeah, sure. That's why my parents left me to go out to a function tonight. She came because I had her down as my emergency contact on my forms and they called her. And how could she say no without looking like the cold, uncaring bitch she is? First thing tomorrow, Ezra, please contact the Kings and make sure I get those forms changed. I want your name as my emergency contact."

"Not a problem. Consider it done."

"Thanks. I appreciate it. I'm gonna call Fallon now. Talk to you tomorrow." I ended the call and hit Fallon's number.

"Oh, jeez, Dev. Thank God. You're okay? I tried calling, but no one answered, and I was going crazy here. You're sure you're all right?"

I waited for him to stop and catch his breath.

"I'll be okay. Sucks that I can't play, but better safe than sorry."

"Of course, of course. You can't take a chance. I don't know what I'd do if you were hurt. I'll make sure you have everything you need once you're home. When will that be? I have to make all the arrangements."

I bit back a smile. Fallon had always been intense, but it made him great at his job. Next to Brody, I trusted him with everything I held close. I'd offered him the position of working for me as my PA, never imagining how much

I would come to lean on him. He, on the other hand, kept himself a closed book.

"Tomorrow morning around ten, after my parents leave, I need someone to come here and take me home. Can you arrange for a car to get me?"

"You're home? Thank God. You think I'm just gonna send you a car? Fuck that. I'll do it myself. But Dev, I think you need a nurse as well. Or some kind of home health care to make sure you're okay and not overdoing it."

"Yeah? I guess...all right. Can you arrange that for me?"

"Consider it done. Anything you need."

"What I need is to get out of here. I'm already feeling smothered." I raked my hand through my hair. Sweat beaded on my forehead.

"Try and rest. A head injury is nothing to joke about. I'll get you all sorted out, and you'll be in your own bed by tomorrow night."

Tears poured down my face. "Thanks," I whispered, furious with myself for losing control. "I've felt so cut off and alone." I huffed out a laugh. "I can't believe I'm acting like a baby."

Fallon made a sound of disagreement. "Don't you worry. I've got you. You know that."

"I do. And I appreciate it." I wiped my face. Now that I was on familiar ground and in touch with people I trusted, that unbalanced feeling would correct itself. "More than you can possibly know."

"Go to sleep, and I'll get everything ready for you at home. See you tomorrow."

I ended the call and sent a text to Brody, letting him know what happened, where I was tonight, and where I'd be going tomorrow. A minute after I sent it, he responded.

Take care of yourself. That's all I care about. Rest and heal. Then a heart emoji.

I took my pain meds and closed my eyes. The last thing I recalled was Brody telling me he loved me.

My parents came to see me at eight the following morning before they left for classes. My mother stood at the door to my room, as if afraid of catching something if she entered. My father stood by my bedside and examined my medicine bottles. "I hope you aren't becoming addicted to these. There's an epidemic of people dependent on them because of injuries. It's a quick slide for you athletes, I've heard."

King of the warm and fuzzies—that was my father. "Don't worry. I feel better this morning, and I don't need them." It wasn't a lie. I'd had a decent night's sleep, and it had made me feel almost whole. All the aches and pains from playing the game, along with the brutal sack, felt manageable. The occasional blurry vision and constant pounding headache had all but vanished, but a dull ache remained, though I still had no memory of what happened on the field leading up to my injury. I knew I'd need to go to the doctor here and get checked out, but it all seemed overwhelming, like a mountain I hadn't prepared to climb.

"Your mother told me about your...relationship."

I crossed my arms, and I could see him checking out my tattoos. "Nice, aren't they?"

He grimaced. "I've never understood the need to desecrate your body like that."

"Then it's a good thing you've never gotten any. I love them, and it's my body. Anyway, about my relationship, you can say the word, you know. *Husband.* Brody's my husband. We're married. In love. Have been for years." I made a rolling motion with my hand. "I'm gay. I've known it since I was twelve years old." With each word, he recoiled farther, until he'd joined my mother by the door.

"I have to leave. The car is waiting downstairs."

Frankly, I was surprised he'd come to see me at all, considering I barely remembered his presence during my childhood. My mother, working toward her tenure at Columbia, hadn't been home much either. Both my parents were raised by full-time nannies, so it was all they knew.

"Good-bye," I replied. I figured after I left today, I probably wouldn't be seeing them again. I could hardly imagine them sitting at the kitchen table with Brody and his mother.

I waited for the front door to slam, then called Fallon. His mouth was running before I had a chance to say hello.

"How was your night? I've canceled all your appearances for the week, but we can put out a statement later for the press so they stop hounding you. Plus, I've got your masseur coming later this afternoon, and I have an appointment set up with a neurologist tomorrow. A nurse is waiting at your place." His warm, reassuring voice was so good to hear, it made me emotional all over again, and I pinched my eyes shut.

"Thanks, Fallon. You're the best."

"Just get yourself home and let us take care of you. Ezra was already here this morning. I'm coming with the car and driver. We'll be there at ten."

"I'll be waiting. Thanks."

I moved slowly, but had no problem walking on my own. I opened my suitcase and tossed in the few items I'd taken out–phone cord and headphones, and made sure to take my meds with me as well. I showered and dressed, then made my way downstairs. Hugo was nowhere to be found, which I preferred. He didn't deserve to be put in the middle. Outside, I set my bag on the top step and sat waiting. I couldn't wait to get home, but the truth was, until Brody came back, it wasn't a home to me.

CHAPTER TWENTY-ONE

Brody

Division Championship Sunday

"Coach, have you heard from Dev?"

I figured I'd ask to make it seem as if I didn't know. In fact, the two of us had been texting and FaceTiming nonstop all week. For me, the excitement of the championship season had vanished, and all I wanted was to go home and make sure Dev was okay.

When I said as much to Dev, he ripped me a new one, telling me I'd better put in a thousand percent on the field today and whip the Bobcats' butts.

"Yeah, he and I spoke, and he said he'll be watching." Coach Jackson chuckled. "He told me, 'Tell the guys to kick their asses, and let 'em know the Devil made you do it.' "

My lips twitched. "Sounds like him."

I finished putting on my gear, and Luke Fontaine walked over to me. "Hey, Blink?"

"Yeah, what's up?" The kid looked nervous as hell, and I couldn't blame him. Stepping in for a future Hall of Famer like Dev wasn't easy during the regular season. Doing it during the playoffs? I had to say, I had total respect for him.

"I know how friendly you and Dev are. I just wanted you to know I never wanted to play like this, and I wish Dev were here today."

"You're a class act, Luke. Wait a sec." I took my phone from the locker and made a call. "Hey. Someone here wants to talk to you." I held out the phone. "Talk to Dev."

Luke froze, and his eyes bugged out. "What? No. He must be so upset. I–"

"Go ahead. It's all good."

His Adam's apple bobbed, and he took the phone. "Hi, Dev.... Yeah, I know.... Uh-huh.... I appreciate that.... Yeah...." A smile curved his lips. "I promise.... You know it.... Yeah, I watched the tape.... We will. This one's for you.... Yeah, sure." He held the phone out. "He wants to talk to you."

"Yeah. What is it?"

"Watch out for him. Make sure those bastards don't hit him dirty."

"I will."

"Love you."

"Same."

"Go bust ass."

I put the phone away. "So, all good?"

Luke nodded. "Yeah. He insisted I was more than ready and that they were in for a surprise if they thought I wasn't. He told me which side they're weakest on and some tricks he used against them in other games." Brown eyes shone with admiration. "Dev's the best. I was nervous, but now I'm pumped to get out there and show him I can do it."

My chest swelled with pride. "He's great that way. Even in college he was always putting the team ahead of himself. He loves the game and winning." I patted him for reassurance. "Now let's go out there and kick their asses. For Dev."

We joined the rest of the team in our usual circle to calm nerves and center ourselves, and today we all recited a prayer for Dev's recovery. One last cheer and we headed into the tunnel to the field, already hearing the roar of the crowd filling the stadium.

"Did you see that throw?" Zeke yelled as we hit the locker room. "Kid's got it locked down."

We were all celebrating our 21-14 win, but Zeke seemed to take particular pleasure in getting in my face to let me know what a great job Luke had done as quarterback.

"He was great," I agreed, and Zeke's smile grew even more malicious.

"Looks like your best friend should think about packing it in."

"Fuck off." I flipped him the middle finger and gave him my back. Luke entered the room, and we all surrounded him. The kid deserved all the accolades—two touchdown passes, over three hundred yards passing. Damn, I felt like a proud papa.

"Luke. Way to go." I hugged him.

"Thanks." Eyes bright and face flushed, he rubbed his face with both hands. "I can't believe it. Everything Dev said was right on point." He blinked, and overcome with emotion, brushed at his lashes. "I couldn't have done it without his support."

"Conference Championship, here we come!" Jonas turned the music on blast, and the reporters started streaming in.

"Get ready for it, kid." I squeezed Luke's shoulder and watched as the press made a beeline for him. It was a rookie's dream, and while I was happy for him, my heart ached, knowing how badly Dev wished he were here. Several reporters from the national news media approached me, and I put on my game face.

"Blink, tell us about the first touchdown from Luke Fontaine. Did it feel different with him leading the team and not Devlin Summers?"

"Luke did a fantastic job stepping into Devil's shoes. And I know for a fact Dev was cheering him on."

"How's he doing? Do you know?"

"From what I've been told, his tests are all good, and even though he wants to play, he understands he needs to take the time to recuperate."

"How strong do you feel going into the conference championship? Do you think the Kings can win without Devlin Summers? Was today a fluke?"

I bristled. "No win is a fluke. Luke Fontaine rose to the challenge, and we defeated a tough opponent. Do I think we can win without Devlin? I think we proved that today. Thank you."

Dismissing them, I walked away to the bathroom, where I stripped and got under the shower. After the standard check-over by the team physician, a stint in the hot tub, and a massage, I got to the hotel, undressed and lay down in bed, listening to the quiet. Normally after a playoff win like this, I loved watching the highlights on television, and Dev and I would go over the plays.

God, I missed him.

Momma knew I needed a low-key night after a game, and we'd agreed to meet later for a dinner, but right now all I wanted was to hear Dev's voice.

"Hey, baby." His raspy purr sent a bolt of longing through me. Even though we never had sex during playoff season, just having him with me on the field and in the hotel was enough to ground me. Without him near, I was lost and lonely.

"Hey, yourself. Did you watch?"

"Do you need to ask? Of course." He paused for a beat. "The kid looked good. Really good."

"He's not bad. Talking to you helped."

Dev chuckled. "Yeah, I watched the press conference afterward. He thanked me repeatedly."

"He was respectful to you. I think it was nice."

"It was." I could tell something was bothering Dev, but I waited for him to tell me. "Dammit, Brody, I missed it."

I was wondering if he'd admit it out loud or keep it to himself. "I know."

"It physically hurt not being there with all of you. I hated not being on the field, hearing the fans cheering and the shit talk from the guys."

Dev was such a fierce competitor, and he loved the game so much, I couldn't imagine how painful it was to sit on the sidelines.

"I hated not havin' you here. How's your head feelin'?"

"Fine," he grumbled. "And before you ask, yes, I went to the doctor, and they gave me all this therapy—oxygen and cognitive...I passed everything." He blew out a breath. "I bet I could play if they'd let me."

"Which they won't. Dev," I warned, "it's only been a week, and you aren't at full speed. You gotta follow the concussion protocol—league rules. Ezra told me he's seen you a couple of times and that you're still getting headaches. You think he doesn't notice, but you're wrong."

"Traitor," he muttered, and I laughed.

"No. He's bein' a good friend. And so is Fallon. We're all watching out for you. Please, Dev. Take the time to recuperate. I need you healthy."

"I just need you, period. Seeing you on the field, watching that cute butt in your uniform, knowing how hot and sweaty you are...*mmm*. I got so turned on."

"Yeah?" My dick stirred. "Tell me more."

His voice deepened to the sexy, husky growl that never failed to get me hard. "You wanna know what I'd do to you?"

"*Mmhmm.*" I palmed my cock and stroked it to its full length.

"I wouldn't even let you shower. I'd get you naked and lay you down all dirty and messy on my bed and lick you."

"That sounds so good." I sighed, my hand moving faster. "Where are you lickin' me?"

"I'd start with that beautiful, big dick, and then I'd open you wide, licking your hole, tasting you. So hot and sexy."

"Oh God, Dev." My hand was a blur on my shaft as my hips jerked frantically. I could feel his mouth on me, so soft and wet, and I moaned.

"Yeah, baby. I'm eating that gorgeous ass of yours, fucking your hole with my tongue. Your cock is bigger and thicker than I've ever seen, and you're jerking it through your fist."

I couldn't answer because I'd just come so hard, I lost my ability to speak. My eyelids fluttered, and I licked my dry lips.

"Dev?"

"*Mmhmm?*" He sounded a bit winded himself.

"That was wild."

"I know." I sensed his dissatisfaction. "But it doesn't take the place of the real thing. You here with me."

I wiped my hand on my boxers. "I know. I'll be home soon enough and we'll have the whole off-season."

"I guess." His sigh sounded ominous. "The doctors want me to take it easy. They said I shouldn't fly yet. Something with my equilibrium and the head injury."

"So we don't. We'll head up to the mountains to the cabin. I'm gonna take care of you, spoil you rotten. And after it gets warm, I'll drive to my house."

"That sounds nice," he murmured. "I think I'm gonna shower and go to sleep."

In an instant I grew concerned. "Do you feel okay? You don't have a headache, do you?"

"I'm fine," he snapped. I stayed silent and he softened his tone, realizing he'd overreacted. "Sorry. But please don't get all smothering on me. I just got my rocks off having phone sex with my husband, and I'm sticky and wrung out. That's all it is."

"Don't get mad at me, Dev. I'm askin' because I love you."

"I know. But it's so fucking hard watching from the sidelines, wanting to play. We worked all season to get here. And now I'm letting everyone down."

"We wouldn't be here if it wasn't for you. Sometimes the big guns need a rest and have to let the little ones show what they can do. I know next season you'll come back bigger and better than ever."

"Thanks. I'll talk to you tomorrow. Say hi to your mom for me."

"I will. Love you."

"Love you too."

I sat in the darkness and could only hope he was telling me the truth. Dev always minimized when he was hurting, shunning any discussion of injuries. He loved the game so much and even gave up his family to follow his dream.

"Nothin' I can do about it until I see him." But I sent Ezra and Fallon a quick text to check on him tomorrow, then took a shower.

Momma was waiting for me at a table in the corner of the hotel restaurant. After talking with some fans and the usual pictures and autographs, I reached her and gave her a kiss.

"Sorry I'm late. I was talkin' to Dev."

Momma's brow puckered with worry. "How's he feelin'? I called him and we talked. He sounded upbeat."

He would, to her. Dev loved Momma and wouldn't want her to worry.

"He was. But you know him. He wants to play, and it's killin' him that he's not." The server came, and I ordered steak and potatoes, while Momma ordered the fish. I wished I could have a beer, but no drinking during playoff season, so it was iced tea for both of us.

"He'll be back next year. You'll come home and rest all off-season."

"I hope so. But there's a little change of plans. Once the season's over, we're gonna go to the cabin and stay there for the winter. Dev's doctor said he shouldn't fly, so we'll come when it starts to get warmer."

Our salads came, and we ate for a few minutes. Momma wiped her mouth. "Can I ask you somethin'?"

" 'Course." I buttered a roll.

"Do you think Dev's gonna play again?"

I stared at her. "What're you talkin' about?"

She met my eyes. "Don't get all riled up. It's just that this is the second bad concussion he's had, and that can be dangerous. I was readin' up on it. I know he loves the game, but he's gotta think of his health, especially long-term."

Our salad plates were whisked away and the mains brought, but I didn't even pay attention. "Momma. Dev's got six months to recover and the best doctors in the world takin' care of him. He's gonna go through the concussion protocol and be ready when the season starts. No one's told him he can't or shouldn't play."

She picked up her fork. "But they don't care about him like you do. You need to sit and have a real serious talk with each other."

We ate our meal and sat over coffee. "I think I'll have plenty of time to see in the off-season how he's feelin'. But ultimately, it's his decision. He's thirty and got a lotta time left to play." I lifted my coffee cup to drink it while it was still hot.

"I know. But if they say he can't, where does that leave you?"

Puzzled, I set the cup on the table. "What do you mean?"

"Would you quit playin' if Dev can't? I know you love him, but you also have to plan for your own future."

"Which is with Dev. If he can't play, he wouldn't stop me. And if I were the one injured, I wouldn't prevent him from continuing. We support each other."

"I hope so."

"It'll all work out. Don't worry. Now I gotta get to bed before I break curfew. The only thing I gotta concentrate on is winning next week's game."

I paid the bill and kissed her good night. She was leaving in the morning for New York, where our conference championship would be held, while I'd be traveling with the team. I couldn't wait, not only because we'd be on home turf, but because Dev would be there to greet us.

The Super Bowl championship had yet to be determined, but it didn't matter. I'd already won at life.

CHAPTER TWENTY-TWO

Dev

Conference Championship Sunday

Clapping my hands, I walked into the locker room. "Hey, guys. Knock them on their asses."

"Dev."

"Yo, Devil."

"How the hell are you doing?"

My teammates crowded around me, and Brody hung back, wide-eyed and confused. I hadn't mentioned to him in our nightly phone call that I'd be coming, but with the game on our turf, I couldn't stay away. Thanks to our amazing security guards, I'd managed to duck the press.

"I'm good. Feeling stronger than I did last week. No more headaches or dizziness." Luke didn't approach me, but I wanted him to know I wasn't there to take the shine off his star. "Dude, you're the bomb. I know you're gonna kill it today."

His smile was tentative. "Thanks, Dev. Are you gonna stay for the game?"

"Heck, yeah. I gotta cheer you on. Keep you all in line." I put a hand on his shoulder and spoke directly to him. "Just keep your concentration. Don't think about anything other than getting that ball to whomever you want. Focus on picking your receiver for passing, and if you're handing off, make sure you don't release the ball unless they've got their hands on it. Lemme tell you what I remember from regular season."

He listened carefully as I went through what I perceived as the other team's weaknesses. "I'll remember. I appreciate it. I'd better go finish suiting up."

From the corner of my eye, I spotted Coach Jackson walking over. "Dev." He hugged me. "You feeling okay?"

God, I hated feeling like an invalid, and it was annoying as fuck to constantly reassure people that I wasn't injured, but this was Coach.

"Yeah. I'm good. Just came by to make sure these bums don't slack off."

"You're gonna sit with us. The fans will love it, and it'll be great for morale." It wasn't a request, but I was glad he'd asked. Being away from the team for the first time since I'd started playing with them had left a gaping hole in my life, especially with Brody gone. Even if I wasn't playing, being in the thick of the playoff race juiced me up, and I finally felt whole again.

"I'm ready." I turned and waved my hands to everyone. "Go get 'em." Before I left, I walked over to Brody and patted his shoulder. "Win it for us," I murmured for only him to hear.

"Gonna do my best."

"Dev, let's go," Coach called out. "You're gonna walk out with us."

With one final meeting of our eyes, I left Brody and joined Coach and the staff. When we jogged out from the tunnel to the field, the moment fans realized I was there, their roar was deafening. Cameras pointed in my direction, and I kept my grin on, knowing they were zooming in. Maybe I wasn't able to be on the field, but this was the next best thing.

We won the coin toss and elected to receive. I swatted each player on their ass as they passed me, and then the game began. Yeah, I cheered and hollered, but man, it fucking sucked to be where I was. I itched to be the one behind the line. To call out the plays and throw the passes. This week wasn't like the last. The Stars were on our asses, and Luke was showing his inexperience and nerves, getting sacked a few times and throwing incomplete passes.

Down 14-3 at halftime, I stood in the locker room and rallied the troops.

"Fuck that first half. Let's do this. You got this."

Coach went over the strategy, and I completely agreed with his plays. The halftime show was completed, and the teams readied to return to the field. I spoke to every one of them, saving Brody for last.

"We can still do this. I wanna make that trip with you to Orlando for the Super Bowl."

Brody frowned. "You're not supposed to fly."

I winked. "You leave it to me. Fallon and Ezra will come too, and I'll make them drive."

His grin matched mine. "Got it all figured out, don'tcha?"

"I always do. Now go kick ass." I lowered my voice. "And don't let anyone put a mark on yours."

He snorted and rolled his eyes, but I didn't miss that cute blush. Suddenly the world looked brighter. If we won, it was only two more weeks until we could be together again. And if we lost—which we wouldn't—I'd be with him tonight, in our bed.

I followed them out to the field.

As hard as it had been to observe the game from the sidelines, watching all the guys celebrate their come-from-behind win was even harder. I was part of the team, and yet I wasn't. And though Brody and some of the others tried to include me, it wasn't the same, and I ended up watching them spray their champagne and listen to the press fawn over the new fan favorite, Luke Fontaine, along with my secret husband. They'd teamed up for the winning touchdown in the last minute of the game. The forty-yard pass that would be talked about for years to come. The fingertip catch by my husband that was already being hailed as one of the greatest in playoff history.

I sat there and clapped, cheering my heart out, but it was a hollow emotion. It had been years since I'd felt this excluded. I watched Brody search the room, and when our eyes met, he joined me.

"Why aren't you here with the rest of the team?" He dropped to my side, and it was hard as hell not to lay my head on his shoulder. Funny how my misgivings melted away with Brody next to me.

"I don't belong there. I didn't play." The words stuck in my throat.

"That's some bullshit, and you know it. Dev, you're the one who got us here. Do you actually think we'd be in the playoffs without your leadership?"

My ego wasn't big, but damn, it was nice to be stroked. "Luke is doing an incredible job. Kid's only been playing for two years, and he's more than risen to the challenge." I darted a glance at the media crush around him and how he was smiling and answering questions. Much more confident than last week. Like a leader. A chill ran through me, and I shivered.

Was this a foreshadowing of the future?

Brody, always attuned to my moods, nudged me. "He's good, but he's no Devil. He's had two years of sitting on the bench, watching the best and learning. He's got a great career ahead of him, but there's only one you."

"I agree that he's gonna be a star. He's got the hands and the instinct. This playoff series has proved it. It wouldn't surprise me if teams made offers for him during the off-season."

"I doubt the Kings would let him go unless they got some huge picks out of it. Anyway, I don't care about him. We're goin' to the Super Bowl, and I can't fucking wait."

I had no chance to answer as microphones were shoved in my face.

"Dev, can you tell us how you feel?"

"How do you think Luke has handled stepping into your shoes?"

"Do you think you'll still be with the team next season?"

That question rocked me, and I pretended to laugh. "Unless you know something I don't, that's the plan. I'm feeling healthy, and I have no lasting effects from the concussion. I'm here to support my team, and I know they're gonna take it all the way." I fist-pumped my arm in the air. "Super Bowl, here we come!"

My teammates' cheering rose around me, and the reporters continued to make the rounds. Brody was pulled away for more interviews, and I decided to leave and go home, but first, I returned to the field. It was empty now, with only the crew picking up the trash from the stands and the groundskeepers tidying up the grass. My gaze swept over the stadium where I'd accomplished all the dreams I'd had as a kid. Clouds had rolled in, and the sky darkened to a somber charcoal. I shivered and zipped my coat up, then turned and walked away.

Super Bowl Sunday

I'd had the choice of sitting in the owner's box or on the field. Brody's mom, Ezra, Roe, Fallon, and Troy, Amber, and Jimmy were our guests, along with Vette and Dora Lee. Dante and Lover joined them as well. Maybe I did belong there more, but I needed to be on the field with my team. And as long as the league allowed it, I was staying.

It had been a roller coaster of a game, the lead changing hands at least four times. Luke had made some good plays and some bad ones, but who was I to judge? My first Super Bowl, I was so nervous, I thought I'd wet my pants. Right now it was fourth quarter, we were on defense, and the Wildcats were on our thirty-seven-yard line. It was third and seven, and I knew they were gonna pass.

Their quarterback faded to the left and threw a perfect spiral. Jarvis Malone jumped up and tipped it so it fell short of the receiver.

"Yeah, baby. Way to go." I clapped furiously.

Fourth down, and they were going for the field goal. It was a long-ass try, but they had one of the best special teams in the league, and they proved it by making it, giving them the lead, 24-21.

They kicked off, and our speed demon, Levar Wilkes, got to midfield. I gave Luke an encouraging clap on the back. "You got this. Doing great."

"Thanks. I'm trying."

I shouted out words of encouragement to everyone, trying to get them pumped up. It seemed to work as Luke hit pass after pass and we scored a touchdown. That revved our defense, and we intercepted a pass from the Wildcats and returned it for another score.

With the stadium shaking, I yelled myself hoarse as the clock ticked away and we'd done it. We were Super Bowl champs. I hugged everyone, and we all ran on the field. This was the only time it was appropriate for me to hug and hold on to Brody in public, and I wasn't about to let that opportunity pass. The press was everywhere, interviewing Luke, who was definitely going to be MVP, and Kendell Watson, who'd intercepted that last pass for the final score.

The field teemed with players, celebrities and others, but I made a beeline for the only person who mattered. I spotted him from behind and jumped him.

"You did it." Laughing, I slid off him, and we hugged. I knew the cameras were taking pictures, but I didn't care. "Super Bowl champion, baby."

Super Bowl hats were slapped on our heads, and damn, it felt good, even if I hadn't played. For the first time since I was injured, I was happy.

"It was awesome. I'm so glad you're here." Brody's big blue eyes met mine, expressing everything we couldn't put into words.

I spied Brody's mom, escorted by security onto the field, and waved to her. With a huge smile, she came running up to us and threw her arms around him. "You did it, honey. I love you."

"Thanks, Momma."

I knew how special this was and took a few steps away for them to have this moment. Marlon and Jonas ran over and grabbed me.

"We did it."

"You sure as hell did."

Marlon's eyes darkened with anger. "Screw that, Dev. You got us here. You're always telling us it's a team effort."

"Yeah, man," Jonas argued. "Fuck that. You think 'cause you missed two playoff games you're not part of the win? No way."

The grandstand had been set up, and it was time for the presentation of the trophy. We all got up on the stand, but again, I hung back, part of me still unconvinced I deserved to be there. I watched as they presented the trophy to Armand Winters and then, as expected, named Luke as the MVP. I waited for him to pass the trophy to Brody or Kendell, but instead, he turned and motioned to me.

"I want to thank Devlin Summers, who gave me the courage to take on the challenge of standing in his place. Without him, we never would've reached the playoffs."

Tears burned my eyes at the sound of applause. Words stuck in my throat, and the best I could do was raise the trophy in one hand and my fist to the sky in the other. I handed the trophy off to Brody, who slung his arm around my neck and held up the trophy, screaming, "Yeah, we did it! All hail the Kingdom!"

When we got down, we were surrounded and gave our interviews to the press. The return to the locker room was jubilant and celebratory, and I made my way to Luke and offered him my hand.

"Thanks, man. That was classy."

"I meant it. I'll never forget how you treated me, and I'm gonna make sure if I'm ever lucky enough to be the starting quarterback, I'll treat my backup the same as you did."

We hugged, and the press yelled at us for a picture. We posed, and a reporter for ESPN asked me, "Dev, how did it feel to sit on the sidelines during the biggest game of the year?"

"Gee, Marv. It felt great. I loved watching everyone play while I twiddled my thumbs." Frustrated, I huffed out a sigh. "C'mon, man. You know I hated it. But I was glad Luke got a chance to play, and now I can concentrate on getting in the best shape to defend our title. The team did great, and I was happy to play a part in the regular season to get us here." I waved at them. "Thanks, guys." And I walked away.

"Devlin, hi." The owner of the team, Armand Winters, stopped me. "Congratulations."

I shook his hand and that of his boyfriend, Hayden. "Thanks. I wish I could've done more, but I'm still thrilled."

Armand looked me straight in the eye. "Take care of yourself, Dev. We want you healthy and happy. You are our franchise quarterback, but football should never take priority over your physical and mental well-being."

Having met Armand many times, I knew he was sincere, but it was still a business and all about money.

"Thanks. I'm doing everything right, and I really feel one hundred percent. The off-season will give me a chance to rest up and get in peak condition for next year."

"I've heard from the coaches you've been a real help to Luke Fontaine, and I'm glad to hear that. I'm sure part of his success was your encouragement."

"It's a team effort. I'm just happy to be part of the team."

"As are we." Armand grinned. "Now go have fun on the roller coasters."

After everyone showered and got dressed, I met Brody, who was hanging with Jonas, Marlon, and Kendell. Vette and Dora Lee were there, as were Dante and Lovell with his fiancée, Vanessa.

"Y'all did it. Fuckin' A." The guys hugged us, and Dora Lee gave Brody and me a kiss.

"That was so exciting," she gushed. "I was on the edge of my seat, screaming."

"Me too," one of Vanessa's friends said, melting brown eyes eating up Brody. "That catch you made was amazing, Blink." Thick lashes batted at him, and he smiled.

"Thank you. All part of the game."

"It must've been so hard on you to sit on the sidelines, Devil." Vanessa's other friend, tanned and toned, dressed in a tight Kings' tank top and a jean miniskirt, cozied up to me. "I'm glad to see you've recovered."

I gazed at her and knew I should play the part, but I didn't want to. Not anymore. I was tired of faking it, and I had no problem using my health to get out of being forced to spend an evening with someone I didn't want.

"I still have to take it easy. Just gonna hang out with my buddies for a little while. No partying for me tonight. Fact is, I'm planning on turning in early."

She laughed. "Seriously? You're the Super Bowl champ. You can't." She slipped her arm through mine. "I'm Aurora, by the way."

"Well, Aurora, I'm afraid I can."

"Y'all ready to head out?" Dante asked. "Cars are waiting to go to the club."

"I'm ready." Aurora left my side, and Brody gave me a face full of surprise.

"I'm not into it tonight," I explained, and Brody nodded.

"Understood."

I knew he would. He always did.

CHAPTER TWENTY-THREE

Brody

With Dev hanging out on the edge of the dance floor, watching everyone celebrate, I had a burst of clarity. He was being true to himself and our marriage, while I continued to play the game we'd been forced to for a decade. Connie stood by my side expectantly, but my focus wasn't on her. It was on Dev who, as if sensing me, raised his gaze to meet mine. God, I wished I could stride right to him and plant a kiss on his lips.

Attuned to me as always, Dev shook his head, turned, and walked to the bar.

"Wanna dance?" Connie cooed.

"Sorry, sweetheart, but I'm crashing right now. Been a helluva day. I'll have to pass." I left her and made a beeline for the one person I wanted to be with.

At the bar, Dev stepped aside and made room for me. That wicked grin kicked up his lips, and I knew he was planning something.

"What's goin' on in that evil mind of yours?"

He widened his eyes at me. "I have no idea what you're talking about. I'm innocent." He smirked, and I snickered.

"You're many things, but innocent has never been one of them."

He sipped his club soda—his doctor had forbidden drinking alcohol. "I'm wounded."

But I knew my husband, and I didn't have long to wait for him to make his move.

Leaning on the bar, I felt Dev's hand slide over my ass and into the back pocket of my jeans. Mother of God, he was going to kill me. But what a way to go. He kneaded the cheek, and I desperately needed to be alone with him.

"Gonna hit the head." Hoping he got the hint, I walked away into the dark recesses of the club to find the men's room. A minute later, Dev followed me and locked the door behind him.

"Dev." I sighed, uncaring that someone might want to come in and they'd find us.

He didn't answer me, just held my face and crushed our lips together. My greedy hunger for him exploded, unable to be quashed. He couldn't keep his hands off me, and I reveled in it.

"Fuck, baby, I just needed to touch you so bad. It's been hell being away from you all these weeks."

Knowing our time was brief, I grabbed him again and covered his mouth with mine. We sucked each other's tongues until I broke away and unlocked the door. "Can't take the chance. But we're gonna be together tonight. Later. Gotta figure out how."

Panting and wild-eyed, Dev traced my lips with his thumb. "Kelsie's parents have a place near here, and they're away visiting her sister in California. She's been here all week for the pregame stuff, but she's gonna stay with her friends tonight and gave me the key. I'm gonna leave in a few, blame it on a headache. Stay a while, then follow. I'll text you the address."

"Perfect. Fuck, I can't wait." The need for him clamored in my blood. I'd been able to bank it for weeks with the playoffs to concentrate on, but now all that tension was released and I needed to let go. With Dev.

"Go first. I gotta make myself look pathetic." A sudden thought hit me and my stomach dive-bombed.

"You don't really have a headache, do you? You promised you'd let me know if you did."

"Absolutely not. I swear." Dev kissed his fingers and held them in the air.

"All right. But I plan on going to bed early."

Dev's eyes twinkled. "Exactly what I had in mind."

I left Dev in the bathroom and returned to the bar. Connie reappeared and linked her arm through mine.

"You sure you don't wanna get out of here and go somewhere more private?"

"Sorry." Luckily, I spotted Luke, Kendell, and Marlon by the bar. "But why don't you let me personally introduce you to some of my friends. You know Luke Fontaine, the MVP? And Kendell Watson and Marlon Lane. Guys, this gorgeous lady is Connie, and she needs some friends to dance with. I gotta go see my momma."

"You all were *amazing*," Connie gushed. She didn't seem to miss me as much anymore.

Kendell grinned. "Thanks. Can I buy you a drink?"

I made sure to lean in and whisper to him, "Keep it wrapped up. You don't need a baby mama this young." He gave me a face filled with surprise but nodded.

"Thanks."

I said good-bye to a bunch of the others and passed through the club. I laughed watching Zeke dance with a woman whose dress barely covered her ass and boobs.

I checked my texts. Dev had sent me the address, and I called for a car, my anticipation rising. It had been weeks since I'd touched my husband, and I couldn't wait.

Dev pulled me into the house and yanked the shirt over my head. He tweaked my aching nipples and bit them. A moan ripped from me, and I fell into the door. Dev popped the button fly and yanked my jeans and briefs, so they fell to the floor. My dick, already hard and aching, thrust out, and Dev wasted no time. Those full wet lips slid down my erection, and I cried out.

"Fuck. Dev, oh God, I missed you."

Dev's tongue danced the length of my dick as he cupped my balls. He sucked and swirled the crown, and my nails dug into the wood of the door as my hips rolled. Dev played along my throbbing shaft, and his fingers slid up my crack to play with my hole.

"Dev, Dev, please."

The tip of his finger slid past my rim, and I came, seeing stars as I exploded. He clutched me hard, digging into my thigh, and swallowed me completely.

From beneath half-lowered lids, I watched him sit on his heels and wipe his face with the back of his hand. "You're amazing. My Super Bowl protein shake."

Even in my drowsy state, Dev made me laugh.

Dev rose, and I stepped out of my sneakers, pants, and briefs and left them by the door. Leading me with a hand at my waist, we walked through the dark house to the bedroom, where I found myself pushed onto the bed. With avid, hungry eyes, I watched Dev strip off his clothes and fondle his erection. I licked my lips.

"Put it in me. Please." My breaths came in short, harsh gasps.

"Baby, I don't want to rush this." He kissed each globe of my ass and ran his tongue along the cleft. "I've missed you so much."

We were used to being apart during the season, but this time, with Dev injured, the separation had been worse. Maybe I'd been hesitant to push him, fearing a setback, but tonight he was completely in control, and I was happy to let him be that dominant alpha man.

On all fours, I gave him my ass, and over my shoulder I watched him pour lube on his dick. He worked his fingers in me for a bit, and my pulse spiked as I pushed hard against his hand.

"Dev, do it," I growled.

He pressed his hand at the base of my spine, lined up the head of his cock at my rim, and pushed. I grabbed hold of the headboard and moaned as Dev split me in two, stuffing me full until I couldn't move.

"Oh, yeah. I've missed this." Dev bit my shoulder, then kissed the sting as he dragged that hot length out of my passage before thrusting in again. And again. He grasped my hips and pounded into me, his nails scoring into my skin. Despite the air conditioning, we were a sweating, slippery mess, and I keened as my cock filled and I began to jack myself off. Dev's grunts added to the creaking of the bed and my own groans.

"Oh God, oh fuck." Dev drove deep, and that brush to my prostate blew me apart, and I came, squeezing the rock-hard dick in my ass.

Hot come filled me as Dev trembled and shook. We collapsed on the bed, and Dev curled around me and kissed my neck.

"I love you so fucking much."

"I love you too, Dev. Forever."

He withdrew, and though he still held me, I already missed him.

"No one compares to you. No one ever has."

I rolled to face him. "I can't believe how lucky we are to have each other. I couldn't wait to leave the bar and come to you. There were a hundred people there, but without you I'm alone."

"I'll never leave you." Dev kissed me. "You're everything I've ever wanted. Smart, sexy, the kindest, sweetest person. Somehow you overlooked all my faults and loved me anyway. And I'll never let you regret it."

"The only regret I could ever have is if I hadn't kissed you back all those years ago."

He nuzzled into my neck. "Let's shower and get some sleep. I know you must be tired as hell. You made some awesome catches but took some hits too." His mouth moved lower. "Tell me where it hurts, and I'll make it better."

"*Mmm*, it might take all night."

We showered and returned to bed. My head barely hit the pillow and I was out.

My eyes opened to pale light filtering in through the curtains. Dev lay next to me, still sleeping. I got up to use the bathroom and, worried that Momma might call my room to go get breakfast and I wouldn't be there, found my pants in the living room and checked my messages.

Momma hadn't texted me, but Zeke had.

I know you and Dev are together. I saw you come out of the bathroom, then him.

A cold sweat popped up over my body, and I practically ran to the bedroom. "Dev, wake up. We've got a problem."

His eyelids fluttered open, and he yawned. "What's the matter?"

"Fucking Zeke, that's what. Look." I handed him the phone. His face tightened in anger, but instead of fear, I saw determination.

"Don't you worry. I'll have him taken care of."

Dev gave me my phone and reached for his on the nightstand. "Ezra?... Yeah. I'm here with Brody, I'm putting you on speaker. Sorry, I know it's early, but there's an issue." He relayed what happened in the bar and what Zeke had texted this morning. "I know for a fact that Zeke isn't paying child support and that he's been physically abusive with those women. He can't prove anything with Brody and me, but I'm sure the team wouldn't like to hear that one of their players is a deadbeat dad and an abuser. What do you think?"

Ezra blew out a long-drawn breath. "It's risky. The last thing you want with someone like that is to get into a pissing match. My advice is to leave it alone. Don't answer that text and ignore him."

"Thanks. Talk soon." After ending the call, Dev got out of bed. "You can leave first and go to the hotel. I'll join you later. I've gotta clean up here and get my shit together."

Catching a familiar twinkle in his eye, I asked, "What are you up to?"

"I'm gonna call Kelsie and have her meet me for breakfast at the hotel. We're going to look very cozy together."

Despite the seriousness of this situation, I couldn't help laughing.

Dev pulled me close. "One day, we're not gonna give a shit and just be free to be ourselves." He kissed me, and I held on to him as the only stable thing in a world spinning out of control.

"I'll see you later." I got dressed and called for a car. When I was halfway to the hotel, I called Momma.

"Wanna have breakfast?"

"Sure, honey. I'll be down in a little while."

"Meet you there."

I was ready for the Dev show.

CHAPTER TWENTY-FOUR

Dev

"So let's go over this again," I said to Kelsie, who cracked her gum.

"Dev, it's not that hard. You want me to pretend to be a girl you've spent the night with." She eyed me, her eyes twinkling. "You're gay but outrageously hot. It's not gonna be a problem for me. You're the one who's gonna have to fake it."

"Listen, sweetheart. I'm gay, not dead. I still find a beautiful woman attractive and sexy." I patted her cheek. "You're gorgeous, and I don't have to get it up, just make it seem as though I can't keep my hands off you."

She giggled. "I went to LaGuardia High School. It might have been years ago, but the acting skills are still there. And this beats the heck out of running errands for you. Not that I don't love doing it, but it's nice to mix it up, you know?"

Fallon had brought Kelsie in to help him with overflow work, and I trusted her to keep my secrets. She showed up looking like we'd had a rough night together—blond hair tousled, makeup smudged, tiny bike shorts, and a tube top that barely held her boobs in check.

I took her hand, and we got out of the car and headed to the hotel restaurant. "Showtime," I murmured and slipped my hand around her small waist. It didn't take long for people to notice me and take pictures and video. "Make it real, babe."

She nuzzled me and kissed the side of my mouth. "*Mmm.* You smell good."

In the restaurant, I spied half the team, including Brody and his mother. I walked over to them, greeted Ms. Faith with a kiss, and slapped Brody on the shoulder.

"Blink. How's it shaking?"

"Doing just fine."

The hostess led us to a table near Luke and Marlon. Jonas was there with his little daughter and his wife. I grinned at them and pulled out the chair for Kelsie.

"Thanks, baby. You're an angel." She patted my cheek. "Makes up for last night when you were such a devil."

"Takes two, baby."

Instead of sitting across, I sat next to her, and we gazed into each other's eyes, making sure people in the restaurant saw us. Brody sat with a smirk on his face. Out of the corner of my eye, I saw Zeke walk in. "Here he comes." I gave Zeke my sunniest smile as he approached. "Morning," I called out to him before turning my attention to Kelsie. "Hungry?"

"Yeah. This morning and last night made me work up an appetite, baby." Kelsie tipped her head against mine.

"What do you wanna eat?" She nibbled on my ear but made sure her voice carried. "I've already had a nice fat sausage this morning, so I'm a little stuffed." Her hand trailed down my chest to my lap and disappeared under the tablecloth. I hummed loud enough for Zeke to hear and spread my legs. Kelsie deserved an Oscar for this performance.

Zeke's eyes narrowed, and I bit the inside of my cheek. I slipped my arm around her shoulders, letting her settle into my chest as I played with the ends of her hair. My eyelids fluttered half-shut. Zeke scowled as he walked past but didn't say anything.

Brody's lips were pressed together, and I knew he was laughing at us. I was glad to see people had their phones out and that this was being recorded for posterity.

I could only imagine the headlines, but for once I'd be happy to be in the spotlight. The server brought us coffee and took our orders. Kelsie sipped hers. "I think that was pretty damn good, if I do say so myself."

"You're perfect. Remind me to give you a big fat raise."

"After you dump me, maybe you can introduce me to your cute friend."

She tipped her head, and I glanced at Luke and Marlon. "Which one?"

"Mr. Very Big, Very Dark, and Incredibly Sexy."

I chuckled. "Marlon is pretty quiet. Not a real party guy. I know he'd like to meet someone and have kids."

"That's okay." She eyed him. "I'm twenty-seven, too old to be in the party life anymore. I wouldn't mind a stable guy who'd treat me right. I wanna have a home and a family."

Our food came, and I drenched my pancakes in syrup. "You know it's gonna be a while until I can say anything about my personal life. But if you wanna break up with me, I'll be okay with that."

"Tired of me so soon?" She ate her eggs. "It's okay. I can wait. Just keep me on the radar."

"You and Fallon are like my family—hell, you're better than my real family. Anything you want, you can have."

Serious now, she put her hand on mine. "Just being your friend and knowing you trust me is enough, Dev."

I'd told Kelsie I was gay after Brody and I were married. I had that sense, like with Fallon and Ezra, that I could trust her with my most personal secrets. Little by little, I'd let people into my life, and they hadn't proved me wrong.

"I do. And I don't trust many people, as you can imagine." We finished our meal and were drinking our coffee. I filled her in on our plans for after the hoopla of the win settled down and we finished all the required promotional work under our contracts, to retreat to the cabin for most of the winter for privacy.

"Excuse me, Mr. Summers?" I looked up to see a boy of about twelve standing with his parents. He wore a jersey with my number on it and was holding a football.

"Hi. What's your name? And call me Dev." I winked at his parents. "That's what all my good friends call me."

"My name's Duncan. I'm sorry to interrupt, but can I have your autograph? You're my favorite player. I'm a quarterback on my team."

"You are? And my number-one fan? I think that deserves more than just my autograph. Hey, guys? C'mere. Duncan here is a big fan. Let's take a picture."

All the guys—even Zeke—came by, and with my arm around Duncan, his parents took several pictures with all of us and after with just myself and Duncan.

"Wow, thanks. That's so awesome." He looked at his parents' phones.

"How about we go outside and play a little catch. Then we can sign your ball?"

I thought Duncan's eyes would pop out of his head. "Su-sure. That'd be way cool."

I took out my wallet and tossed two fifties onto the table. "Let's boogie."

For the next twenty minutes or so, we were in the parking lot, throwing the ball, and it might've just been me throwing to a child, but it was as good as being in the Super Bowl. My arm felt good, my shoulder was fine, and there was no problem with my vision or any headaches.

After we all signed the ball and Duncan left, I walked hand in hand with Kelsie to her car. Knowing everyone was watching, I gathered her close. "Put on a good show."

"Ohh, baby," she purred, and I grinned, tipping her chin up.

"I'll talk to you later."

We kissed, and I watched her leave, then retraced my steps to the restaurant, where Luke and Marlon waved me over. Brody and his mother were talking to Jonas, his wife, and his daughter.

"Man, she's gorgeous." Marlon sighed. "Where'd you meet her?"

"I've known her for a while. But it's nothing serious. You know how it is."

"Nah. Lemme tell you something. If I had a lady like that, I wouldn't be sittin' around with you jokers. I'd snatch her up and put a ring on it."

Luke snickered. "You shoulda heard Marlon. He was sayin' he wished she wasn't your girl, that he'd go for her in a heartbeat."

This would prove better for Kelsie than I thought. "She's not my girl. We were just having fun. To tell you the truth, it got annoying 'cause she was kinda more into meeting you than being with me." I shrugged, watching Marlon's big brown eyes grow wide. "So if you want her number..."

"Say what? You looked really into her."

"Kelsie's a great girl, but I'm not into getting serious with anyone. She wants the whole family thing—house, kids. That's not my style." I grabbed a muffin from their basket. "I was gonna bow out, so if you're interested..." I raised a brow.

"Hell, yeah," Marlon declared.

"What about you, Luke? You have a girl?"

His cheeks turned pink. "Yeah, her name's Dawn, and she's a schoolteacher. She and I have been dating since high school. Her mom's in a wheelchair, and Dawn takes care of her. That's why she doesn't come to the games."

"Sounds like a special lady. You gonna get married, you think?"

Why I'd decided everyone needed to couple up now that Brody and I were married, I didn't know, but I guessed when you were happy, you wanted all your friends to share in that joy.

He nodded, growing bright red. "Yeah. That's always been the plan, but I wanted to wait to make sure I wasn't gonna be cut."

"I think it's pretty obvious that's not happening."

Luke dipped his head. "I'm hoping." He seemed nervous, and I wondered what was going on. "Can I tell you something?"

"Yeah, sure." I glanced at Marlon, who shrugged.

"My agent called and said he's gotten some calls already from teams wanting to make me their starter."

Not unexpected. Luke had come in for me late in the games after we'd amassed a lead we couldn't blow or after we'd secured a spot in the post-season. Or, simply if I needed to rest. Each time he grew more confident. And now that he'd led a Super Bowl team and was in his third year of the four-year rookie contract, it was natural after his spectacular play in the post-season for teams to want to snatch him up.

"What are you thinking?"

"I don't know...I love the Kings organization, but I don't want to be a backup forever."

I understood. I was drafted because the Kings were in desperate need of a quarterback, and I was a player from day one. I couldn't imagine the frustration of being a second-round pick like Luke had been and then being forced to sit on the sidelines for three seasons, only filling in when we were far enough ahead.

"You do what's best for you, but I'm sure the Kings are gonna do whatever they can to try and keep you."

"Except make me the starter," Luke stated frankly.

"Yeah, well, that's kind of taken at the moment." Ezra and I hadn't yet begun to discuss renegotiation of my contract, but maybe I needed to think about it.

"Why's everyone lookin' so serious over here?" Brody and his mother came by our table.

"Just talking shop." I rose to my feet. "How was your breakfast?"

"Just fine, thank you. Are we all goin' to the parks today? I haven't ridden a roller coaster in years."

I rubbed my hands together. "I'm ready."

As we left the restaurant, Brody pulled me aside. "Do you think you should be goin'?"

My brow puckered. "What're you talking about? Why not? Is it because I didn't play?"

"Of course not." The concern in his face was real. "But it's only a few weeks since the concussion. You should still be recoverin'."

I beat my chest in mock play. "Look at me. I'm fine." My eyes twinkled. "I was pretty damn recovered last night, don't you think?"

"Shut up." Brody covered his face as if it could hide the pink of his cheeks from me. "Just wanna make sure you're okay."

"I'm perfectly fine. Stop bein' such a worrywart."

Two hours later, after doing promotional football and theme-park videos and taking pictures, including with fans from all over the country who'd won radio and advertising contests to meet the winning Super Bowl team, we were ready to take to the rides.

We took the easy ones first, and it was nice to simply sit and ride through a fictitious world where everyone got along. Pleasant in theory, but sadly, it didn't all work out that way. Next was the haunted house, and it was fun to see some of the guys actually get spooked. Jonas sat with his daughter, and it was sweet to watch her experience it all for the first time. We bought her stuffed animals and a cute hat to wear.

"Who's ready for some of the big coasters?" Kendell yelled, and I pumped my fist.

"Let's go."

We hopped on, got strapped in, and off we went, zooming fast, then climbing slow only to drop at a speed that sent my stomach hurtling to my throat. I held on and yelled, so damn happy to be alive. My vision blurred for a moment, but I ignored it.

We got off, and all of us needed a minute to get our legs under us. Ms. Faith, who'd decided not to ride any coasters and stayed with Jonas's little girl, came to me with a worried face. "Are you okay? You look pale."

I brushed her off. "I'm fine. Don't worry. Do you need some water?"

She held up her bottle. "I'm good, thanks. But I think one big ride is enough for you."

I knew she was only trying to be helpful, but I refused to show weakness in front of my team.

"Nah, I'm good. I've got one more."

We headed to the coaster built into the mountain, and it was a little less enjoyable as the beginning of a headache thumped behind my eyes. I shook it off, refusing to quit. We had lunch, and after some food, tons of water, and an energy drink, I felt better. I'd stopped in a little convenience store and bought some massively overpriced pills to help my head, and they worked.

The gang suggested the Star Wars ride next, and I was all in. One of my favorite movies ever. Brody and I sat together, and just being with him, living our best life, made it all worthwhile. Lights flashed, and the rides spun. The longer the ride went on, the worse I began to feel. My head throbbed, and all the colors melted together.

Fuck, I'm going to be sick.

I sat praying I'd hold on until the ride was over, my eyes closed and hands gripping the rail. Everyone else was too enthralled to notice me, and I sucked in a breath of relief when it was finally finished. Careful not to fall on my face, I climbed out of the ride. Once outside and in the fresh air, I thought I'd feel better, but I quickly found a trash bin and threw up. Brody and several of the guys raced to my side and helped me to a bench.

"I'm all right. I'm okay. Must've been something I ate." I rested my head on my arms and concentrated on taking in fresh air. "I just need some water."

Brody crouched in front of me. "I told you it was too soon. I hope you didn't hurt yourself."

"I'm fine," I responded, sharp enough that they all stared at me, and I realized we were in a public place and people were eyeing us. "Sorry," I mumbled. "I'm just gonna hit the bathroom. You guys go on ahead." I forced a smile. "Ms. Faith and I will catch up with you in a bit."

Of course they all followed me inside. I rinsed out my mouth, and Jonas gave me a juice from his daughter's bag. I drank it all down. "Thanks. I feel better now."

I was telling the truth, but my reaction to the rides meant I wasn't as recuperated as I'd thought. And that scared the hell out of me for the future.

CHAPTER TWENTY-FIVE

Brody

Three months later

"Yeah, for sure I'll take it," I told Ezra, who called me early that morning to let me know the Kings wanted to extend my contract and were offering four more years at more than fifteen million a year, guaranteed. "I'd be crazy to say no."

Laughing, Ezra agreed. "Well, yeah. Obviously, the Super Bowl win and your performance in the playoffs made them realize they need to lock and load you. I can't guarantee a no-trade clause, though. They're really stingy with them these days, even for superstars. I'll get the contract to the lawyers and let them review all the fun stuff, like salary cap and incentives. But you're gonna end up being one of the highest paid tight ends in the league."

"Not too shabby for an old man of thirty."

"And you're thrifty with the money, that I know. Dev said he monitors all the finances."

"He's great like that." From the glass doors looking out onto the yard, I could see Dev, striding up the path. Every morning, no matter the weather, he took a five-mile walk. Alone. He said it cleared his head and the fresh air helped his recovery.

"I'm glad he's got something to fall back on when he's no longer playing."

"What do you mean?" A chill ran through me. "Why are you sayin' it like that? Did you hear somethin'?" A second passed without Ezra responding, which was a second too long. "Ezra. Tell me what's goin' on."

"Nothing at the moment. I swear. But I gotta tell you, the Kings don't want to lose Luke Fontaine after his performance this post-season."

I grew angry on Dev's behalf. "So they wanna trade Dev? Are you fuckin' serious?"

"I'm not saying that's what's happening. I promise you I haven't had any outreach from management, and I wouldn't lie. He still has time left on his contract, and a lot can happen. But between you and me, he didn't do himself any favors with that amusement-park trip and getting sick on the roller coasters." Ezra's sigh matched my own.

As we'd feared, Dev's "incident," as we called it, had made the rounds of the sports news: "Is *the Devil too sick to return? What's the real story behind Devlin Summers's injury?*" Of course people had taken pictures of him getting sick over the trash bin and cradling his head in his hands, us surrounding him with worried faces. The press was only too eager to plaster them everywhere.

The speculation made us so damn angry, and it hurt Dev to his core. Fallon had done a masterful job of keeping the media at bay by putting out statements from Dev and his physicians. There were carefully timed releases this winter showing Dev up here in the mountains, either snow tubing, or on his walks, fresh-faced and clear-eyed. On his forays into the city for PT or medical exams, he'd always do a little shopping, and again, a positive photo of Dev would pop up, looking fit, skin glowing, always with a smile on his face.

But the bottom line was money and whether he could play with the same fierce intensity he was famous for. Two bad concussions were enough to give the team pause to think, no matter how Dev behaved in the off-season.

"I'm not gonna argue with that, Ezra. I warned him it was too soon. But he's been doin' great up here. Resting and following up with his doctor appointments online. He went to the city and had the tests, and they all came back normal."

"That's great. I'm sure he has nothing to worry about. Dev's the best in the league, one of the greatest ever. They know his worth."

"I hope so," I grumbled. "The kid was good, but he's still unproven. A few playoff games and even a Super Bowl win doesn't make him a replacement for someone like Dev."

"Exactly my feelings."

Dev began his return to the house, waving his hands at me. Even from here I could see the joy on his face. He loved living in the mountains during the winter, and I had to admit, as someone who didn't grow up in cold weather, there was something to be said for getting snowed in with the one person you loved more than anything.

"I'd better go. Thanks for tellin' me the contract news."

"Say hi to Dev, and we'll talk after I've reviewed all the paperwork."

I tossed the phone aside and went to the kitchen to pour Dev a cup of hot coffee. After depositing coat and boots, he came inside, his color high and eyes glowing, cheeks cool but lips warm against mine.

"*Mmm.* Thanks. This is the best. Like you."

"How was the walk?"

"Great. Saw some deer, coyotes, and a fox. I tried to get pictures, but they were too fast for me."

"You're becoming a real mountain man," I joked.

"You know, it's not such a bad life. No noise and traffic. Even when the weather sucks, it's still beautiful. I can wear the same clothes, and no one cares."

"Now wait a minute. I care if you don't shower and do the laundry."

He chuckled and sipped the coffee, looking totally relaxed on the sofa. "This is the life. You and me, alone in the middle of nowhere. Just the two of us."

"Nice, isn't it?" I sat in the club chair and put my feet up on the ottoman. "Let's have a fire tonight."

"Sounds good to me." He drank more coffee. "Who were you talking to?"

"Ezra. The Kings wanna extend my contract and raise my salary. Probably gonna be some shifting around with the cap, but Ezra thinks it's a good idea."

"Yeah? Raise it? By how much?" He set his cup on the rough wooden table between us and sat up, eyes intent.

"Over fifteen million a year."

I could see his brain working. "Make sure you find out the incentives."

"Ezra knows."

"Good." He picked up his coffee cup again.

I figured I'd test the waters. "You have any thoughts on your contract?"

His brows drew together. "Like what? There's still a while to go."

"I know. Just wonderin'."

But Dev was no dummy. "Did Ezra say anything?"

"No, 'course not. He wouldn't discuss your contract with me. Anyway, what's on the agenda for today?"

Still lost in thought, Dev stared into his mug. "I've been hearing things."

"Like what?" I asked guardedly.

He narrowed his eyes. "Like Luke is angling for my spot. Now, I don't believe that because he's too nice a kid and wouldn't cut me off at the knees like that. At least I hope not. But I have a plan."

"What're you talking about?" I shifted forward in my chair. "You never mentioned anything." A little hurt that he was keeping things from me, I frowned. "What's goin' on?"

"I just thought of it on my walk in the woods. I was gonna discuss it with you."

Mollified, I nodded. "Okay. So what're you thinkin'?"

"I need to show them all that I'm in good shape because I don't think those little trips to the city are enough. I'm gonna call up my friendly reporters and give them exclusives. Let them interview me on television so people can see how fit I am." His eyes twinkled. "It's one of the reasons I'm doing all this walking. I want a nice, healthy glow. I know it's off-season and time for us to let go a little, but I have something to prove." He pulled out his phone. "Matter of fact, I'm gonna call them right now."

I watched and listened as he was put through to the head of the sports department at one of the major sports networks.

"Joe, I've got some free time and was wondering if you'd want an exclusive on my off-season recuperation and plans for next year."

An exuberant voice burst from the tinny speaker. "Yeah? I'm listening."

As Dev outlined his ideas, a sense of foreboding settled in my chest. As excited as Dev was, I suspected Ezra knew something he wasn't yet willing to share. And keeping that knowledge from Dev hurt my heart, but my husband would be devastated to hear the team he gave his soul to would so easily trade him.

"So?" Sparkling eyes met mine. He'd ended the call while I sat lost in my head. "What do you think?"

I gave him a thumbs-up. "You're gonna rock it."

We hadn't been together for so many years without knowing each other inside out, and Dev frowned. "What's going on?"

"Nothing. I swear." Lying didn't come easily to me on a good day, and keeping the truth from Dev was going to take Herculean effort, but I'd do anything to protect him from the eventual fall, for as long as I could. "I'm still waitin' for the coffee to kick in."

"You sure?" Concern furrowed his brow. "Do you think it's a bad idea? You'd tell me if you did."

"No," I rushed to reassure him. "It's great. You're in peak condition, and the fans should see that you're ready to roll." My gaze remained steady on his, and Dev nodded.

"Thanks. You're gonna come with me, right? I need my emotional support Brody." He leaned in to kiss me.

"You never cease to amaze me. You're always thinkin' ahead."

"I'm always thinking about us. I want us to be set for the rest of our lives whenever we decide to retire."

Curious because we'd never had this discussion, I left my chair to sit by him. "Is that somethin' on your mind? Retirin'? I thought you were fightin' to stay in the game."

"I am. I love playing football. And when I was younger, I thought it was all I ever wanted." He chewed his bottom lip. "Then I met you. I don't wanna wait until I get so badly injured that I have to go out that way. I want to be able to enjoy our lives and not worry about long-term problems. I know I've been lucky to avoid something big—and no, I don't consider the concussions big. But if they offer me a four- or five-year deal? Yeah. I think I'm done after that."

"What're you gonna do after?" All of this was a surprise to me.

He ran his foot over mine. "Be Mr. Devlin Summers-Martin. Your husband."

Would I be ready? Retiring at thirty-five or so wasn't such a bad gig. We'd already achieved the apex of the sport and had more money than we knew what to do with, so what would I be playing for? And traveling or fishing, doing charity work and simply being with Dev, that sounded pretty damn good to me.

"Not too shabby."

His smile was a warm hug. "Haven't you been thinking about what we're going to do with the rest of our lives?"

"I'm busy with the day-to-day. Keeping my eyes open to the present and what we see right in front of our eyes. You're the planner." In our relationship, Dev was always a step ahead, while I lived more in the moment. It was why he was so good with our finances and investments.

He settled into the cushions. "So tell me, since you're in touch with our surroundings, any rumblings of the Kings wanting to trade me?"

I should've known Dev wouldn't let it go so easily. "I haven't heard anyone on the Kings say they're lookin' for a trade. I swear."

It wasn't a lie.

He laid his head on the sofa cushion and stared at the rough ceiling beams. "I just want to leave on my terms. After everything I've given them, all the wins and playing my heart out each game, I'd hope they'd give me that." His lids fluttered shut, and for a second I thought he'd fallen asleep. Then he popped up and jumped to his feet. "Let's do some practice throws." He wiggled his hips. "I need to make sure I've still got all my moves."

On my feet, I slipped my arms around his waist and pressed a kiss to his neck. "Trust me. You've got it all. I don't know what I'd do if I didn't have you."

"Good thing you're never gonna have to find out."

Laughter rumbled from his chest, and I wanted to hold on to this moment for whatever the winds of change might blow into our lives.

CHAPTER TWENTY-SIX

Dev

Mid-season

Damn, I loved the game. And on home turf? Nothing better than the roar of the crowd to get the juices flowing. Once again, we were on top of the division and looking to add another win. The score was14-3 in the fourth quarter and we were on the opposing team's twenty-yard line. I'd thrown one pass for a touchdown, and we'd run one in. Normally I didn't keep track of my stats, but I hadn't thrown any interceptions, and I knew my yards thrown were good.

"How's the head, Devil?" Terrance Leeks, a defensive end from the San Diego Sharks, called out as we took our positions.

"Hard as ever," I yelled, and my team and several of the opposing one laughed outright. I crouched to grab the handoff from the center.

"White 80, White 80. Set. Go."

I put the ball in Marlon's hands, and he threaded the needle to run the ball and score a touchdown. As I celebrated, from the corner of my eye, I watched Leeks come barreling through, and before I had a chance to step away, he plowed into me as if the ball was still in play. I flew into the air and heard the screams. I rolled and fell hard, the wind knocked out of me, but I wasn't hurt.

Just fucking pissed off.

The whistle blew, and the ref called a flag on the play for unsportsmanlike conduct. On my feet, I stormed over to Leeks and ripped off my helmet strap. "What the fuck was that?"

He shrugged. "Just doin' my job."

"Your job is to play football, not try and injure me. Asshole."

He shoved me. "Watch it, pretty boy."

"Fuck you." I spat and walked away to the cheers of the crowd, while Leeks continued to run his mouth. On the sidelines, I waited for the special teams to make the extra point. Coach Jackson hurried to my side.

"You okay? Fucking bastard. I want him suspended for that."

"I wouldn't say no."

"How's your head?"

I rolled my eyes, but aware the cameras were on me, I held out a hand to show I was steady. "I'm great. Not a problem."

"Good. Rest up." He called Luke. "Fontaine. You're goin' in."

Outraged, I jumped up. "You're pulling me? Why?"

Those dark eyes narrowed. "Because I said so. You're done, Dev. Take the win."

I knew better than to argue, but I wasn't happy. I wanted to take it to the end. But it was a team effort, and I sat and cheered as Luke drove the team down the field and we scored another touchdown.

"Good run," I congratulated Luke when he returned to the bench.

"Thanks. Tough call to take you out."

We watched as we kicked the ball, and to my shock, their receiver fumbled the ball on his thirty-five-yard line. Our guys were on top of it, and the ref signaled a turnover.

"Damn. Can't believe it." I jumped to my feet. "Yeah, let's go." I was almost at the point of putting my helmet back on when I remembered I was no longer playing. "Go get 'em, Luke."

He threw me a quick nod and jogged onto the field, where in succession, he threw two passes to Brody and we scored again. The crowd went wild, and we won, 35-3. To my shock, the Sharks quarterback, Patrick Sloane, came over to me.

"Dev. Listen, I'm sorry about Leeks. That was a shit move."

Trick Sloane was a few years younger than me but a hell of a quarterback, and my respect for him grew even more with his apology for his teammate.

"Not your fault, but I agree. Pissed me off. But I guess I'm a target now."

Sloane's lips thinned. "I'm gonna make sure he doesn't do that again. Play to win, yeah. But not dirty."

He stuck out his hand, and I shook it. "No worries. I appreciate it."

Sloane walked away, and it was nice to know that a player I wasn't close with understood.

In the locker room, the media was loving up on Luke, and this time, I wasn't feeling so hospitable about it. Of course at the press meet afterward, I was all smiles and praise, but inside I seethed with annoyance. Yes, we'd won, and that was ultimately the goal, but it pissed me off that I wasn't allowed to finish the game.

And for the next few games, the pattern repeated. In the fourth quarter, if we were leading, I was taken out, each game earlier and earlier. It began to mess with my head, and I started anticipating when Coach would give me the signal. Then the ultimate fuckery happened—I threw a rare interception and heard boos from the crowd for the first time.

Brody sat by my side while defense was on the field.

"What's goin' on, Dev?"

My gaze remained on the field, watching the Flames move the ball, but I shrugged. "I don't know, but something's not right. I feel like I'm slowly being squeezed out."

Brody nudged me. "No way. You're the backbone of the team. Let's get back on the field and kick their asses."

I grinned. One thing Brody always managed to do was drive away my bad mood. "You're right." I clapped my hands and whistled. "Let's do this."

We blocked their attempt at a field goal, and I was putting my helmet on, but Coach Jackson stopped me. "Take a seat. Luke will play the rest of the game."

"What? Why? One interception and you're benching me? C'mon, Coach. What's really going on?"

"Summers, sit. Fontaine, take his place."

I didn't care if it would cost me a fine. I stormed off the field and went to the locker room. Something was going on behind the scenes, and I didn't like it. For several minutes I paced the room before deciding not to play into their hands and returned to the field. The offensive coach, Tim Downs, wasn't happy and chewed me out for my bad behavior.

"You don't like the call? Too fucking bad, Devlin. What happened to the team player you're supposed to be? I have half a mind to fine you."

"Go ahead. Maybe if I felt like I wasn't being pushed aside, it would make sense. Is that what's happening?"

He didn't answer, but I saw a flicker of something in his normally stoic expression that sent a chill through me. I bit my tongue and remained silent.

"Don't throw a temper tantrum. Just do as I say."

Seething, I followed instructions and sat on the bench. For the rest of the game, I ignored all the shit floating around in my brain and concentrated on the plays going down. We ended up losing, and Coach took a lot of heat from the press at the aftergame conference for removing me. Several questions were tossed my way.

"Devil, how did it feel being taken out? Do you think the Kings would've won if you'd stayed in?"

"Dev, do you think you're playing at a hundred percent?"

"I'll answer that last question first." I gathered my thoughts and waited for my anger to pass. "No, I'm not playing a hundred percent. I'm at least at a hundred and fifty percent. I always give my all. Just as important, I'm not here to second-guess my coach. I just follow the rules. Obviously, I would've liked to finish the game, but as always, I'm a team player."

Once we'd gotten changed and took our post-game treatments, I waited until I was home to call Ezra.

"Tough loss," he sympathized. "Were you having some words with the coaches?"

"Kind of. That's part of why I called. I don't like the signals I'm getting."

"Signals? Like what?"

"That's what I need you to find out." I pinched my eyes shut. "Please, Ezra. It's bugging the hell out of me. If there's trade talk out there, I want to hear about it before the rumor mill gets it. I know the deadline is next week." The lock clicked, and Brody walked in, sporting a grim face. "Let me know what they say."

"Will do. Talk to you soon."

I tossed the phone aside, and Brody sat next to me. "You okay?"

I shrugged. "I dunno. I'm feeling weird."

Brody's brows pulled together. "Weird how? Something physical?"

And I could see his fear that my head was bothering me. "No. Not at all." Only to Brody would I voice this. "I feel like they're testing the waters of the team without me."

"No way. You're our leader."

"Well, then someone is staging a *coup*. Brody, I'm telling you, the Kings are gearing up to trade me."

Nothing in Brody's face indicated that he wasn't telling me the truth. Of course I didn't think he'd lie to me, but I also knew he'd hate to hurt me if there were rumors. "No fucking way. You're young and in your prime. Best in the league. A Hall of Famer."

Hearing Brody's outrage on my behalf, I put my arm around him. "I can't imagine they're really gonna trade me, but it's upsetting that they're finding it so easy to toss me aside week after week."

"They aren't," Brody insisted. "I refuse to believe it."

Two days later, Ezra called. "Dev? We need to talk."

Instantly, I went on alert. Brody and I had come home from practice and were in the living room of my place, studying tapes for the upcoming game on Sunday.

"What is it?" Sensing the tension in my voice, Brody swung his legs over the side of the couch and sat up.

"I'd rather talk in person."

"Ezra. Just tell me. I can already guess, but I need to hear it."

"The Kings have received some offers for you. Draft picks, players...pretty good ones obviously. You're worth a hell of a lot."

I ignored the ego stroke. "Not enough to keep me, though, despite so many playoff and Super Bowl appearances and wins. Four championships in ten years isn't a goddamn joke." Even though I'd hate to be away from Brody, it could be doable if the team was close. We could deal with it for four years or so. "Okay. Where to? East Coast, right?" Brody rubbed his nape, sadness emanating from his eyes. I held out my hand, and he took it.

"Not exactly. The Oklahoma Bisons and the Utah Peaks."

Panic rising in my chest, I shook my head. "Oh, no. No, no, no. No fucking way. I can't live away from Brody for that many years. I won't."

It wasn't easy for Ezra either. "Dev...I'm trying to do what's best for you, but you don't have a no-trade clause in your contract. I'm afraid the head injury last year has made you vulnerable in a way you've never been."

Exactly as I feared. "And there's no such thing as loyalty. I know, I know. It's a business, and it's all about the money."

"Yes. All I can do is get you the best deal possible."

"Thanks, Ezra. I know it's not your fault. Talk to you soon."

I ended the call without waiting to hear what he had to say and stared off into space. Brody remained quiet. Waiting.

"It's across the country," I stated, sick to my stomach.

"How far?"

"Utah or Oklahoma. I'd rather retire. That I can do, at least."

"But you shouldn't have to. It's not fair. Dammit, you're young. You've got years left to play." I'd never seen Brody so angry.

"I know." Frowning and frustrated, I ran my hands through my hair. "Be honest with me. Do you think I've fallen off my game? Have I been screwing up?" I knew no matter how much he loved me, Brody would tell me the truth.

"No. I haven't noticed anything different in your play. Don't let that interception freak you out. It's not the only one you've ever thrown; you're just hypersensitive to every move."

"Maybe, but I think I have a right to be, especially now when I see they're ready to trade me." I had a wild idea, but I needed Brody's consent. "I want to ask you something. Are you willing to let me try something that would require us coming out, but it would definitely still remain a secret?"

"That doesn't make any sense. How can we come out if it's still a secret?"

"Trust me?" I gazed deep into those beautiful blue eyes.

"Yeah, of course."

I kissed him. "Let me tell you what I have in mind."

Dressed in my best suit and hoping my nerves didn't show, I strode into the business office of the Brooklyn Kings. I greeted the receptionist.

"Devlin Summers."

The young man nodded. "Yeah, of course, sure. Mr. Summers. Pleasure to meet you."

"I'm here for Armand Winters."

"Let me ring him." He picked up the phone and spoke quietly, then glanced up. "His assistant will be out in a second."

True to his word, the door opened, and Hayden walked out to greet me.

"Hi, Dev. Follow me." The guy was ridiculously good-looking, and I recalled there was a bit of a scandal with him, but I couldn't remember what about. "Can I get you coffee, espresso, water?"

"No, no thank you."

"Armand is ready for you." He gave one knock on the door and opened it. "Devlin Summers is here."

Armand Winters waited in front of his desk. "Come in, Devlin. Please sit." He shook my hand and we all sat at the conference table. "Do you mind if Hayden remains with us? I have him take all my notes as his recall is exceptional."

"No. Not at all."

Armand Winters wasn't much older than me, and I hoped the fact that he was in a same-sex relationship would help my case. In the times I'd met him, Armand had struck me as a nice guy—much different than his father, who'd been the old-school, business-only type. In the years since Armand had taken over the team, the Kings had set up mental-health clinics for the players to help cope with stress and depression. I also knew the team contributed to many LGBTQ causes. It boded well for what I had to say. At least I hoped so.

"I'm a little curious about this meeting, especially because it's you on your own—is your agent or attorney coming?"

"No. This is completely my call. It's personal. And first of all, thanks for agreeing to meet so early because of my training schedule."

"Not a problem. I sensed it was something urgent. Are you in any kind of trouble? Do you need help?"

I shook my head. "No. I'm going to be frank with you. I've played with the Kings my whole career, and I love the team. I know my concussion's raised concerns that I'm not one hundred percent, but that's just not the case. The doctors said I'm fit to play and that there are no lasting effects."

Armand's eyes reflected sympathy, and he sighed. "You've heard about the trade talks. Honestly, I was a little surprised about it myself, but I have full faith in my coaching staff that whatever they decide is in the best interest of the team."

Listening to Armand speak so casually about my future made me wince, but I'd never shied away from a challenge.

Here goes nothing.

"What about my best interest? The person who brought you four Super Bowls and a winning season ever since I joined the team. Don't I get a chance to make my pitch to stay?"

Armand's gaze shifted to Hayden, who'd sat quietly, typing on his iPad. The man's lips twitched, and he said, "I think that's very telling. It isn't often a player cares so much about where he plays, rather than how much he's playing for."

"Hayden's right. And I agree we owe you the opportunity to make your case." Armand nodded. "Go ahead. I'm listening."

I laced my fingers together so tightly they hurt. "I'm gay." Two sets of brows, one dark and one blond, shot high. My turn to smile. "Surprise. And my partner is also with the Kings." Their gazes remained intent, and under their scrutiny, I blew out a breath. "It's Brody. We've been together since college, and last year we got married in California."

Armand blinked and rubbed his chin. "Uh, okay, wow. This was *not* what I expected to hear."

For the first time, my laughter was genuine. "Yeah, I'll bet. It was one of the reasons I turned down an offer a few years ago to move to the Rockets for *a lot* more money."

"I have to say I wondered about that. Obviously, I was glad you stayed with us, but we were all surprised. Not many people would walk away from that kind of money." Armand's expression was endearingly sweet. "However, now it makes sense."

"Yeah. I did it to stay with Brody. I didn't want to be separated from the person I love more than anything."

"That's really beautiful. And thank you for sharing your story with us, but I'm still not sure how it relates."

I had to make my point before something pulled him away and the moment was lost. "I'm asking for that kind of grace from the Kings as an organization. I came to you because I figured as a gay man in a relationship, you would have a better understanding of my feelings. I love the Kings—you're the only team I've ever wanted to play for, and which I'd hoped to retire from. But I love Brody more. Please don't trade me. I know you're listening to the coaches and their fears that I'm not the quarterback I once was, and for you, as the owner, it's only about business and the bottom line. Maybe it's true, but I've given you everything I have my whole career, and I hope I have your respect so you'll listen to me. It's not business to us. It's our lives."

Armand seemed uncomfortable. "I usually don't get involved in the trade negotiations. I trust my coaches to steer the team in the right direction."

"I'm coming to you—and coming out to you—because I thought you'd understand more than anyone how difficult it's been to live in this world that wouldn't accept Brody and myself as partners. I've lived my entire career under a shadow of fear that I'd be outed and have to give up what I love doing. Because you know for sure, if I came out, I'd never be able to play."

Armand sighed. "I hate having to agree with you, but you're right. I remember when Keller Williams came out, and he's a high school football coach now—not even active. The press hounded him and his partner."

That had been a shock to me as well, but obviously, I shouldn't have been surprised. "Exactly. Even though it shouldn't, the focus becomes the player's sexuality, not the game."

"Okay, Dev." Armand hitched his chair closer. "So what is it you want me to do?"

"I'm asking you to reconsider this trade and let me stay for five more years. Be the franchise quarterback, as you've called me, and let me bring home more Super Bowls."

"And Luke Fontaine?" Armand posed the obvious question. "What about him? He wants to play and has proved he can. He's going to be a free agent, and we'll lose him."

"Maybe so, but I'm the proven entity. I've been the one to get the wins and lead the team. I'm the one who's brought you all the championships. Trade him for great draft picks if you can. If not, then he stays my backup, and I don't mind if he plays some, but not because you feel I'm washed up. Look. I still keep my eye on the college scene, and there are a few kids coming up in the ranks with incredible potential. Remember, we also need young, fast running backs, wide receivers, and tight ends. It's a circle of life—eventually everyone on the team will turn over. But I'm only thirty-one, and that's not so old for a quarterback."

"What's to say we won't be having this conversation again in five years?"

A fair question, and at least he hadn't dismissed me outright. "I'm giving you my word. By that time, I'll have had enough. Brody and I want to be able to enjoy our lives. Hopefully we'll have more Super Bowls to add to our collection, and I'd do everything possible to make that happen."

The phone rang, and Hayden jumped to answer it. "I'll tell him," he stated and hung up. "Armi, your meeting is ready."

Thankful I'd been able to get this much time to plead my case, I stood. "I appreciate you seeing me and listening to my story."

We walked out together. Armand shook my hand. "Thank you for sharing your personal life with me. You're a great player, Devlin, and whether you stay with us or finish your career elsewhere, you're a role model and someone I'm proud to know."

"Thank you."

Of course I nodded and said the right words, but as I took a car to the field for practice, I had no idea where I stood. I met with the offensive coaches, and both Luke and I went through game planning and preparation. I didn't get any vibes from them whether I was staying or going. There were no messages or emails from Ezra or anyone.

Four days passed, and my nerves were on edge, but I'd about given up hope. We broke practice around dinnertime, and in the car home, I checked my messages, Brody's first.

Be over after I shower and change. I'll bring dinner.

Warmth rushed through me. No matter what happened, I'd never be alone as long as I had him.

Fallon had sent me a bunch of texts.

US Sports Network, NFL This Week, and Football Daily all want to know if the trade rumors are true. What's going on? What're they talking about?

I responded with two words: Nothing. Yet.

What do I tell them? They're not the only ones. Local TV stations are asking too.

The fact that I hadn't heard a peep from the Kings or Armand wasn't a good sign. But I'd always been lucky with the Hail Mary pass, and this one was the biggest of my career.

Just say I don't comment on rumors.

I lay on the couch, waiting for Brody to arrive, when I got a call.

"Ezra? What's up?"

"Turn on *Sports News Network*. What did you do?"

"What do you mean?" I grabbed the remote. I saw Coach Jackson flanked by all the coaching staff. The door lock clicked, and Brody walked in with two bags.

"What's goin' on?" He set the bags on the table. "That's Coach."

"Ezra's on the phone. Said I needed to watch."

"You do," Ezra called out.

Coach adjusted the microphone. "Today we made a trade deal with the Oklahoma Bisons. We've traded Luke Fontaine for future draft picks and All-Pro wide receiver Jerrod Bermiester. We have full faith and confidence in Devlin Summers as our franchise quarterback and the leader of our team."

"I'll call you back," I said to Ezra, and set the phone on the table. "It worked. Armand Winters must've spoken to the coaches."

"I guess. I hope he didn't say anything."

"There's no way he would. Are you upset that I did? You said it was okay to tell them."

Brody looked down at our entwined hands. "No. I'm just...overwhelmed. Relieved. I guess you were right goin' to the top." He lifted our fingers to his lips. "I should know by now that you always get what you want."

When I'd told Brody I wanted to talk to Armand Winters because he would be the one person to understand our predicament, he'd been hesitant, but I'd asked him to trust me.

I held his face between the palms of my hands. "Only if it's important. And that's you. The most important thing in the world to me."

We listened to a little bit more of the news conference, but there were no other startling revelations. My phone was blowing up with texts from friends on the team. Fallon sent one that was a line of hearts and clapping hands, and I laughed at Kelsie's.

Now that you're staying, time to introduce me to your hot friend.

Of course. I live to give you a sex life.

She sent me a kissy-face emoji and a heart.

I put my phone facedown to concentrate on Brody.

"I'm so glad to have this settled."

"You think they're gonna sign you for the full five years you were talkin' about?"

I picked up the remote and turned off the set. "I don't know. I'm hoping, but I'll call Ezra and see."

Ezra didn't even bother to say hello. "What did you do without talking to me first?"

"I took one chance to shoot my shot, and it paid off. I spoke to Armand Winters."

"It sure the fuck did. They sent me over a contract. Five years, eighty million dollars. The usual incentives and such."

"Won't say no to that. You think I can get a no-trade in there? I agreed to retire after the five years."

Ezra's snort almost broke my ear drum. "You're pushing it. No. Lemme ask you, what the hell did you say to Winters?"

I laid my head on Brody's shoulder. "I spoke from the heart, hoping that as a gay man, he'd understand my feelings. How hard it is to live a closeted life in sports. And that I could play for another five years, but not if I moved away from Brody. I reiterated my stats and what I've done for the Kings, and that I wanted to stay with them because it's a family. And that it would mean everything to me to be with the man I love."

"I have it on good authority Armand Winters personally made this request, so it's basically a done deal. I'll have all the paperwork to you tomorrow. Get some rest."

I set the phone on the table, and Brody grabbed me in a bear hug. "Ow. Don't crush the merchandise." But I couldn't stop laughing and kissing his face, over and over.

"I love you, Dev."

After all these years, it came down to the end game. A life of love with Brody.

EPILOGUE

Brody

Five years later

I was never one for calling press conferences—all that attention on me wasn't something I enjoyed. But after nearly fifteen years in the NFL, it was necessary, more for the fans than the media. And as we'd decided, Dev joined me. After all this time, we had to do it together.

"Hello, everyone. Nice to see y'all. We wanna thank the Brooklyn Kings for giving us this time and the use of their offices to have this press conference. Now that the season is over, Dev and I are here today to announce that we're retiring."

"We waited until we could bring you one last Super Bowl championship," Dev interrupted. "You're welcome."

I chuckled, and Dev grinned, but from his bouncing knee, I could see how nervous he was. Ezra and Momma sat side by side in the front row, along with Lizzie, Fallon, and Kelsie. I leaned into the microphone.

"We've loved every single moment of our time with the Kings. I joined the team after Dev, but I'd always heard the talk about how they operated as a family, and when I got here, I realized it was true. And yet, it could still be damn lonely sometimes."

We'd orchestrated how we wanted to do this, and decided for the big announcement, Dev would tell the world. I gave him a nod, and he pulled the mic to his face.

"You all know that five years ago there was talk of trading me. Aside from wanting to remain on the team I'd played with for my entire career, I had a much more important reason for staying. So I decided to throw the biggest Hail Mary pass of my career and went to the Kings' owner, Armand Winters, and we talked, and I want to thank him for listening. For being more than just the team's owner."

Armand stood in the back and smiled at Dev's acknowledgment.

"Armand Winters made today possible. The reason I wanted to stay, that I needed to stay, was because I wanted to be with the person I loved." He took my hand, laced our fingers together, and placed them on top of the table for everyone to see. "The man I love. Brody Martin and I have been together and in love since college. Now we're ready to start the next chapter of our lives, out and proud."

Shockingly silent as Dev spoke, the room erupted with cameras and shouts from reporters. I winced, but Dev's eyes twinkled.

"You're enjoying this, aren't you?" I murmured.

"I sure as hell am. Look at these vultures, ready to pounce." He pointed to a reporter who'd always treated us well. "Darla? You have a question?"

She stood. "I-I think we all do, Dev. So, you're gay. You and Brody Martin?"

I wasn't about to sit like a statue and let Dev have to answer all the questions. "Yes. I knew if I wanted to play professional sports, especially football, I'd have to keep quiet about my sexuality. I never expected to find someone like Dev, but–"

"I'm one of a kind, what can I say?" Dev chimed in, and the entire room laughed. "And in case you're wondering, I made the first move the night we won the Orange Bowl. I fell for Brody the first time I saw him because, well..." He nudged my shoulder, and my face grew hot. "Aside from the obvious, he's the kindest, sweetest, most loving person I've ever met. I don't have a family to speak of, and Brody and his mom took me in and made me their own. They cared about me."

Time for me to interrupt Dev. "And Dev's bein' modest. I never thought I'd find someone who made me a better person, but his unrelenting love and support for me and our relationship allowed me to hope for a moment like this. You can't imagine how it was growin' up where I did, thinkin' I'd have to be alone my whole life, but Dev just barged right in and told me we could do it. Together." He squeezed my hand, and my eyes burned with unshed tears.

"Any other questions?" Dev asked.

"Are you going to get married?"

"Do you plan on having kids?"

"What do your teammates have to say?"

"What're your plans for retirement? Are you going to go into broadcasting or coaching?"

I cleared my throat. "We were married in California, in a confidential ceremony, eight years ago," I answered, and it was funny to see everyone's reactions. "Only family and a few close friends were present. Now that the secret's out, we'll be doin' it up right, here in New York."

Dev took the other questions. "We haven't discussed children yet, but that's a private matter between Brody and me. As for our teammates?" He paused, and I knew it was emotional for him because Dev had never liked hiding who he was, even though he understood the need for it. "A few close friends know, but we kept it from everyone else, and I hated lying. I hope they forgive us and realize we did it for our own protection. I truly value my friends and teammates as my family."

I watched as Momma wiped tears from her eyes. "I came out to my mother years ago, and she was nothin' but supportive and lovin'. We hope that by tellin' our story, it might help kids strugglin' with their own identity. Plus, maybe it will put to rest the idea that gay men can't play competitive sports. Our plans right now are to go down to my hometown in Georgia and help with some projects we've been involved with. After that? I don't know."

Dev squeezed my hand. "Thanks, everyone. That's all for today."

The questions continued to come, but we shut off the mics and walked away to join Momma and Ezra. She hugged me while Ezra spoke to Dev.

"That was very brave of you two," he said. "I'm very proud."

The crowd of reporters hovered, hoping for extra sound bites, but we knew better. The Kings had hired security for the event, and they ushered out the press quickly, until it was just the four of us, Lizzie, Fallon, and

Kelsie. Armand Winters and Hayden joined our group and shook our hands.

Armand smiled at us. "Congratulations to you both. I know how hard this must've been, but you handled it with grace. It's not easy being gay in a professional sports environment."

I'd heard some of the gossip about Armand and how he and his father didn't get along before he took over the Kings. It sounded like he and Dev shared that type of background, and I knew I was one of the lucky ones.

"Thank you for making it all possible." I didn't think I'd become emotional at leaving, but stepping away from a huge part of my life was like buckling in for a roller-coaster ride with no end in sight.

"The Kings aren't going to stop their contributions to your causes, in case you were concerned," Hayden stated. "In fact, we were wondering if you'd be interested in setting up a football camp for high school kids where you grew up, Brody. Maybe you and Dev could hopefully recruit some of your fellow athletes to help."

Warmth settled in my chest. "That'd be great. I think we'd like that. We usually spend summers down south, so it'd be perfect. I'll talk to some of the guys."

"Great. We'll be in touch." They said their good-byes and left.

"Let's head to Dev's place for lunch." Ezra pulled out his phone. "I'll get the cars for us."

Dev nudged me as we walked out of the offices. "You okay? I thought it went as well as could be expected."

"Yeah. I'm just curious what the guys are gonna say." The elevator came, and everyone got in but us. "We'll take the next one and see you there. Momma's got a key."

We waited for the doors to close. "Me too," Dev agreed, grim-faced. "My phone was vibrating like hell in my pocket during the press conference."

"Did you look yet?"

He shook his head, an expression on his face I'd rarely seen since I'd met him.

Fear.

"And I'm not going to. I want to have a nice afternoon with the people closest to us. If people are going to shit on our happiness, it can wait."

It made sense. These were friends we thought had our backs, and I preferred to think they'd be supportive. I put my arm around him and gave him a hug. "It'll be okay. I know it."

The afternoon was all we could've hoped for, and Ezra went above and beyond by ordering from Charles Pan-Fried Chicken. He then spent most of the time on his phone, eating in fits and starts. I wondered what was going on.

We feasted on fried chicken, ribs, pulled pork with mac and cheese, yams, and string beans. Momma had baked two cakes—carrot and devil's food—and Kelsie had made cupcakes.

"Oh God," Dev groaned, rubbing his stomach. "It's a good thing we don't have to play this Sunday. I may never move again."

"Will you miss it?" Finally off his phone, Ezra joined us, and I nodded.

" 'Course I will. Football's been my life from when I was thirteen and went away to camp. I can't say how I'll feel once training camp gears up."

"What about you, Dev?"

Stomach woes forgotten, Dev sat up and pinned Ezra with narrowed eyes. "All right. What's the offer?"

Ezra cracked up laughing. "Damn, you're good. Okay. It's tentative, but as you can imagine, my phone's been on fire. *United Sports Network* is interested in hiring Brody for commentary, and NFL *Weekly* wants you. I told them I'd consider it for you both as long as you'd always be in the same city, covering the games."

"And they have no problem with our announcement today?" I had to ask.

Ezra whipped out his phone, scrolled for a moment, then read. "We'd be thrilled to have Blink Martin join us. He's a role model for young people and players alike."

My eyes smarted with tears. "I just wanna be happy."

Dev wrapped his arms around me. "As long as we're together, we will be. I think it's a great opportunity for us. And like Ezra said, people need to see that gay men can play football. And win. Seven damn Super Bowls and twelve winning seasons in my career. No one's ever gonna take that away from me."

God, I loved his passion. It was the first thing I'd noticed about him on the field all those years ago, and it had never waned in all our years together.

The buzzer sounded, and Dev kissed my cheek and went to answer it. I heard him murmur into the speaker box. He met my eyes with an odd expression.

"What's wrong? Who's that?"

"Jonas and Marlon are here." For the first time that afternoon, he pulled out his phone and checked his messages. A muscle ticked in his jaw, and I ran to him.

"What is it?"

He held it up so I could read the screen. Zeke had texted him.

Fake-ass man. I knew it. Sick perverts.

"Screw him." I read farther.

Jonas and Marlon had each texted: *We need to talk.*

Dante texted: *What the fuck man? You couldn't tell us?*

Lovell was the last: *Whoa, dude. You serious? I never knew.*

I couldn't tell how Lovell and Dante actually felt, but for now it would have to do. At the knock on the front door, Dev opened it, and Jonas and Marlon stood waiting.

"Man, you coulda come to us." Jonas grabbed Dev and hugged him. The relief almost made me dizzy.

Marlon grinned. "You make a cute couple." I snickered, and he hugged me. "Good for you. Just so you know, Kelsie never told me about the two of you. I know she was doin' what you needed, and I don't care who you love."

Marlon slung his arm over Dev's shoulders while Jonas talked to me. "Happy for you, bro. You and Dev are the best. Glad to see you're okay."

"Yeah, we are. Thanks for coming by."

Marlon walked past me. "I see you've got my favorite sweets." But he bypassed the cakes to join Kelsie, who was hanging out with Momma, Lizzie, and Fallon. They'd gotten engaged the year before, and they greeted each other with a kiss. Kelsie had never looked happier.

"Did Kelsie say when the wedding is?"

"In the fall," Dev answered. His brow furrowed. "Fallon's gonna be bored as hell. I'll have to figure out something more for him to do. I'm afraid I'm not going to need him in the same capacity as before, but I can't fire him." He nibbled on his lip. "Maybe I can find another guy on the Kings to hire him. I can't just leave him out in the cold."

"You'll figure it out," I reassured him. "He's family, and we take care of our own." I scratched my chin, thinking about this new step in our lives. "It's gonna be a hell of a difference being up in the booth talking about the game instead of playin' it."

"And you can keep your hair long year-round. The way I like it." Those green eyes twinkled. "Speaking of weddings..." Dev took my hand and pulled off the wedding ring. "I think we can do it publicly now. What do you say?" He slid it down my ring finger. "Invite everyone. I'm ready to throw the ultimate touchdown and win the Super Bowl of life with you."

I removed his ring, placed it on the correct finger, then kissed him. "First and goal forever."

Thank you so much for reading *End Game*. I hope you enjoyed Dev and Brody's story and you'll see them again in *False Start*, Book 3 of the Brooklyn Kings series.

If you're interested in Ezra and Monroe's story, that can be found in The Promise, which is part of the Lost in New York series. It can be read as a stand alone.

If you join my newsletter, I'm writing a serialized story for Josh, the receptionist. I think he deserves a happily ever after too!

NEWSLETTER
https://tinyurl.com/y85e69ab

FELICE STEVENS writes romance because what is better than people falling in love? Her favorite part of a romance novel is that first kiss...sigh. She loves creating stories of hopes and dreams and happily ever afters. Her stories are character-driven, rich with the sights, sounds, and flavors of New York City, and filled with men who are sometimes deeply flawed but always real.

Felice writes gay romance because she believes that everyone deserves a happily ever after. Having traveled all over the world, she can safely say that the universal language that unites people is love.

Felice has written in a variety of sub-genres, including contemporary and paranormal, and she has a mystery series as well. You can find all her books listed on her website.

Felice is a two-time Lambda Literary Award nominee and a Lambda Award winner in Gay Romance for her book *The Ghost and Charlie Muir*.

BOOKBUB
https://www.bookbub.com/profile/felice-stevens

NEWSLETTER
https://tinyurl.com/y85e69ab

READER GROUP
https://www.facebook.com/groups/FelicesBreakfastClub/

FACEBOOK AUTHOR PAGE
https://www.facebook.com/felicestevensauthor/

INSTAGRAM
https://www.instagram.com/felicestevens

GOODREADS
https://www.goodreads.com/author/show/8432880.
Felice_Stevens

WEBSITE
felicestevens.com

PAYHIP STORE
https://payhip.com/FeliceStevensAuthor

www.ingramcontent.com/pod-product-compliance
Lightning Source LLC
Chambersburg PA
CBHW030124010826
48973CB00002B/419